ABOUT

David Thompson was born and grew up in Consett, County Durham. He moved to London in his early twenties and lived there for 14 years, during which time he made 3 short films and wrote 3 feature-length screenplays. In the late nineties, he moved with his wife and children to Cumbria, where he obtained a degree in English Literature and History at St Martin's College, Carlisle. He was a founder-member of Tree-house Orchestra Recordings, a music and arts collective based in Carlisle, which has had 80 music releases to date. He writes and records music as part of the bands Old Weird and The Dead West and through his solo project, Cat of Tomorrow, under which persona he has performed in local clubs and bars. He has also written reviews and sleeve notes for many of Treehouse Orchestra's releases. He lives in Carlisle with his wife and daughter and has a son who now lives in London.

STRANGE~
LOVE
PLACE

DAVID THOMPSON

To Carol

With Best Wishes

David Thompson

First published by Romba Press 2021

ISBN 978-1-7399554-0-3

First Edition
This paperback edition first published in 2021 by Romba Press
www.rombapress.com
Enquiries to editor@rombapress.com

For Ron Delves and David Jones

And with love and thanks to
The Basement Hacks (they know who they are)
I couldn't have done this without them

STRANGELOVE PLACE

Ok, so Janie didn't die – I'll give you that. But it's not always easy to be certain about these things.

I appreciate that you might be thinking 'what kind of cold-hearted bastard doesn't know whether his girlfriend is alive or dead' but, if my experiences of late have taught me anything, it's that life and death are states that are less separate or clearly defined than we might believe.

I've never been a great one for details and I do tend to exaggerate, but my life has become so fucked up recently that making some kind of sense of it all is not going to be easy. The world's gone wrong and I can't be the man I used to be while walking around in it.

Telling my story though, is what I need to do, and the sense I can make of it is the thing I'll be left with – the truth that I'll take with me.

Where to begin though, that's a bugger for starters. Our lives seem determined to resist taking shape or committing themselves to anything as convenient as structure. We can look back at certain periods and say, "yes, that was when this thing was coming together and I can see that it led to that, as it was somehow meant to do," but, when looked at another way, it all falls down. Cause and effect, I go with that totally, but how far back do you go – when was the cause and how long did it take before the effect began to be felt in any meaningful way? Shit happens, but why does it happen so often and why does there have to be so much of the stuff? You can maybe get some idea now of the problem I have with details. The problem being that I just don't trust them. They say the Devil is in the details. Maybe God is in there too, if you believe in such things. Put them together and you get the 'bigger picture', something we might call the truth. But, in the end, details are just the things that people notice, that they consider as being somehow important, usually after the fact. It all depends on how these things are assembled and remembered, as well as who's doing the assembling and remembering. It's the same with autobiographies and memoirs, where people recall their lives in great detail – who they met on any particular day, what they had for breakfast, what they were wearing, exactly what they said and what was said to them. Let's face it, who remembers all that stuff, exactly as it happened? Total recall – no such fucking thing. Memory is a construct – fragments of events recalled dimly that we put together to try to make sense of who we are and what our relationship to the world might be.

I've heard storytelling described as taking a really long piece of string and choosing where to make first one cut then another. You're left with a shorter piece of string, but it's your piece. So where shall I make my first cut?

Well, Janie didn't die, as I think we've already established, though these days it's hard to tell. It sometimes doesn't seem like we're together anymore, though there was no leave-taking, no real end to it. I looked back one day, and she was gone. Maybe my looking back caused her going but, to be honest, the cause and effect don't seem to belong to the same family tree. Whatever, and for what it's worth, I want to go back to a point when she was most definitely alive and when we were very much together. I'll take it from there and when I've told you all I need to, I'll stop and cut the string. Maybe then it will make some kind of sense. For sure, I'll have another piece of string, slightly shorter, but all my own.

Janie and I were fucking. It was a morning in early November. The television was on in the background in our bedroom, the sound down low:

"What's the story in Balamory – wouldn't you like to know?"

The good people of Balamory were busy trying to figure out what the story was but we weren't too bothered. Janie was sitting on top, moving steadily, with me inside her. Miss Hoolie was singing. My hands were on her breasts as her movements started to get faster and more deliberate. There was a problem with flowers, a problem with children. My left hand moved up to her face, caressing her right cheek, my fingers finding her mouth as her movement intensified. There was an unusual vegetable competition. My other hand moved down to her belly and onto her left thigh. It was a bright sunny day, but something was missing. The postmistress was perplexed. She was moving down on me harder now. I could feel myself coming, without ejaculating, a steady wave of pleasure that was sustaining itself, beyond the point where it should have broken. Janie started to come too, losing

3

her rhythm and out of breath, slowing down and finally stopping, then leaning slightly forward. There was a misunderstanding, much relieved laughter, and yellow paint everywhere.

You know sometimes, when you come, it's a good, clean shot – you feel spent and satisfied. That's you for a while. Other times, you ejaculate but you don't really have an orgasm. It's a reflex action and you feel slightly embarrassed about the whole thing – perhaps you just imagined it. And it doesn't really satisfy you. It's a bit like a Chinese meal, you're hungry again very soon after.

This was not like any of those. I felt drained. I had been sucked dry. It was a warm, heady feeling and I tingled all over. Janie sat for a while on top of me, catching her breath, then leaned forward and kissed me on the mouth. The inhabitants of Balamory had finally sorted everything out. Janie eased herself off me and lay down by my side.

"That was better than sex," I said,

"Yeah, and how would you know?"

"I read books."

"I'm sure you do, pet," she said, cuddling up to me. "But sometimes there's no substitute for experience."

"So, you would recommend an empirical approach?" I said.

"Don't get saucy."

She kissed my chest then sat up and opened a drawer in the bedside table. She pulled out a packet of cigarettes. I pulled a face.

"I thought you were giving up," I said.

"It's a work-in-progress. Don't rush me." She took a cigarette out of the packet and put it in her mouth.

"Wouldn't dream of it, darling," I said.

She lit up and took a long drag.

"I'm so glad to hear that you don't have a problem with it," she said.

"No, not me, baby, I'm just a passive smoker."

"Well, maybe you should be more assertive."

"Shall I spank you, then?"

She smiled and shook her head. "No, I might enjoy that too much. Possibly not the deterrent you're looking for."

She was sitting up in bed, out of the duvet, and she looked great. Much as I hated the sin, the sinner was hot, even as she indulged in her vice, indeed perhaps because of it. In fact, strangely enough, all of my girlfriends, bar one, have been smokers. Maybe I'm addicted to them. Sure, the reality is not good but the image works. You can shoot me dead for saying it, but a naked woman smoking a cigarette is horny. Actually, a naked woman doing just about anything is horny. I started to stroke her pubic hair. She blew smoke in my face.

"Maybe I'll just die right here and now," I said, coughing and spluttering melodramatically.

"Aaaah...my poor baby."

"That's me."

"You have it so hard, don't you?"

"Too right I do."

She began to laugh.

"Go ahead," I said. "Mock the afflicted".

She stopped chuckling and attempted to look serious and sympathetic.

"And what affliction would that be, pray tell?"

"You know, the usual...being a man."

"Ah, right, bit of a bummer, that."

"Ever so faint smell of not being taken seriously," I said.

"Since when did being taken seriously ever do a man any good?" she said.

"Try it sometime. You'd be surprised."

She stubbed her cigarette out in an ashtray by the bed.

"Ok, baby, just show me where it hurts, and I'll tell you who to call."

"Look for the swelling," I said.

She pulled up the duvet and peeked underneath.

"Ah yes, pretty serious, I agree, though I thought we had that particular condition sorted out."

"Oh, you know, it comes and goes."

She slipped a hand under the duvet and addressed the problem.

"Chronic, would you say?"

"Pretty much. It's just a case of relieving the discomfort every now and then."

Janie moved over towards me and started to kiss my neck gently.

"Guess I'll have to operate, then," she said, pulling away the duvet. She continued to kiss my body, moving down from chest to stomach to groin.

Now, I realise that this may all seem somewhat gratuitous and perhaps a little self-indulgent on my part. What's the story here, you may be asking. Well, *this* is the story. I'm the story. Janie too. This is the start of my piece of string and from here on you can see for yourself what the story might be. For now, I'm taking the time to remember Jane, to hold her like that in my mind, the way she was, the way she felt. And selfish nostalgia and titillation aside, this does all serve to underline one important point that you need to understand – my life was never going to be this good again.

CHAPTER TWO

I was sitting up in bed a little later, playing my acoustic guitar, while Jane took a shower. I was letting my fingers find chords that pleased me. The minor ones are always winners, particularly E minor – God, I love that chord. Once there, I wandered into *Albuquerque* by Neil Young, from *Tonight's the Night*, one of my favourite albums of all time. A strung-out number, ragged but strangely uplifting, from a record that's full of songs like that. An album about death and loss that makes you feel good to be alive, while acknowledging those who've passed on, feeling both the happiness and sorrow of remembering lost friends and lovers. Slide guitar and harmonica fill out the picture of open highways, truck stops and everything else you might pass by on the way. A wilderness both longed for and thrust upon you, a future uncertain and down the road somewhere. All this from a few chords played in my bedroom on a chilly November morning in South London.

Jane came back into the room, a bath-towel wrapped

around her and her red hair tied back. She smiled over at me as I played.

I found a new chord sequence, this one more urban and street-smart, a cocky strut rather than a languid road trip into the unknown.

"Sweet Jane...sweet Jane..."

A love song and a come-on. God bless Lou Reed – the miserable old sod. Jane smiled and gave me a little shake of her backside. She took off the towel and finished drying herself with it, under her arms and between her legs then up and down each of them.

She threw the towel onto a chair and went over to the chest of drawers, a little wiggle in her walk. She opened a drawer and took out a pair of knickers and a bra, keeping time to my playing and singing. Bending over, she drew the knickers up her legs slowly, looking over at me with a half-smile, then she stood up and started putting on her bra, in an exaggerated fashion, a little drama in itself.

She went over to a clothes rack at the far end of the room and took out the rest of her clothes.

"...Sweet Jane...sweet Jane..."

Soon she was dressed, and the show was over – a reverse striptease that left me hard again and more in love with her than ever. She walked over and kissed me on the lips, then went to the door, turning to blow a kiss and, with one last little wiggle, she was gone...only to pop her head around the door, moments later.

"Don't forget to put the rubbish out," she said. "And the kitchen floor needs a good going over too."

CHAPTER THREE

I was in the front room by the gas fire playing my guitar, this time a tune of my own that I'd been working on for a while, though I have to admit, not very successfully.

When I'd had my shower, I noticed a kiss mark in lipstick that Janie had left on the glass door. It made me smile. I left it there.

Janie and I had been together for nearly three years. We'd met at a party, and hit it off straightaway. Nothing had happened for a while, though we kept meeting at other parties, often thrown by my friend Michael, the Andy Warhol of Strangelove Place. Whether these affairs turned out to be happenings or piss-ups, or a mixture of both, they tended to involve the same crowd of people, with everybody knowing everybody else, or at least knowing them while inebriated at parties. I was going through a bit of a black patch, pretty morose and negative to tell the truth, particularly when drunk, which was so often the case back then. Jane was seeing someone else at the time, a guy called Keith, and he would be there too, a little aloof, not really part of the scene. Packed in the kitchen, Janie and I would invariably end up having long, bizarre, and charming conversations, usually by the fridge. I always left thinking about her and wanting to see her again, hoping that Michael would throw another party and we could take up where we'd left off.

But, of course, I have to tell you about Michael's parties. They had become legendary around these parts, admired (and sometimes dreaded) for their strange mixture of high spirits, intellectual curiosity, artistic élan, and general debauchery – much like Michael himself, as a matter of fact. For these affairs were an extension of the man, built around his character and enthusiasms, a vision all his own that he shared with those he deemed worthy. They were his works of art, and the people his materials, so they had to be right.

At these events, Michael's bedroom would be the hub for a particular group, with the Two Daves' cod-underground movies unfolding, without mercy or the need for any sort of narrative logic, on a TV screen, while big spliffs were rolled and smoked and heavy dub reggae pounded from the hi-fi by Michael's bed. You might find Yani in there, taking in the dub and dope in equally profound measures. Yani's a French-Algerian, who grew up in Paris and, although he's lived in London for years, he's still retained his accent and an unmistakable air of Gallic cool which I, for one, would dearly love to have. Always colourfully dressed and invariably with a big smile on his face, Yani is an aficionado of music, with a wide but impeccable taste. He is also a pretty good saxophone player.

In the spare bedroom beside Michael's boudoir, others might sit and talk, drinking and indulging in other drugs of choice. Walking on towards the kitchen, you would come to the living area, dimly lit, and again buzzing with bodies standing around with drinks in their hands, some lolling on or around the one sofa in there. A different kind of music would be playing here – blaring out from an old beaten-up stereo in the corner. It might be a compilation of sixties girl groups, some John Lee Hooker, Howlin' Wolf, early rock and roll, like *Sun*-era Elvis, Chuck, Buddy, Little Richard, Sweet Gene Vincent or good old Jerry Lee, the Killer. This was music for dancing to and Michael would often demonstrate this by suddenly jumping onto a vacant piece of floor space and throwing himself around wildly, sometimes blowing randomly into a harmonica like some honking demon in heat.

In the kitchen, people would be gathered around, picking at salad or other snacks on the table while whatever Michael was cooking up bubbled away in a big pot on the stove – chilli maybe, or some kind of intense stew, but always something that was punchy, substantial, and democratic. Again, there'd be more bustle as people passed through to grab a drink from the fridge or one of the plastic bags lying around here and there, maybe lingering a while to talk. At the other end of the kitchen were the bathroom and toilet, fairly basic and just about hygienically acceptable. People would often be standing in the bathroom too, with someone sitting on the edge of the bath, perhaps Maddy, looking both weary and amused – the Mona Lisa was an open book compared to her. Maddy and I had once had a fling – or at least that's what I think it was. Anyway, we had a great time as well as a drunken, confusing, and sometimes downright odd one, until the fact that we were so totally different meant we decided to end it. We remained firm friends, though we were fairly haphazard as lovers. Maddy is an artist – a very gifted one, crazy and intense – turning out big sprawling, vivid canvasses full of colour and mystery. On the long side wall of Michael's living area, you could see one of her works – a commission for an earlier party and a gift to Michael, who'd been there through many a bad time for her, and indeed the rest of us in St Ragnulf's.

As Maddy sat there on the edge of the bath, smoking and laughing away, she might be talking to Ray – lead singer with X-Ray und die Hand mit Ringen, a Lambeth-based band you'll never have heard of – or maybe Rudy Rauss, originally from Dusseldorf and also a painter, though his work was so extreme that the term 'abstract' could never do it justice and the man himself was often extreme to the point of insanity. On the windowsill in the bathroom was a large mirror with a huge crack down the middle, the result of a particularly drunken argument between Michael and Rudy over the merits of Joan Crawford's performance in Nick Ray's *Johnny Guitar* that turned into a brawl.

While wandering through these scenes, you would also probably bump into one, other, or both of the Two Daves, armed with endlessly whirring super-8 cameras recording it all. They were both called Dave, it's true, though their respective surnames are lost to me now, if I ever really knew them in the first place.

Welsh Dave was a native of Swansea – a stocky individual with a plump face and a general air of melancholy, who did not talk much. When he did though, it tended to be in short, gnomic utterances or, occasionally long rambling anecdotes which were dry, understated and gradually hilarious in their unassuming accumulation of absurd detail, made even more improbable by his accent and soft, sing-song voice. His partner-in-crime, who we referred to as Posh Dave, was tall and thin. Posh Dave was a Londoner, the product of a well-to-do middle-class family and the public school system, but one that had turned out wayward, mercurial, and rebellious. He talked all the time, in an impeccable accent and usually with flamboyant hand gestures and a beaming smile. His father had been very much part of the British establishment, in Military Intelligence, or something of the kind I believe, though there was Portuguese ancestry on his mother's side which gave him a Mediterranean effusiveness and a slight swarthiness to his skeletal features. These two disparate individuals had met on a film-making course and, despite being different in so many ways, had instantly bonded due to their shared love of avant-garde cinema, reggae, and a wide variety of illicit substances. While their work showed on the TV in Michael's boudoir, they went about their business, capturing the context of their film's presentation and reception, creating another movie around it, to be edited together from their separate footage and shown again at some later party – one more shell of an ever-expanding matryoshka of self-referential art.

Michael's parties were pretty common, in those days – hardly a month seemed to go by without one. After a while, they started to blur into one long drunken, dancing, hazy entity – the gap between them like a sort of waking dream which served only to punctuate the madness that gradually began to feel like normality, eventually losing much of its strangeness and excitement in the process. But, back then, they were events – artworks – one never the same as another, though largely populated by the same cast of characters.

One particularly memorable occasion was Michael's 19th century Russian literature night. The idea was that everyone would come dressed in costumes inspired by the great works of that country in that particular period – the age of Pushkin,

Dostoevsky, Chekhov, Tolstoy, and Gogol. It was a winter's night too I remember, very cold and with a slight falling of snow, which added to the atmosphere, as if the evening air of London had been infiltrated by a chilly wind from Siberia. I made my way down to Lambeth on the tube in costume – a black greatcoat, with ornate buttons, that I'd pick up from a charity shop, a peaked cap, fingerless gloves, and a pair of Doc Marten boots. It wasn't too different from what I normally wear to tell you the truth, and my defining accessory – a small, plastic axe – was tucked away in my duffel bag, along with two bottles, one of red wine and the other of vodka. So, as I sat reading Dostoevsky's *Notes from the Underground*, I received no more strange looks from my fellow travellers than usual.

I'd headed off late so, by the time I reached our local, The Ship, the pre-revolutionary revellers were already coming out of the pub and taking to the streets on their way to storm Michael's place, since the Winter Palace isn't on the main bus route from Lambeth. I found myself swept along by serfs, Cossacks, anarchists, and others in more mysterious-looking garb. Maddy was rigged up like a playing card, specifically the Queen of Spades, in homage to Pushkin's story. She wore a vintage evening dress, slashed in several places, and a slightly tattered crown that made her seem regal, but in a shop-soiled, punkish way, rather like Miss Havisham as dressed by Vivienne Westwood. Setting this off was a strange rectangular structure that framed her, with a white border and two black spade symbols in opposite corners. She was puffing on a cigarette and distinctly merry, chatting away to me as our motley group descended on Strangelove Place. As we approached Michael's front door, I looked up at the roof, imagining that I might see a fiddler there, jigging in the snow in a precarious but life-affirming manner. Sadly, but perhaps predictably, this did not turn out to be the case.

There was a fiddler inside though, wandering around Michael's flat, playing Yiddish folk music with exaggerated Slavic gestures and a melancholy expression on his face. Michael himself greeted us as we entered the living area. He wore a pale blue smock – at least a couple of sizes too big for him – and a pair of baggy black pants. On his head was a furry Russian hat and he was sporting a splendidly luxuriant – though rather wayward – false beard. He had on each shoulder a papier-mâché head, decked out in much the same fashion as his own while, out of each side of his smock, there protruded two extra arms, which waggled impotently but added considerably to the general effect. In the leg department, however, I counted only two.

"Greetings!" he bellowed, his arms wide and ready to embrace, which he did, kissing me heartily on each cheek. "Good to see you, generic angst-ridden Russian student type, perhaps with anarchist tendencies, maybe even a Bolshevik in the making?"

"What if I said I had a small axe in my bag?"

"Ah, Mr Raskolnikov, how could I have failed to recognise you? It's most wonderful to see you. I must introduce you to my landlady – I could do with a cut in my rent."

"Happy to oblige. And you, of course, have chosen to pay homage to that obscure, nightmarish story about the mad Russian scientist who carries out strange genetic experiments on serfs."

"Well, I've never heard the Brothers Karamazov described that way before, but your reading is as valid as anyone's, my dear."

He led me to the kitchen, where more refugees from the

Great Russian Novel stood chatting, skulking, or otherwise indulging themselves. There was also a nice selection of food on the table – katleti, Olivier salad, blinis, smoked meats, yoghurts, and cheeses – and a big pot of borscht on the stove.

Michael produced a bottle of vodka from the icebox in his fridge and poured us out a healthy glass each.

"To life!" said Michael, raising his glass.

"To love!" I said, raising my own.

"To the steppes!"

"The Volga!"

"The Urals!"

"The fleshpots of St Petersburg!"

"To your health!"

"And yours tovarich!"

It was a good night, with bursts of song and misguided attempts at Cossack dancing, as well as much consumption of vodka, inevitably preceded by extravagant toasts and musings on the meaning of life. The costumes of the guests ranged from the prosaic to the inventive and beyond that to the downright baffling. Yani wore an extravagant green kaftan with cherries stuck to it, in a nod to Chekhov's orchard, while the two Daves were War and Peace – Welsh Dave in combat khaki with a toy machine gun and Posh Dave dressed as a hippy, straight out of Haight-Ashbury in the Summer of Love. Rudy Rauss took his inspiration from Oblomov and typically turned it into performance art. He installed himself in the spare bedroom for the evening, lying on one of the beds with drink and cigarettes within easy reach. He had dressed in his own clothes because he couldn't be bothered to find a costume, and chatted to any visitors to the room, occasionally sending them off to the kitchen to get him some food, and all this between exaggerated bouts of inertia. Elsewhere, there were huge papier-mâché noses, large overcoats that threatened to engulf their wearers, people dressed as seagulls and a Taras Bulba that owed more to Yul Brynner than to Gogol.

It was only later on that I bumped into Jane. I hadn't seen her for a while – she'd missed the last couple of Michael's parties, and I'd begun to worry that maybe she'd moved on. I was in the kitchen, fixing myself another drink, when I felt a tap on my shoulder and turned to see her standing there, smiling.

She was wearing a rather creased wedding dress and her red hair was tied back. In one hand she was holding a copy of *Hello!* magazine and, from her other wrist, hung a small bottle labelled 'Rat Poison'.

"Hi," she said.

"Hello, good to see you. It's been a while."

"Sure has."

"Madame Bovary, right?"

"Got it in one. I'm impressed!"

"Me too. Very nifty indeed, though somewhat geographically inappropriate."

"I know, but I always get her mixed up with Anna Karenina – you know, silly spoiled cow, unhappy with her life, has an affair, kills herself."

"See what you mean. Same story really."

"Yeah, I've always thought so. Anyway, Michael gave me a special dispensation so... here I am."

"You look lovely."

"Nice of you to say so."

"Besides, we've already got one Anna Karenina kicking about. I saw her earlier, in a black evening gown and with a piece of railway track strapped to her back."

"Hard lines for her," said Jane.

"Well, what do you expect? You get stuck in a big, depressing novel by Tolstoy – it's always going to end badly."

"You're not wrong. You want to buy a girl a wodka?"

"I'd be wery honoured."

I found a glass and poured her out a drink.

"Thank you kindly," she said.

"Keith not with you?" I said, looking around the kitchen.

"No, that finished a good while ago."

"Sorry to hear it," I lied.

She shrugged.

"These things happen," she said.

"They do indeed."

"No use worrying about it."

"Not at all. So, what shall we drink to?"

She looked into my eyes, a wistful smile on her lips.

"To the future," she said, raising her glass.

"The future. Yeah."

We ended up going back to my place, a dingy little bed-sit in Willesden Green – two characters from 19th century European fiction, escaped from their mother works and off to create a joint future in an entirely different time and context. We spent the rest of the weekend together and, before you could say Ivan Ivanov, we were in the same novel, and on the same page. It was a novel of our own and we were going to write it ourselves.

My landlady at that time was a crazy spiritualist who held séances downstairs and gave me the evil eye every time she saw me coming in or going out. When she finally tired of my playing My Bloody Valentine's *Loveless* and The Velvet Underground's first album loudly late at night after too much red wine, she kicked me out and I ended up moving south of the river to Strangelove Place, where I lived for a good while on Michael's couch. Eventually, a flat a few doors up from him became vacant and I took it on. Not long after, Janie moved in with me. We got a couple of cats, Banana first, then Louie shortly after. I was the happiest I'd ever been.

Janie took some of the waywardness out of me. I felt more grounded with her. In fact, the first thing that struck me about her was her natural serenity, a calmness that she seemed to both emanate and inhabit. Having said that, she had the dirtiest laugh I'd ever heard coming from a woman and a capacity to drink me under the table if the mood took her. She loved to dance and we often found ourselves jiving, stupidly and with wreckless abandon, whenever we had the chance. Music was important to both of us, and Janie liked the songs that I was coming up with.

When I write a song, the words usually come first though, with what I consider to be my most successful efforts, the melody follows very soon afterwards – it can feel almost simultaneous – when the stars are in a favourable alignment and the gods are looking down on me with an approving smile on their faces. In most cases, it is a phrase or a line that is the spark and, more often than not, this will end up being either the title of the song, or the first line or else it will turn up in the chorus or as some kind of lyrical motif that runs through the whole piece. The important thing for me is that this phrase contains an idea which, once I've heard it and it's planted in my brain, kind of explodes – suddenly I know that there is definitely a song there and, on my better days, I pretty quickly know what it will sound like. It's only a seed but I have a good idea of the kind of plant or tree it will grow into – it's all there in that tiny fragment and you just have to work on it and tease it all out with love and patience.

I do think songs are gifted to you – ideas come if you are tuned in and ready to receive them. You have to be open to what the song wants to be and try your best to help it get there. It takes talent and musical ability, to be sure, but I believe that it's best not to know too much about musical composition and all that stuff. In my opinion, if you get too hung up on technique, musicianship, and a set idea of what your 'style' might be, you are more likely to end up with a generic song – even if it works and is passable – and in the process, you will probably have squeezed out what life and personality the thing might have possessed in the first place. Just like the education system when I was growing up.

That may all sound like airy-fairy mystical-schmystical bullshit, but it's been my experience of the process. Although I'm trying to explain it, there is a part of me that doesn't want to analyse song-writing too closely – I'm always afraid that the songs won't come any more if I do.

As I've said, the best songs for me are the ones where words and music come to me more or less at the same time, but there are the other occasions where I have an idea for a lyric and write it down, as if it were a poem. I usually don't finish it, but I'll return to it now and then if it interests me enough until I finally get it to a point where I think it needs a tune.

That morning, after our sensational Balamory sex session, I found myself with just such a problem. I had tentatively called this problem *Baby Wolf Song* and, if I remember correctly, it was a case of the opening line coming out of nowhere and the remainder of the first verse following quickly but then nothing. I didn't want to force the song out – that can be very much like trying to get a little more toothpaste out of a tube that's squeezed flat and just about empty – and so I kept coming back to it periodically. I'd tried various melodies on for size but nothing I was happy with and now it was time to try again. This was the lyric:

Baby Wolf in the woods -
Keep the lights on at all times,
Make sure that the clock still chimes.
While rain outside outlives the fog,
The hearth is hungry as a dog.

Darling spirit lost in rhyme,
Trees fall punch-drunk to the ground.
In a clearing bluebells sound.
Having thoughts of homemade snow,
Jam and candle burning low.

And so the tale begins –
The hornet stings and the spider spins.
Needles, tacks and rusty pins –
While all around are drowsing in their dreams.

Phantom sweethearts ill defined –
Let down by the shifting dawn,
Windswept and woebegone,
Of their own haphazard choosing,
While not winning never losing.

And still the yarn unwinds,
To chart the mazes of our minds.
The moon can sometimes be unkind
And catch us lonely in its ancient beams.

I really liked the words – I must have been going for a spooky folk vibe – but setting them to music was proving tough and this was not the first time I'd tried. I had toyed with the idea of using an alternate tuning for the guitar, which would maybe free me up from just playing the usual chords and encourage me to let my fingers do the walking and find the melody another way. As it was, I left the tuning alone and let my finger slide down the A-string, while picking the rest. I ended up with a descending progression in the verse which sounded a bit like an early Pink Floyd song called *Cirrus Minor*, which is almost archetypal late sixties British Psychedelia – dreamy and melancholic, drifting down the Cam in a boat in the early morning, the dew still on the grass, while stoned and reading *The Wind in the Willows*. For the chorus though, I shifted to the chords of A minor and E minor, which retained the melancholy but took it into early R.E.M. territory, which was fine by me.

I felt that I was finally near to cracking it and started to play it through again when I noticed someone hanging around outside the window. A black shape that lingered for a while, then moved out of sight. I went over to the window to see what was going on.

There was a knock at the front door, and I moved out into the hall. I could hear a voice, distorted and nasal. There was something about it that made me feel uneasy and my heart began to beat faster. Nevertheless, I opened the door.

There was a despatch rider standing there in a motorcycle helmet and leathers, with a clipboard under his arm. He had a radio in a holster slung over one shoulder and this was the sound I'd heard. The volume was up a little louder than it needed to be, and the disembodied voice continued to rattle on, barely intelligible.

"Take the next one to Jericho and prepare it for reception. It's a special so don't let them slow you down," the voice seemed to say.

"That's a roger. It'll be delivered sweet and proper," the man said through his helmet. I couldn't make out much of his face behind the visor, but his eyes stared at me as he spoke.

"Hello, have you got something for me?" I asked him.

"You Frank Brand?"

"Not the last time I looked."

He continued staring at me for a moment, almost as if he hadn't heard what I'd said, then glanced down at his clipboard.

"It says here Brand, number twelve. This is number twelve." He nodded at the number on my door, which was indeed '12'. That I couldn't deny.

"I can't deny that," I said, "but I'm definitely not Frank Brand. A guy called Frank does live a few doors down, at number six, though I'm afraid I don't know his second name."

The man looked at me some more, still seeming not to take in what I was saying, as if I was speaking Urdu.

The radio barked out again. "Birds fly south for the Winter, then lose their feathers for want of desire." At least that's what it sounded like. I chuckled nervously.

"He's just giving me directions," he said, obviously sensing my bemusement. "Another address south of river that's been giving him stick over the wire. Sounds pretty urgent."

"Right," I said, meeting his gaze. The pause was pregnant, perhaps expecting quintuplets.

"Number six, you reckon?" he said.

"Well, there's a Frank living there. I can't promise that Brand is his surname, but you might catch him in though."

He pondered this for a moment.

"Cheers, mate," he said.

As he walked away, I caught a glimpse of the name of his company on the bag slung over his shoulder – Swift Despatches – and I watched him as he stopped in front of Frank's door. He stood there for a while, as if in contemplation, then looked back at me, holding his stare. I held mine. The radio croaked into life again. It sounded like an angry crow, cursing the sky at the break of dawn. I couldn't decipher the message. The man turned away and started speaking into the radio. Again, I was unable to figure out the instructions he received but he turned away from number six and headed down the path and off towards the street, out of my sight, without looking back again.

When I got back into my front room I flicked through the Yellow Pages and found the Courier Services section (see also: Delivery & Collection Services); the Delivery & Collection Services section (see also: Messengers); the Messengers section (see also: Despatch Riders) and the Despatch Riders section (see also: Courier Services, Delivery & Collection Services & Messengers). I did not find Swift Despatches under any of these headings.

I turned on the PC and googled 'Swift Despatches' ("Do you mean Swift Dispatches?"). I tried both and though I was pointed in the direction of much interesting information concerning *Gulliver's Travels*, nuclear warfare, data handling, and black holes, I found no courier company with either name. After trying other search engines, Swift Despatches still remained stubbornly elusive. If this was a commercial company, it was difficult to see how they could attract customers and have any kind of financial success, unless they did so in a particularly arcane fashion. If they weren't operating on any established business model, then they were doing their own thing, effectively working as a covert organisation. Or else they didn't exist.

CHAPTER FOUR

I was still feeling a little uneasy about this episode when I left the house a couple of hours later. It was very cold outside now, with a definite chill in the air. I had on my big black coat and black fingerless gloves, a black corduroy cap (very early-sixties Dylan) and my guitar case slung over my shoulder. As I got to the door of number six, I noticed it was slightly open, which seemed a little odd. I stopped and listened for a moment at the door but couldn't hear anything. I gave a knock and waited but there was still no sound of any movement. I knocked again, a lot harder this time, with a sick feeling growing in my stomach. I heard a cough and some muttering. The door opened just far enough for Frank to stick his head out. He looked pale and dishevelled, his eyes squinting against the light.

He coughed again and blinked at me, getting his bearings.

"Where's the fire?" He croaked.

"No fire, Frank. Just checking you're ok. Sorry, did I wake you up?"

He blinked again.

"Ah, Stevie, it's you."

He opened the door wider now. He was wearing a vest and a shabby pair of trousers. His feet were bare.

"Afraid so," I said. "You alright, man?"

"Me? Yeah, I'm fine, son. Right as rain. I dozed off for a bit, that's all."

"Your door was open."

He looked puzzled, as if he really had to think about that one.

"Oh yeah, thanks son. You know me. What time is it?"

"Half-elevenish."

"Half-eleven, right...and it's Friday?"

"It is indeed."

He nodded contentedly. The world wasn't going mad after all. It kept time and played fair with the order of its days. He could trust it for a little longer.

"Good lad. Where are you off to?"

"Got to sign on, then I'm rehearsing with the band."

He smiled now and almost burst into a chuckle, stopping himself when he realised that I wasn't joking.

"Ah, alright. Good on you, son. You keep at it."

"Don't worry. I will."

"Aye, you keep at it."

He was looking a bit blank now and his voice sounded thin.

"Are you sure you're alright, Frank?"

"Yeah, sound as a pound." The stain said hot, the label said not.

"You take it easy," I said. "See you later. Down The Ship, maybe."

"The Ship? Yeah, sounds as if it could be arranged. I'll ask the missus."

I nodded and started to move away.

"Bless you, son...bless you."

His voice trailed off. I raised my hand in parting and walked on, looking back once to see him, still standing there, blinking into the daylight, making sure that the world wasn't going to change its mind and pull a fast one.

The truth was, Frank didn't need to ask his wife's permission to do anything, since she'd been dead for nearly two years. Cancer – a long and painful business that had left all of us in Strangelove Place pretty shaken. Frank had taken it hard, and he'd hit the bottle even harder. He was in his late sixties now but looked older, his body shrunken and his spirit diminished. He had seemed younger than his years before then. As a young man, he'd done a bit of boxing and had always kept in good shape. He'd been a market trader, a ducker and a diver, maybe not always on the right side of legal but not a crook either. He was a proud man, generous to a fault – he'd sort things out for you and sling a few quid your way if you needed it. Most of all, he made sure that his Mary wanted for nothing. He treated her like a princess, even to the end, when she was racked with pain and didn't know who he was anymore.

Frank had lived on Strangelove Place forever, long before most of the rest of us had turned up or even heard of it. I was probably still living up North in the town where I was born, saying my prayers like a good boy, and Janie was most likely a

Girl Guide and reading *Smash Hits*. I can't speak for the rest of our cast, but you get the general idea.

Nevertheless, we observed Frank's fall and had to put up with him while he fell even further and got drunk and stupid just to try and dodge his grief – the pain of being without the woman he adored.

CHAPTER FIVE

I turned up at the Jobcentre Plus office and went through the usual process of justifying my existence, recounting all my efforts to address the thorny issue that was my lack of gainful employment, so that I could grudgingly be paid my modest portion of Jobseeker's Allowance. After the chat with my work coach, a rather dour individual called Colin, during which I produced my little notebook detailing my (fictional) efforts to find a job in the past fortnight, along with bogus 'thanks, but no thanks' letters, I walked to Lambeth North tube station with a strange, unsettled feeling in my stomach. A chill had set in and my breath, visible in the air, looked alien to me. It wasn't mine anymore, just another lungful of life, lost in the wind, part of the atmosphere, along with everyone else's. I could still breathe in again, of course, out too, keep the cycle going, but it was not the same. The world was older and so was I, one breath closer to the last one. God, I was feeling really morbid – where did that come from? It wasn't the result of having to jump though the required hoops for my JSA – no, I'd gotten used to that and it brought me neither shame nor sadness. More likely it was because I'd been thinking about Frank and his wife – could well be that idea of change and loss. How it comes out of a clear blue sky, and we never know how it's going to hit us until we're lying flat out on the floor and have to decide whether we're going to get up again or not.

As I walked on though, I couldn't quite shake off that whole business with the despatch rider. It might mean nothing, but I had the strange feeling that something wasn't quite right; a suspicion that the guy was trying it on. After all, the company he worked for didn't appear to exist, or else it was going to great lengths to prevent anyone from finding out about it. For whatever reason, the chill I felt wasn't just the cold November wind – autumn making its inevitable way towards winter. It was deeper than that.

As the Waterloo Line train rattled on from station to station, everything was far from hunky dory, and I was feeling more than a little low. At Embankment, a woman got on and sat opposite me. She must have been in her late fifties, and she bore a remarkable resemblance to the late, great, Ingrid Pitt – the Scream Queen of such cult classics as *The Vampire Lovers*, *The House That Dripped Blood* and, of course, *The Wicker Man*. She wore a white trouser suit, with matching fedora set at a provocative angle. She was carrying a Biba tote-bag and pulled from it a thick, dog-eared book, which she started reading. It was *Our Mutual Friend* by Charles Dickens.

The train rattled along, its motion strangely reassuring. I continued to watch Ingrid as she read her novel, which was a book I knew well. Though never a big Dickens fan, I'd been drawn to that particular work and found it captivating. It is one of the great books about London, I think, capturing the phantasmagorical side of the city and the pungent whiff and energy of the Thames, both of which have always appealed to me. I was born elsewhere, in a small town in the North-East, but I'd lived in London for twelve years or so and the place never ceased to fascinate me. It felt like home and Dickens' book reminded me of why I love this city so much. It was also about the connections between people, the invisible cords that bind us together, sometimes restricting us, sometimes making us feel less alone. And it was about death...and life. And how the two are inextricably linked, sometimes indistinguishable.

Dickens' book made me think about David Bowie, in the seventies, when he was at the top of his game, bringing out one cracking album after another – a purple patch that few other artists have equalled. The albums that sprang to mind were those from the start and end of that decade – *The Man Who Fell to Earth* and the 'Berlin Trilogy', *Low* and *Heroes* in particular. These works shared that same sense of a hybrid state, somewhere between life and death, a stop between stations. An intermediate state, with forces working on us – influencing our lives – of which we aren't always aware. But there is always a chance to transform our lives, our identities, a chance to redeem ourselves. If we're always crashing in the same car, as Bowie sings on *Low*, maybe it's time to change cars, or else pack in driving altogether.

The train stopped at the next station. Some people got off. Others got on. The doors closed and the train moved away again. The woman's eyes shifted from her book to me, an almost imperceptible change but I felt it nevertheless. The noise of the train stopped being reassuring and put me on edge, like cotton wool between my teeth. The woman continued to look at me. I felt that maybe I should say something to her, if only to feel less self-conscious. Perhaps she wanted to impart some information and I needed to give her permission to do so. The train continued towards the next station. Its rattle made me feel far from home. I was going somewhere but I was not sure where that might be. I lost the question that was on the tip of my tongue and looked away for a moment. When I looked back at her, she was reading her book once more. The train slowed down and came to a standstill. It was my stop and I got off. The doors closed behind me, and the train headed off into the tunnel, carrying with it a woman who looked like Ingrid Pitt.

I stood for a while on the platform, feeling a little nauseous. The platform was empty, and the place was quiet. After a while, I headed off looking for an exit.

I soon found myself walking down a long corridor and, though I'd passed through this tube station many times before, a strangely unfamiliar one. Again, there was nobody else about – no one passing me, no one walking behind. There was a slight wind against my face as I continued on, increasingly uncertain that I'd taken the right way. I could now hear a guitar playing faintly, somewhere further down the corridor. It was a busker, obviously, but I couldn't make out the tune. I came to another passageway – it was marked 'Way Out', and I followed the arrows.

I was still feeling sick to my stomach and a little light-headed. The music seemed closer now with a wailing blues harp joining the strumming. What's more, the tune was familiar and, as I moved closer to the music, I realised that it was the song I had been playing around with earlier that morning, the one I couldn't figure out how to fix. The harmonica too, sounded like me, it was my style, if you can call it that – the way I blew, the way I bent notes.

My pace quickened. I was determined to track the musician down. I wasn't sure whether once I found him, I'd give him some money, stop to talk and compare notes, or just punch him in the face. I took a turn down another corridor, starting to run, the music coming ever closer. There was a set of stairs. I hurried down them and turned left at the bottom to find myself on another empty platform. The music stopped. I looked along the platform to see a man in a big coat, with a guitar case over his shoulder, turn off into one of the exits. I started off towards him, but I needed to sit down on one of the seats. My head was pounding, and I closed my eyes tight shut.

A train came out of the tunnel. I looked up as it slowed to a halt and the doors hissed open. People poured out and moved off in different directions. The doors closed with finality and the train was sucked down the tunnel on its way to its next point of call. The thudding in my head continued and I still felt weird, but I got myself together and wandered off after the last stragglers who were also looking for an exit. I was desperately in need of some fresh air.

CHAPTER SIX

When I arrived at Strength of Strings – the studio in Paddington where we rehearsed – I was extremely late. The other guys were already there, and I might have got some dirty looks if they weren't already immersed in the customary music-related dispute. It was never a dispute about our own music, you understand – not a bout of 'creative differences' that threatened the stability of the group – but rather a disagreement over the relative merits of a particular artist or album. In this case, it was Bob Dylan's '80s output – not for the first time, I might add.

The guys were all sitting around, behind or beside their instruments, and holding cans of beer. When Hal noticed me, his expression turned from mischief to concern.

"Hey, Floyd. You alright, mate? You look like shit."

"Yeah, fine. Had a bit of strange journey over here, that's all."

"How about a pick-me-up? I've got some beers in the fridge."

"A cup of tea would be great for now, mate. A strong one."

"Fuckin' hellraiser! Coming up."

The others nodded over at me as I settled myself down in a chair, but they didn't skip a beat in their interchange.

RJ, our bassist, was conducting an impassioned defence of certain albums from the Big Zim's lost decade. I'm a huge Dylan fan, but I'm not a completist and I have no desire to hear bad Dylan albums, or indeed bad albums by anyone else, including other artists I admire. I myself had begged to differ with RJ on a previous occasion over *Shot of Love*, which he held in high regard. This was an album that I had borrowed from the local library – its return being very hasty indeed. It seemed to me, with the exception of the sublime *Every Grain of Sand*, to be a muddy, laboured, and unconvincing record. It is often lumped together with *Slow Train Coming* and *Saved* to form a kind of 'born again' trilogy and, to my ears, it is as underwhelming as those two records – heartfelt and impassioned, to be sure, but well below the standard set by Dylan's best work. To make things even worse, RJ was now singing the praises of 1988's *Down in The Groove*, which for most of Dylan's fans would be regarded as the dictionary definition of fighting a lost cause.

Chips, our drummer, felt obliged to play the *Oh Mercy* card. This was the album after *Down in The Groove* and a critical and commercial success for Dylan – the bright beacon in that dark decade of the soul – and generally regarded as an emphatic return to form. RJ was having none of it.

"That's so predictable, Chips mate, but so fucking wrong. Christ, that record is so fucking overrated. It's like everyone was so desperate to find a Dylan record they could like, after having missed some of the great songs that were on the ones that they hated. So, here comes Daniel fucking Lanois to sprinkle his fucking pixie dust on a bunch of passable

Dylan numbers and lo and behold, it sounds like sodding U2, so we can like that a lot. Granted, it's not bad, I'm not saying the record's shit, man, but it doesn't sound like a Dylan record."

Hal came back from the studio kitchen and handed me a cup of tea.

"Rip it up, mate," he said.

Chips grinned and took a swig of lager from his can.

"If you're having a go at *Oh Mercy,* you're in the 'Twilight Zone', mate, away with the bloody fairies. Yeah, so the production is a bit Lanois-heavy, the polish laid on a tad thick, but it's hardly the fucking *Joshua Tree,* for shit's sake! There are some damn fine tunes on there, RJ. *Most of the Time, Ring Them Bells, Everything's Broken,* top stuff. If you're gonna say that *Oh Mercy* isn't as good as *Blonde on Blonde, Blood on the Tracks* or *Love and Theft* even, fair play to you. But *Down in The Groove*? You're having an absolute fucking giraffe."

Chips was our drummer by the way, so called because he liked chips, and the straightforward origin of his moniker was fitting for the man. I've not always found myself in accordance with Chips' beliefs and observations but, on this particular occasion, he was right on the money.

"Stevie's here by the way, chaps," said Hal.

"Yeah, we know," said RJ. "Wotcha', mate."

"God, you look sick as a pig," said Chips. "You alright?"

"Yeah, I'm fine." I couldn't tell them about my journey, about what had happened to me, or what I thought had happened. It would only burst on the air, like a bubble, in the telling and they'd all be staring at me as if I was certifiable.

RJ's invitation for me to join the circle did the trick, though, and Dylan's dark period was forgotten, for the time being anyway. We had a bit of banter and caught up a little, then I set my guitar up and we got to it.

At this point you should know that I am describing a gathering of Return of The Thumb – the group that I'd formed with these three disparate characters, and which had been extant for eight months now. The band's name had come from a comic book I'd read. The Thumb was a criminal mastermind from another dimension who had been vanquished by The Quantum Squad – a superhero team who travelled through time and space fighting crime. It was a really awful comic, to tell you the truth, but I had a soft spot for it and bought a few issues. The stories were fairly lame but the artwork – by JT Kresky – was pretty fantastic. *Return of the Thumb* was the story where the imprisoned super-villain escapes from his captivity in the Shadow Continuum, bent for revenge. I'd always thought that it would be a great name for a band and, when we got together to attempt to conjure up a kind of ramshackle psychedelic country music (that's what we called it anyway), everyone agreed that it sort of fitted. Well, actually, Chips couldn't understand it and thought it was shite, but he was the drummer and so Return of the Thumb it was.

We rehearsed a couple of times a week and it generally went ok. We'd all been in bands before and had collected our fair share of bad experiences, enough to know that the present set-up was pretty equitable. We fancied ourselves as a 'cosmic country' band, our main reference points being '70s Neil Young and Crazy Horse, Gene Clark, The Flying Burrito Brothers, late '60s Byrds, early Flaming Lips and Mercury Rev. Hal and I wrote most of the songs, but we also came up with material just jamming together. We'd played a couple of local gigs, both fairly ragged and not especially enjoyable, and our rehearsing on this particular day was with a view to performing again. Once I perked up a bit, we started working on one of my songs, called *Inca Spaceship*.

Civilisations come and go –
Ask the Incas, they should know.
The Aztecs and the Mayans too,
We still don't know the things they knew.
Wisdom ancient but fresh off the press,
The pulse of dormant consciousness.
Retrospective and futuristic,
Supersonic and shamanistic.

Like an Inca Spaceship heading for the stars,
Taking all that knowledge with me,
Of the Carter Family and the Shangri-Las.
Good Vibrations and radio stations
Will help us reach our destination.
Tuned into the infinite,
Without the need of medication.

It was all very *Rust Never Sleeps* and we had developed an extremely strung-out version that gave Hal plenty of opportunity for wigged-out solos. Mr Young could probably have sued but it sure was a whole lot of fun and an hour passed by quickly and with a fair amount of hilarity. We spent another hour working on one of Hal's songs, a grungy number called *Interesting Times,* that was punchy and bellicose, before deciding to call it quits for the day.

Hal and I went for a pint afterwards at a nearby hostelry – The Moonflower Arms. I got a text from Janie on the way over there. I hate mobile phones, but Jane kind of needed one, being a nurse and all, and when she upgraded, I inherited her old one. Guess she liked to know where I was and what I was up to. While Hal was getting in the drinks, I read her message:

'Hi honey. Still sore? I'm not surprised :) x'

Bless her heart and all the bones in her lovely little body, I thought to myself. I must have been smiling too.

"What're you grinning at, Floyd? You on a promise or something?"

"None of your business. Where's me Guinness?"

"It's the black stuff in the glass in my hand, Brainiac. Left hand – the other one's mine."

I took my drink. "Cheers, mate," I said, raising my glass.

"Bottoms up, you spiky old sod. How is Miss Livingstone, anyway? Haven't seen her for ages."

"She's fine. Just checking up on me."

"Too right," he said, lifting his glass. "To Syd."

"To Syd," I said.

"What was the matter with you today, anyway?" he said. "You seemed really fazed when you turned up."

"Just had a weird episode on the way over. Can't really explain it. Seems silly now just thinking about it. Got the fear for no reason at all."

I told him about getting lost in the tube station and, rewinding a little, about the despatch rider and his non-existent employers.

"You do seem to have had a bit of a freaky Friday, Floyd. I'd lay off the mescaline if I was you, mate."

"Thanks for the tip," I said.

40

"I've got to have a piss," he said, and followed that thought out of the bar.

Left to my own devices, I got up and wandered over to the jukebox – The Moonflower has a particularly good one, as it happens. I fed it a pound coin and punched in my selection. C19 – Elvis Presley: *The 50 Greatest Hits – One Night*; M6 – Nirvana: *In Utero – Dumb*; J2 – The Beach Boys: *Pet Sounds – You Still Believe in Me*; Q10 – *The Sound of the Smiths – What Difference Does It Make?*; T13 – The Flaming Lips: *The Soft Bulletin – Feeling Yourself Disintegrate*.

I returned to my seat, my work done. Hal came back and sat down with a sigh.

"Fucking Elvis," he said.

"He always speaks well of you, you know."

"Between huge mouthfuls of Big Mac, I'm sure."

"Elvis loves you, Hal. Never forget it."

"I suppose you didn't put any Clash on, then."

Kurt followed Elvis, then the Beach Boys chipped in.

"I'm not sure how you do it, Floyd, but you always manage to be both predictable and random at the same time. Can't go wrong with a bit of Brian though."

"Well I can think of someone who might disagree. He might even advise Mr Wilson on how to put it right."

Hal started to smile; he knew where this was heading. He put a hand on my shoulder.

"It's not worth going there, mate. You'll only get upset."

"You're right," I said, looking suitably chastened. That way lay madness.

"I mean," I continued, "all you have to do is turn up at the fucking studio and do your bit. You've got a really top-class meal ticket, touring around the world, great hotels, all the girls you want, hit records with your stupid mug on the cover

– all courtesy of a genius that just happens to be your cousin. You're in a band with him, you've kind of lucked out. Everything's peachy, so just get down on your fucking knees and thank God every day of your fucking life. But no, you have to shoot arrows at the goose that lays the golden eggs, so you turn up for work and suggest that the genius is not producing appropriate music. Do you think that this is appropriate, mate? God, this is really inappropriate, right?"

"See what I mean, Floyd," Hal said. It was a Mike Love thing.

"Yeah, alright. Bloody great track though."

"If I could hear it, yes." He raised his glass. "To Brian."

"To Brian," I said, and took another drink.

CHAPTER SEVEN

I made it back home and had a shower. The couple of pints of Guinness with Hal had made me a little groggy and I needed something to eat. I grabbed a sandwich and put on the Flaming Lips album, *The Soft Bulletin*, along with a DVD of the film *The Incredible Shrinking Man*, with the sound turned down. The message of both was the same – the universe doesn't make sense, bad luck and bad science will always let us down and we're all going to die in the end anyway. But, regardless of all that, we still have our time, it's precious and we all mean something, as small as we are, in the general scheme of things. I soon felt a lot perkier.

I headed off to The Ship. It was around 8 o'clock – Janie was working a long shift but she was going to come along later. The Ship was our local – our uber-local, in fact. It was actually called 'The Battleship Potemkin' and the sign that hung outside depicted a set of stairs with a pram hurtling down them. At least it did until the brewery told the landlord that it would not stand for such nonsense and insisted that the name be changed and a pub-sign showing a sailing ship, steadfast and reassuring, be put up in its stead.

I stepped out of the cold November night into the warmth of the bar. It was a true local. A front room away from your own front room. I took off my big coat and hung it on a coat rack by the door, nailing my colours to the mast, so to speak. The place was fairly busy, even at such a relatively early point in the proceedings.

"Evening, comrade," said the landlord. He was in his mid-fifties, his face a little haggard but still handsome, like a shop-worn Stanley Baker, a trace of those late '50s hard man roles still visible in his features. His name was Eric – Eric the Red to his regulars, due to his political beliefs, which were old school hard left, to say the least.

"Evening, Eric," I said. "How's it going?"

"Not so bad, son. Where's the princess?"

"She'll be in later. Long shift."

"She's a great girl. Mother of the nation, boy. But you can't stick a plaster on a burst artery. Fucking NHS – great idea, in the hands of idiots."

"Pint of Guinness, Eric mate."

"On the way, lad."

I looked around the room. "It's starting to fill up."

"Yeah, it's gonna be a good night."

I looked over at the space in the far corner, where there was a makeshift stage – a vacuum with flashing paraphernalia and bad karma.

"Smells like Karaoke, man," I said. "What goes on?"

"I know, lad. It's a departure. The brewery tried to sell it to me a few years ago and I put my foot down. Don't mind the idea so much now."

"It's a bit Twentieth Century, Eric, that's for sure. Actually, it manages to be both archaic and futuristic at the same time. A combination of medieval torture chamber and disco, you might say."

Eric handed me my Guinness.

"I like it," I said, and took a drink.

"So, you'll get up and give us a number later, lad."

"No way, Eric," I said.

My fingers were curled around the microphone. I was caught in a trap but, for the life of me, I could not get out. It was something to do with loving someone so much but never truly trusting them. A flashing screen told me the words I had to sing, though I knew them anyway. I had sung them before, while dancing around my front room with an imaginary mike and a theoretical guitar, in front of an invisible Las Vegas audience with a phantom chorus of black ladies singing in the background. This time though, it was for real. Well, far from Vegas, but real all the same. Very much like life in general.

The song trailed off and there were faint traces of applause from around the room. I saw Janie at the bar, armed with what looked like a very large G & T. I headed towards her, and I blessed her cotton socks when I spotted the Guinness that she'd bought me.

"Oh damn," she said, "I was just about to whip off my knickers and throw them at you. Get back on."

"How was your day?" I asked her.

"Baby, it was shit. I so need this drink."

We moved over to the table where Michael, Maddy and a couple of others were sitting.

"Well done, Stevie," said Michael. "You had me wondering for a moment whether I was in Heaven or Las Vegas."

"I thought that was your normal state, Michael," said Maddy.

"Aren't they the same thing, anyway?" I said.

"They are to you, Floyd," was Maddy's response to that. I pulled a face and shrugged. She stared back at me for a moment, then picked up her Bloody Mary and took a sip.

"That's because young Stevie is an Angel of the Ersatz," Michael said, with a big grin on his face. "A winged messenger between two worlds, at home with both the Cosmic and the Kitsch. Blessed Stephen of the Ironic Gesture."

"God, Michael, you are so full of shit sometimes," said Maddy.

"Pot-kettle interface, darling," said Michael, with a smile that was nevertheless accompanied by a steeliness in his voice.

Maddy was most definitely in one of her snappy moods – I'd seen them many times before, when everything got batted back at you, with extra edge and spin. Those times when her natural joie de vivre turned sour and her instinct to needle everyone around her came to the fore. Michael could always handle her when she got like that, and their little exchange seemed to quieten her down a bit. After that, she sat, saying nothing, though I noticed her glancing over at me occasionally.

I saw Frank over in the corner, looking fairly jittery. I tried to catch his eye, but he was miles away.

Michael decided to get up and treat us all to a version of *Kiss*. I couldn't decide what he was trying to do with it – I don't think he knew either. Just when I was thinking that he should act his age and not his shoe-size, I noticed a guy at the bar who was a stranger to The Ship, yet somehow familiar. A guy in leathers, with near shoulder-length black hair and a bemused expression. I studied him for a while until the penny dropped. The last time I'd seen him, he was wearing a crash helmet, but I was pretty sure it was the same man. I got up, walked over to the bar, and stood beside him, watching Michael do his thing.

I looked over at the man. He carried on watching the show.

"What do you reckon – Prince or Tom Jones?" I said, so he could hear me.

"As a general principle or just this moment?" he said, still looking forward.

"Say what you see."

"I'd say more like P.J. Proby. On a bad night."

"Get you. If he splits his trousers, I'll split the difference with you."

"You're on."

"Would you like a drink?" I said.

"No thanks, I'm good. I'm going to buy you one though."

I felt a little strange – surprised, embarrassed, I'm not sure how to describe it.

"No, you're ok..."

"I know I am," he said, "We don't need to argue about that."

He motioned to Eric and got his attention pretty quickly.

"Jack Daniels. A double."

"Ice or water with that," asked Eric.

"No, keep it simple."

Eric poured and faded. The man pressed the drink into my hand.

"Enjoy."

"Thanks very much."

"Catch you later," he said, and headed for the door.

He was out of the pub before I even registered it. I made off after him and stepped outside. The air was chilly, a heavy frost not far away. I looked both ways down the street, but he was nowhere to be seen. A motor-bike engine revved up somewhere in the near distance, and I heard it pull away. I felt my nose run and wiped it against the back of my hand. I looked down and saw that my hand was streaked with red. I hadn't had a nosebleed since I was a kid – I used to have them all the time back then. I stepped back into the bar, feeling a little stupid. I pulled my handkerchief out and attempted some damage limitation.

"Where were you?" Jane asked when I got back to our table.

"I'm not entirely sure," I said, looking over again at the door.

Janie must have had a really bad day, the way she was knocking back the G & T's. It was a good night though. Quite a few people got up to sing, including Frank, though that didn't turn out to be the greatest of ideas. His rendition of *The Street Where You Live* probably had 'For Sale' signs going up as he sang and, though less than rapturously received, he insisted on treating us to another – a version of *Come Fly with Me* that never really got off the ground.

When closing time came and Jane and I were heading

home, we saw Frank leaning against a wall, catching his breath. He was struggling and didn't sound too good.

"You ok, mate?" I asked him.

"Sound, son. Just having a little breather." He was only about fifty yards down from the pub and his flat wasn't that much further to go. "Give me a couple of minutes to get myself together."

We did more than that. Taking an arm each, we helped him along the street and into St Ragnulf's. We were far from sober ourselves, but our efforts still qualified as help. When we got to Frank's front door, an unseemly fumbling in his pockets eventually yielded his keys and we got him indoors and onto his bed. Jane put him in the recovery position and placed a pillow at his back. Once she'd assured herself that he was going to be ok, we let ourselves out, leaving him fast asleep, still fully clothed.

When we got ourselves home, we were both very drunk and dog-tired. It didn't take long for me to get to sleep, and when I did it was deep and murky, troubled by dreams of Elvis, mushroom clouds and human sacrifices.

CHAPTER EIGHT

Janie was up well before me the next morning and out to work pretty sharpish, an early start and another long shift. I don't know how she managed it – I was only vaguely awake enough to grunt something approximating a farewell at her and this was little more than a Pavlovian response to her goodbye kiss on my forehead.

It was much later when I finally surfaced. I'd not had what you might call a 'proper job' for a while now. I'd had too many of those in the past and found them more and more soul-destroying – grim transactions that warped my mind and kept me from my real passion, music. For the last few years, I'd managed to stay afloat by busking and helping out a friend of mine on his record stall in Charing Cross when he needed it, while still signing on. It kept me going and helped preserve a sense of myself as a bohemian musician, an itinerant minstrel, whether that was true or not. As a result, I'd kind of come unstuck from the normal run of things, disengaged from the way society operates. Fanciful or not, I sometimes didn't feel that I belonged in the world at all.

It was only when I found Strangelove Place, and later moved there, that I felt I had finally come home, since Strangelove Place didn't seem like part of the world either. In fact, it always seemed cut off from that bigger world, both geographically and psychologically, by physical location and temperament. You won't necessarily find it on a map. True places never are, as someone once said. But, if you're interested, head south down Kennington Road from Lambeth North tube station, cross over Lambeth Road, passing the park, to your left, where the Imperial War Museum stands. Further down on the same side there's a pub, a fish and chip shop and a grocery/off licence.

After passing the row of shops, cross over to the other side and take a right turn along Cherry Tree Avenue. Fifty yards or so along, on the left, there's a primary school. The last house before that school has a passageway straight after it and, if you turn into that, you'll pass through a stairwell and into a long, enclosed area with a pathway leading up the length of it to a high brick wall. To your left is a wooden fence, beyond which is a large area of wasteland all the way back up to the main road – a forlorn expanse of ground with a digger and a crane, both abandoned and left for dead, forever waiting to be discovered again so that the development of this land, once planned and promised, can one day begin again.

To the right of the pathway is a row of terraced houses, the fronts of the buildings weather-blown, crumbling and in need of rendering and at least a couple of coats of paint. These front doors lead alternatively to downstairs and upstairs flats. If you stop and look back, you'll see another group of flats above the entrance and perpendicular to the main terrace. These are accessible via the stairwell you've just passed through. You can also use the stairs to get onto the flat roof of the terraced buildings and walk down their length to the wall if you wish. God knows, I have.

It's not really called Strangelove Place, of course. The good people of the borough named it St Ragnulf's Place, after an obscure confessor and martyr. That's pretty apt, in many ways, but my pet-name sums the place up for me in a more satisfactory manner. This is all academic, of course, and my directions somewhat redundant – Strangelove Place isn't there anymore and, as it happens, St. Ragnulf wasn't the only martyr.

It took three cups of extraordinarily strong tea to get me started that morning. I drank the third one outside. It wasn't as cold as it had been, and the sun was shining. I still had a big jumper on though, but it was good to get out into the fresh air. I was feeling cooped up inside.

At the back of the terrace was a large communal garden. No fences separated it into individual plots, but each resident knew where their patch began and ended, and the others largely respected such easy-going territorial arrangements. Each section reflected the needs and inclinations of its particular tenant, as well as how much time or energy they were willing to spend on its maintenance. There were swings and climbing frames, for those with kids, and washing lines, garden ornaments, and little plots of flowers or vegetables, courtesy of the relatively green-fingered residents. Our section was one of the more overgrown areas, though Janie had once kept a herb garden and I was known to mow the grass when the inspiration took me. We had a plastic table and some chairs out in most weathers, and it was pleasant to sit outside and chat to whoever was around. Everybody tended to get on with each other.

That morning the garden was almost empty. I sat down with my cup of tea and Greil Marcus' book, *Invisible Republic*, which is about Bob Dylan and *The Basement Tapes*, among other things. I had read it twice all the way through and certain sections many more times, but I had been listening to *The Basement Tapes* a lot recently and so, had a hankering to visit Kill Devil Hills again.

The Basement Tapes is the name given to a series of recordings made by Bob Dylan and the Band in Woodstock over the late Spring, Summer, and early Autumn of 1967. Dylan had holed up in the area with his family, initially recovering from a motorcycle accident the previous summer but also taking the opportunity to escape the intense public scrutiny he'd attracted during his 'Wild Mercury' period, as well as the personal, often drug-induced madness that had become his natural habitat. The sessions were part therapy, part fooling-around, part making music for its own sake, though there was some idea of putting together a demo of fresh Dylan material for his publisher to offer to other artists. To my mind though, this was Dylan going back to the well for refreshment and inspiration, which he always seems to do when the batteries are running down, and he feels embattled or compromised as an artist. And so, he returned to the roots of American music – the mother lode of the nation's imagination.

The sessions started off with the musicians covering old material, from traditional folk numbers to songs made famous by Hank Williams, Johnny Cash, Elvis, and others, but then new songs, sometimes improvised as they played, started to take shape. Fourteen of these Dylan originals were featured on an acetate which was made available to certain acts and yielded hit records such as the Byrds' *You Ain't Goin' Nowhere*, Manfred Mann's *The Mighty Quinn* and *This Wheel's on Fire* by Julie Driscoll, Brian Auger and the Trinity. The Band themselves cut a version of *This Wheel's on Fire*, as well as two other basement numbers, *Tears of Rage* and *I Shall Be Released*, all of which appeared on their debut album, *Music from Big Pink*.

The acetate was widely bootlegged and these tracks, along with the other basement recordings, became the stuff of legend – a lost project, rock's great unfinished text, comparable only, I suppose, to the Beach Boys' (contemporaneous) *Smile* sessions. CBS finally released an official version of the Basement Tapes in 1975, collecting together most of the songs from the acetate, cleaned up and with, in some cases, overdubs. This overdubbing was somewhat controversial, as was the inclusion of some tracks featuring The Band without Dylan that were recorded later on and not part of the original basement sessions.

I loved this official version from the first time I heard it and wore down the grooves of my vinyl copy, though I usually skipped the Band-only songs, which seemed out of place to me, diluting the effectiveness of the record. When I learned about the existence of *The Genuine Basement Tapes* – a five CD Japanese bootleg of nearly all the basement recordings, unembellished and with all the tape hiss, false starts, mistakes, and chat between the musicians intact – it became an obsession to track them down. Since I couldn't afford to buy a full set, at fifty quid or so, I bought the individual CDs one by one from market stalls and at record fairs, whenever I came across them and had the money to spare. It was a long process, but I finally got all the discs and was mighty happy indeed. Of course, Columbia later brought out an official release of the sessions, as part of their Dylan 'Bootleg Series', and this claims to be the complete sessions. It's an impressive collection, but it's also pretty expensive so I haven't gone there. I prefer the version I collected myself, painstakingly and over time. It's also a genuine bootleg – hard won and somewhat illegal – and the best way to listen to these wayward, ghostly, and sometimes inexplicable songs. Being able to go into a record shop and buy them or order them from Amazon and have them delivered to your front door just doesn't seem right.

Needless to say, the complete collection of songs is a beautiful thing – a bunch of musicians with a genuine love of music, mutual respect, and trust, playing for themselves, just for the crack you might say, with no real intention that this should ever be for public consumption. And the Dylan originals stand apart from the rest of his work, though they can be seen now as a natural link between *Blonde on Blonde* and *John Wesley Harding*, and do find some echoes in his later albums, such as the much-maligned *Self-Portrait*, the two records of folk covers, *Good as I Been to You* and *World Gone Wrong* and some of the tracks on *Love and Theft* and *Modern Times*. But the basement tunes really have an identity all of their own – deadpan, witty, melancholy, mischievous, enigmatic, and sometimes just downright puzzling. Events and characters are often inexplicable, and the world invoked is one of visions and foreboding, despite the casual, good-natured manner in which it's presented. Tracks like *Million Dollar Bash*, *Lo and Behold!*, *Clothesline Saga*, *Open the Door, Homer* and *I'm Not There (1956)* are more tall tales than songs and their upside-down logic sets out the way this world works, or at least the way it keeps unravelling. This is the 'Old, Weird America', as Marcus terms it, an alternative country, the hidden track playing under the song that we think we're listening to.

I thought about all of this as I read Marcus' book which, despite some fanciful passages and occasional straying off the track, is one of the great books on music, up there with Ian MacDonald's book on the Beatles, *Revolution in the Head*. I was so caught up in the prose, my body in Lambeth but my spirit in a basement in Woodstock, New York State, that it took me a while to realise that I was not alone.

A few yards away, not far from the wall at the back of the garden, a little girl sat by herself on a grassy mound. She had not been there when I came out into the garden, I was sure of that. Her name was Grace, and she was eight years old, the only child of Tom and Lydia, a couple who lived two doors down from us. They tended to keep themselves to themselves, not really part of the main scene, which is to say Michael's scene, with all that entailed. Lydia was a nurse and worked at the same hospital as Jane. They were good friends, so we'd been over to Lydia and Tom's place a few times for dinner and gone out together for the occasional drink. Tom was nice enough, although he and I didn't have too much in common. He was heavily into IT – it was both his job and his hobby – but as long as we stuck to music, science fiction movies and paranoid conspiracy theories, we got along fine.

Grace was autistic and pretty much in a world of her own. She didn't really interact with anyone but her parents. She was just there, detached and apparently disinterested in what was going on around her. If something unexpected happened or anything was out of place, she'd get unnerved and have a panic attack, maybe flapping her arms about or hitting her head with the palm of one hand. Other than that, she would come in and out of the room, get what she wanted, do what she needed to do and leave again, or sit in the room with us, quietly engaged in some activity, usually simple and repetitive. She was a very pretty kid, despite the blankness that undercut that prettiness and the fact that she never smiled. And she had the longest, most beautiful eyelashes I've ever seen.

I walked over, stopping a few feet away from her so that she'd get used to the idea of me being there and not be alarmed. She was busy, putting one seashell after another down, a couple of centimetres apart from each other, in a row on the mound beside her. She was wearing purple dungarees over a thick pink sweater, with black slippers on her feet. Her blonde hair was tied back into a ponytail.

"Hello, Gracie," I said softly. I knew that she wouldn't answer but I wanted her to hear my voice anyway. I sat down on the ground beside her, looking off towards the backs of the houses. I could see her mum through the kitchen window. She was pottering around inside. When she looked out to see if Grace was alright, she saw me, smiled, and waved. I waved back.

Grace put the last shell into its place. There were ten in all. She stopped for a moment, perhaps to consider what she'd done. Then, she put a hand into a pocket of her dungarees and took out a harmonica – a blues harp, key of C – put it into her mouth and started to play. When I say play, I mean that she simply blew and sucked, blew and sucked, slowly and methodically, producing the same two notes in a steady rhythmic pattern. I mentioned that Grace didn't interact with people other than her mum and dad but, at that moment, I believe that she was interacting with me, albeit in a very

Gracie kind of way. I had given her that harmonica as a present, when her parents had mentioned that she liked listening to certain kinds of music, mainly instrumental pieces, and had a recorder that occupied her for long periods of time. She had said nothing when I gave her the harp and there was no flicker of interest on her face. In fact, she had left the room more or less immediately, but every time after that, when Janie and I came over to their flat and she was in the room, she'd produce the harmonica at some point and play it for a while, always in the same way. I counted this as a relationship and us sitting there in the garden like that, her playing and me saying absolutely nothing, was a conversation, as far as I was concerned.

That's when everything blew up.

I heard the muffled blast and a window shattering. A couple of other windows shattered too, either in aftershock or sympathy. Lydia came out of her back door, looked around to try and figure out what was going on, then ran over towards Grace, who had stopped playing the harmonica and started to flap her arms. Lydia sat down beside her daughter and put an arm around her shoulders. I got up and ran towards the window that had broken first and was bleeding black smoke out into the cool morning air.

It was Frank's flat. No mistake. I couldn't see anything through the window when I reached the back of the building – there was too much smoke. Nevertheless, I felt compelled to get inside, even though every ounce of sense I had was telling me not to.

His back door was not locked. I turned the handle, moved

to one side, and pushed the door in with a sharp jab of my elbow, pulling my arm quickly out of the way. More smoke escaped but no flames, no backdraft, no follow-up explosion. I don't know quite what I was expecting, but it didn't happen anyway. I leaned a little into the doorway to get a look, but it still wasn't easy to see what was going on in there. I did catch the smell though, difficult to describe but totally unpleasant. I pulled a handkerchief from my trouser pocket, took a deep breath and put the hankie over my mouth. I stepped inside.

There was still smoke in the room, though most of it seemed to have escaped through the window and door. The walls were blackened in patches, the scorching mingled with streaks of dark red. I stumbled over something but managed not to fall. When I looked down at the floor, I saw a leg, or part of one, starting from a little below the knee, with stubborn remnants of trouser, material and skin blackened, a smoking slipper at one end and a piece of jagged bone sticking out of the other. I froze and began to gag. I stared at the floor for a few moments, taking in the implications of what I was looking at. I had run in, almost on automatic pilot, to see what was wrong and to help someone, if I could. Now I was inside, I knew that I had entered something else. It was not a door I had planned to go through.

My eyes began to take in bits of flesh, lumps of person, scattered around the room, of which my mind could not fully take inventory or truly give labels to the items in stock. That might have been part of a scalp sticking to the side of the toaster, over there a thumb, fused with a scorched plastic curtain, on the draining board a smouldering nose, with some face still attached. It seemed like either a grisly jigsaw puzzle, scattered and missing a lot of the pieces, or else a gallery of unrelated exhibits that never belonged together in the first place, that never were a complete human. Never had a name.

The stench of scorched and burning flesh made me weep and retch. I began to feel faint. I stumbled outside, fell down onto my knees and threw up onto the grass.

CHAPTER NINE

The emergency services arrived promptly. The vehicles couldn't get into the Place – we were off the road – so their occupants had to come in on foot, carrying whatever equipment they needed. Firemen saw to the smouldering mess in Frank's kitchen, making sure there was no danger of fire or further explosions. The paramedics could do nothing for Frank – they couldn't even find all of him – and, though the neighbours that had been around at the time were suffering from shock and disbelief, nobody else had been hurt. The police moved about slowly, but purposefully, asking questions of the residents and conferring with their fellow professionals, trying to put together the bigger picture and, presumably, to figure out if there'd been any foul play. They questioned me in my front room – I'd been taken there and given a cup of hot, sweet tea. I'd regurgitated most of the previous three I'd had.

There were two police officers – a man and woman – both a few years younger than me, I'd guess, perhaps in their late-twenties, though the woman might have been even younger.

They were calm, reasonable and didn't try to rush me. I heard their questions and answered them the best I could but, to be honest, the words I said seemed to be coming from somewhere else, with me mouthing them like a ventriloquist's dummy. I didn't feel I owned the words and so didn't feel I could be blamed for what they meant or how they impacted on these people, doing their job, or indeed on anybody else in the world. They asked what my name was and how I made a living. They wanted to know why I was at home, who else lived with me and what I was doing in the garden. I accounted for my actions and told them what I'd found, what I'd seen, any details that particularly struck me as relevant. They asked about my relationship to the deceased and when I'd last seen him, his state of mind, anything he might have said that might be pertinent or helpful.

A man I knew, not very well but well enough, a neighbour, a man with whom I'd shared a drink and had a laugh, with whom I'd commiserated and who I'd looked out for after his wife had died (as we all had), had now been taken himself. That person was no more, literally no more because he'd exploded (again literally) for no apparent reason. And I'd found what was left of him. There was nothing I could say that was pertinent or helpful. How could there be? The answering of these questions, which I'm sure was necessary and part of some procedure that had to be followed, could not put Humpty Dumpty back together again or heal the rift, the tear in the fabric of my universe that had been caused by that explosion, that horrific and inexplicable occurrence. Stuff was escaping out of that breach too, like the black smoke from Frank's shattered window. God knows what it might be – logic, certainty, decency, the right of a person to fix breakfast or lunch in their own kitchen without being blown to bits. Whether it was one or all of these things, or something else that was crucially important but that I couldn't put my finger on right now, it had escaped and had vanished into the ether. The world had gone wrong.

It was tragic and funny, both at the same time, as well as being pointless too. I excused myself and went into the kitchen to be sick again. I was losing tea all over the place today, four cups now and I couldn't keep any of them down. At this point, Jane arrived – Lydia or someone must have phoned her. She put her arms around me.

"Oh my God, Stephen. You alright?"

"Not really."

She moved back a little and examined my face. She ran a hand through my hair.

"You're still in shock. Did the paramedics have a look at you?"

"Yeah. They told me I was in shock."

She shook her head and made to give me a kiss.

"Be careful," I said. "My breath smells of sick."

She kissed me on the forehead. There was movement in the kitchen doorway. The policewoman was standing there.

"We'll be off, Mr Floyd. Thanks for your assistance. I understand that this can't be easy for you. We will need you to come down to the station tomorrow though, to make a statement. If you could come in the afternoon, I'll be around. Ask for me at the front desk. P.C. Swann. It's just a formality. I'll say good-bye now. Get some rest. We'll let ourselves out."

Maybe it's the old Catholic thing again, but I always feel guilty around the police, even when I've done nothing wrong. I always have the impression that they're going to pick up something from me – my inner badness levels or an inkling of the heinous crimes I might commit in the future if left unchecked. Perhaps I've read too much Kafka.

I remember once, when I was living up on the tenth floor of a tower block in Westbourne Grove, I heard some movement in the corridor outside my flat. There was a peephole in the front door, and I looked through it to see what was going on. A police convention seemed to be taking place out there, with a dozen or so officers gathered for the event. I opened the door. Freed from the distorting qualities of the peephole effect, I could now see that there were only five of them and that their attention was directed towards the flat directly across the hall from me. They were having difficulty getting a response, despite repeated knocking and shouting through the letterbox. At that point, one of the officers turned around to me and said, with a wry smile:

"It's alright. We haven't come for you today."

The smile may have been meant to be reassuring and the remark was perhaps only an example of urbane police humour. Hell, he might not even have used the word 'today' – that might be my memory playing tricks again. Even so, the whole thing seemed pretty surreal – a bizarre ritual specifically designed to unnerve me. To scare me into a blameless, law-abiding life, in case I had ever considered taking the other path. For all I know, they might do this kind of thing on a regular basis, during their slack periods. Maybe they picked an address at random, perhaps using a computer or set of balls, like the National Lottery.

The two officers left, and we heard the front door close. Janie smiled at me in that way of hers.

"I think that she really meant it when she said it was only a formality," she said. She knew what I was thinking. I'd told her the police-outside-the-door story too.

"Shall I get you a cup of tea?" she said.

"No, better not. I'm not having any luck with tea today. A large Scotch would be good though."

"I'll get the bottle," she said.

We both sat and drank Scotch in the front room. Janie was great. She let me talk and, Lord knows, there was a lot to get out my system. I went over the events of the morning, close to tears at times. It seemed unreal, as if I'd dreamt it all. But I hadn't – Frank was gone, and I was the chief witness to the ghastly manner of his passing. I felt as if I had been summoned to the event for that very purpose without ever realising that I'd received the invitation. I did not understand why but I had the weirdest feeling that things could never be the same again.

CHAPTER TEN

I made it to the police station the following day and gave my statement. Janie came with me and the whole thing was fairly painless, though I probably wouldn't have noticed if it had been otherwise, since I was still feeling pretty numb, inside and out.

I wasn't much good to anybody for the next few days. I slept a lot and didn't want to see anyone, other than Jane, though Lydia came over. Michael too. Hal phoned to ask how I was doing, and we spoke for a little while. It was nice of them, but it was a hell of an effort for me.

I didn't feel much like eating – didn't even want to pick up my guitar or listen to music at all. I just watched a lot of crap telly and slept.

There was, of course, the small matter of Frank's funeral to sort out. He had one grown-up child, a daughter, but there had been little or no contact between them for many years.

Nobody really knew why. There had been a kind of truce when Mary was seriously ill and immediately after her death but visits and phone calls petered out, and they were soon back to square one. Frank's daughter was contacted about what had happened and she made the necessary arrangements for the funeral through a local funeral director.

The service at the crematorium was perfunctory. There was not much of the man in the coffin, to be sure, but there was even of less of him in the ceremony. This was how Frank's daughter wanted it. She did not attend herself.

The people of Strangelove Place were there, though, plus a few of Frank's old mates from his market days. It was right that we were all present, though it felt like a travesty and certainly wasn't how we had wanted to see Frank off. We turned up, looking suitably sombre in our funeral clothes, wearing our funeral faces. The service was short and, as the coffin disappeared behind the curtains, I couldn't help feeling that this was the second time in the space of a few days that Frank would go up in smoke.

The post-mortem had made it all as clear as mud. It had without doubt been a freak accident. There was no suggestion of foul play or that Frank had taken his own life. A verdict of death by misadventure had been arrived at, though they could have just as easily called it a quirk of fate or an Act of God. I think that he'd just blown up. I'd seen the result. Frank was wiped out and it didn't matter what the reason might be.

Since we had no control over the service, the residents of Strangelove Place had chipped in and planned a more suitable send-off afterwards. We were having a wake at The Ship and were determined that Frank would be there, in one shape or form. Whatever that shape or form might be, helped into being by our feelings and our memories of the man we knew, that was what we would honour and raise a glass to.

When we left the crematorium and headed to The Ship it had decided to rain. It was already cold and windy. A fucking awful day – to be cremated, to be attending a cremation, to be doing absolutely anything for that matter. I was still feeling sick. I was not up to this at all. And I was not alone. The faces of the people of Strangelove Place seemed to me like white plaster masks concealing secrets, perhaps even from themselves. Getting to the cars was a dumb show, as was leaving them at the other end and going into the pub. The conversation improved once inside, in the warmth, after a few drinks, but the malaise was not totally shaken off.

"So, she didn't show after all," said Michael.

"What a bitch," said Maddy.

"We don't really know what happened between them, so it's maybe not for us to judge," said Jane.

"Must have been pretty fucking bad, not to turn up at your own dad's funeral," said Maddy.

"Well, we'll never know now," said Janie.

"I still figure that Frank deserved better than that," said Yani.

"So he did," said Michael.

Everyone was silent, some nodding in agreement, some lost in thought. I got up and wandered over to the jukebox. Frank, despite his recent demolition job on *Come Fly with Me*, had been a big Sinatra fan and, largely due to his urging, The Ship's jukebox featured a generous selection of the man's work. I put a pound into the machine and punched in the numbers of five songs. *I've Got You Under My Skin* started up as I made my way back to our table.

Eric had provided a fairly good spread, laid out on a table at one side of the bar, as well as closing The Ship for the afternoon.

"Nice one, Stevie," said Michael, "Frank certainly loved Old Blue Eyes."

"Yeah," said Yani, "He told me that he'd seen Sinatra a few times in Vegas, including a gig at the Sands with Count Basie in '66. He had his picture taken with the Chairman of the Board after one of the shows."

"Yeah," said Jane, "I heard that too."

"We all did," said Michael, "Anyone ever see the picture?"

There was general shaking of heads around the table.

"Me neither," said Michael. "Oh, what the fuck. Here's to Frank. God rest his soul and let's hope that him and Sinatra are hanging out together now in that big casino in the sky."

"To Frank," we all echoed, raising our glasses, but somehow the gesture felt empty – a grasping for something that was beyond our reach. *I Can't Get Started* began to play on the jukebox now.

The others carried on talking, trying to create something meaningful out of the whole business, to pick up the pieces. I had nothing to say – my head was spinning, and my tongue was too heavy to make any kind of useful sound.

The room around me was familiar, as were the faces of the people sitting at the table with me. But there was something that was not quite right. Not the same. Even Sinatra singing a George and Ira Gershwin song – usually a world-beating combination and a tonic for the most shell-shocked of troops – could not make it so.

The talk continued, as did the music, and the drink carried on flowing too but, despite all of this, the malaise never really went away. Worst of all, I felt as if that malaise was coming from me, that I had infected all the others. Perhaps they were all looking to me to take the lead. The one who had found him, who had probably last spoken to him, the night before, with Jane, when he was still alive, still Frank. If I could raise a glass and find the strength, the cheer, to celebrate his life and help us to summon up that life, then they all could too. But I did not have it in me. I could not dispel what I had seen, no matter how hard I tried. Even with three large scotches inside me, I knew in my heart that Frank was gone, not just dead but wiped out. Obliterated. What was left could not be reassembled into anything meaningful, certainly not by me. I was the naysayer, the prophet of doom, the Jonah on this particular voyage of The Ship. I knew that they felt that too – I could see it in their eyes. And yet they did not throw me overboard, as I perhaps deserved. No, Frank went into the waters of oblivion instead.

Janie and I left early. I couldn't handle it anymore. The others said goodbye and carried on keeping watch. What had started as a wake had turned into a séance that left us all unbelievers. As much as we wanted to invoke Frank, we could not conjure him up, no matter how hard we tried.

CHAPTER ELEVEN

A week or so passed and, although we all achieved a little distance from the events surrounding Frank's demise, something still hung heavy in the air. Normality, a slippery customer at the best of times, obstinately refused to return. *Haven*, the housing association that owned the houses in St Ragnulf's Place, had sent some people to clean up Franks' flat and clear out what was left of his stuff. The place was to be painted and decorated at some point, we'd heard, but for now it was just gutted and disinfected. What's more, they seemed to be taking this as an opportunity to give the whole estate a make-over.

There had been talk of it for a while – a complete renovation of St Ragnulf's, with all the flats to be redecorated, refurbished, and modernised. Needless to say, there was considerable resistance from the residents, most of whom had lived there for many years and liked the place exactly as it was. Moreover, such plans were seen as a prelude to putting up the rent – which had always been absurdly reasonable – and a sustained effort to drive out what they might perceive as the more undesirable elements.

Much as *Haven* had been fairly benevolent and understanding of their tenants over the years, mainly by honouring an old rent agreement and leaving them well alone, they had long regarded many of these people as more than a little odd. We were, by and large, a bohemian lot in Strangelove Place – artists, musicians, filmmakers, and writers – people who were not necessarily nine-to-fivers and who valued a different kind of environment. This was, after all, what drew me there in the first place. I was one of them. There had, however, been a change of management at *Haven* and all the old tensions between landlord and tenants were resurrected. They looked at their residents and the way they lived, then they looked at the other streets and estates in the area, most of which had been redeveloped and now housed people with markedly different lifestyles and aspirations, and who, not coincidentally, belonged to higher tax brackets. Frank's accident gave *Haven* an excuse to do something about it. It didn't matter that his death was not caused by the outdated heating system, the kitchen not being fitted or the absence of double-glazing. Regardless of the facts of the matter, commercial considerations and health and safety concerns would be marshalled together to work hand-in-hand, in a briskly efficient manner, to drag Strangelove Place, kicking and screaming, into the 21st Century.

The residents were understandably worried, and that anxiety was seasoned with indignation and paranoia. There was talk of action and a meeting of the residents' group was arranged. Jane and I attended though I can't say I contributed anything to the debate or offered any suggestions to the calls for resistance. There was a time when I would have been as upset and ready for a fight as the rest of them, but that time had passed. To tell you the truth, I had fallen out of love with Strangelove Place.

It had been happening for a while. When I had first arrived there, the place and the people had excited me. I had grown up in a small industrial town in the north-east of England, a place where one of the by-products of the local steelworks had been a red dust that periodically filled the air, leaving buildings, streets, and the washing hanging out in gardens, coated with a rusty deposit. This phenomenon had moved locals to refer to the place as 'Redtown'. What's more, this nickname had persisted, even after the works were shut down, the cooling towers had cooled off and men like my dad were no longer required to clock on and put in a shift.

I had always felt like a stranger there. It never seemed to be a place where I really belonged, and the older I got, the more I couldn't wait to get out. After I moved to London in my early twenties, I rented a number of flats and bedsits in various areas of the city before I happened upon St Ragnulf's and, for the first time, I felt that I was home, or at least somewhere as near to home as I was ever going to find in this world. When Jane moved in, that sealed the deal.

But something had changed. I was thirty-six now, with my thirty-seventh coming up in January, the clock ticking on towards the big four-o. I was constantly aware that whatever aims or ambitions I might still have, remained stubbornly beyond my reach, elusive and unfulfilled. Music had always been my passion. I had listened to, played, and obsessed over it since I was a kid. This interest exploded when, in my mid-teens, I got my first proper guitar, a jumbo acoustic from

Windows, a music shop in Newcastle. I learnt to play guitar from the Beatles songbook I bought the same day, and it wasn't long before I was writing my own songs, though these early efforts were predictably naïve and derivative.

I didn't just want to make music, though, you understand. I wanted to make great music. My models were the iconic figures of popular music – Hank Williams, Dylan, Lennon and McCartney, Brian Wilson, Bowie, Syd Barrett, Johnny Cash, Neil Young, Lou Reed, Ray Davies, Morrissey, Nick Cave, Kurt Cobain – some of rock's most distinctive voices, the true originals. But such overarching ambition was combined with a congenital laziness and an unerring susceptibility to being distracted. Life just kept getting in the way. I drifted with it and found myself further down river and still far from home.

I continued to write and play but the music that I had in my head was always better than the stuff I managed to produce. Between thought and expression, as Lou Reed put it, lies a lifetime. Well, sometimes that didn't matter – it was enough for me to keep doing it, to be creating something. I'm a Capricorn, I reminded myself – we're slow learners, late developers and we tend to get better as we get older. Other times, I could only see a shortfall – the chasm that stood between achieving something and failing. I wasn't getting any younger and it was beginning to scare me. Maybe it was an early mid-life crisis, though Janie often joked that I was just having an ongoing life crisis.

What's more, Strangelove Place, which had always been a sanctuary and an inspiration, was now becoming a straitjacket. I felt stifled and I was beginning to get restless. There was a world out there, stuff going on, stuff still to do. For the first time in ages, I felt that where I was and where I wanted to be were not the same place. Frank's death, the way that it had happened and the fact that it had, in effect, happened to me too, had made that clear. It was as if a thought or a feeling, long suppressed, had finally been spoken out loud. It was out there now – it couldn't be unsaid and, more importantly, it couldn't be ignored.

CHAPTER TWELVE

Janie had been very supportive through all of this. She'd given me as much attention or space as I'd needed but my spirits remained stubbornly low. I'm a moody sod at the best of times but I suppose that she had grown used to it. We are quite different people in a lot of ways, with extremely contrasting temperaments. Maybe that's why we worked together so well. She's an uptown, up-tempo lady and I'm a downtown, downbeat guy. I can be frivolous sometimes and see the absurd side of life, but I do tend to think about things an awful lot, perhaps too much, and I get a little obsessive when things aren't right. Jane has a really positive approach to life. To her, there is no such thing as a bad choice. A choice can't be right or wrong, good or bad, in her mind. It's just a choice. You make your decision, follow that path, and face the consequences. Whatever will be, will be. She loved that old Doris Day song and used to hum it or sing it all the time. Drove me round the bend. I hate that fucking song. Sometimes, when she couldn't make her mind up about something and it was just a matter of choosing one option or another, she'd flip a coin and go with that, however it fell, heads or tails. Sometimes, if we were trying to sort out something between us, she'd suggest that we used the same method. This also used to drive me mad.

Maybe it was down to our respective upbringings. She's a Londoner and her parents are resolutely middle-class – both of them teachers. She grew up in a household where rationality and the sensible exchange of ideas and opinions were the norm. It had given her self-confidence and a strong set of values, though I know that she'd clashed with her parents at times and had been pretty wild in her teenage years.

My home, growing up, was vastly different. We were northern working-class and Roman Catholic to boot – a potent cocktail, I can tell you. It was a very loud household, even when there was no disagreement. An outsider might overhear us and think that there was a drama, on the way to being a crisis, perhaps plates might get thrown or bones might be broken but no, it was just the normal way we interacted, our usual manner of discourse. Maybe there was a touch of the Italian in us, that noisy, passionate Mediterranean streak, I don't know. Or maybe it was more of an Irish Catholic thing. I always thought of Redtown as an Irish town, despite its location in the north-east of England. At school, my classmates tended to have Irish names such as Kelly, Rogan, O'Rourke, Rooney and so on, and many of their families, somewhere down the line, had come over from the old country to work in the steelworks or the local coal mine. We also had a taste of religious conflict, a rivalry with the local Protestant schools that never spilt over into anything too horrible, though there were occasional punch-ups and snowball fights in winter. I've strayed off the track a little, though. I don't have time here to talk about my childhood or my youth too much, except that I came out of it guilt-ridden, obsessive, paranoid, with both a massive chip on my shoulder and a similarly-sized inferiority complex, at once opinionated and yet often lacking in self-confidence. So it goes.

In spite of all that and as hard as it might be to believe, Janie always insisted that I was an easy person to live with. She recognised my moods and obsessions and generally knew how to deal with them, or at least when to leave me alone. She also knew when to take the piss out of me. Despite being one of the most understanding and non-judgemental people I know, Jane also has a very mischievous sense of humour, and she would wind me up when she thought I needed it. Lord knows, she got down herself sometimes, especially if she'd had a bad day at work. Being a nurse and working in A&E she saw some fairly horrible shit on a daily basis, and she'd built up a way of dealing with that – a hard-ness you could call it – but it was really a form of self-defence, a way of protecting herself and allowing her to get on with her job. Nevertheless, it got to her sometimes, partic-ularly if it had to do with children. But all this just gave her a sense of perspective on things. There were life and death situations and, if they fell on your watch, you dealt with them. Then there was the small stuff, and that you did not sweat. You just had to be able to distinguish one from the other and act accordingly.

As good as it was between Janie and me, recent events had begun to put a strain on our relationship. We hadn't talked about it much. With Frank's death and its aftermath, we'd just tried to get through things as best we could. Even with the change that was in the air at St Ragnulf's, we'd not gone into it in any detail or examined how it was going to affect us. I found that I wasn't able to focus on that side of things anyway. Maybe, the way I was thinking around that time, it was small stuff to me and so I didn't give it much thought. Plus, they were really short of staff at the hospital where Jane worked, and she was working long shifts. We never seemed to spend any time together and so didn't get the opportunity to discuss anything.

I'd gone back to working on Yani's market stall, behind St Martin-in-the-Fields, off Trafalgar Square. He used to live at St Ragnulf's too, once upon a time, but he'd moved off to a flat in Brixton a year or so ago. He was a few years older than me, in his early forties, but we'd always got on very well. He was a cool dude – a flamboyant dresser, very laid-back, and never far from gentle, bemused laughter. In all the time I'd known him, we'd never had an argument. He was a film-maker – short, strange, experimental stuff, a lot on Super-8 but lately more hi-definition digital work that was equally far-out. I'd been in a couple of his films, most of his friends had, and I'd also come up with some soundtrack music for them.

It was a very cold day and business was slow. Yani generally dealt in bootlegs and rare stuff – a wide range that covered folk, psychedelia, surf music, post-rock, French pop, with some hip-hop, ambient and dub thrown in as well.

"How are things going, Chief?" he asked.

"Oh, you know, man. The dust blows forward and the dust blows back…"

"I do indeed."

He pulled out a hip flask and offered it to me.

"To clear the dust," he smiled, "and keep out the cold."

"Cheers, man. Don't mind if I do," I said. I took a sip and shivered. It was cognac.

"Good shit," I said, handing it back.

"Bien sûr." He took a drink too. "How's Janie?"

"Still Janie, though she's working very long hours these days. I said I'd meet her at work for lunch when I finish here."

Yani went quiet and looked around the market.

"You should go now. I'll probably pack up soon anyway. It's pretty dead today."

"You sure?"

"Sure I'm sure. Allez maintenant, you crazy bum."

I rang Janie from Charing Cross Station and she said she'd meet me in forty-five minutes. I took the tube up to Paddington – Jane worked at St Mary's. I wandered along Praed St and took a seat in the main waiting area.

Invisible Republic had become my constant companion and I read it until Jane appeared. We went up to the hospital canteen, which wasn't too busy. Unfortunately, the only hot food they had left was something that purported to be shepherd's pie and chips. I wasn't too sure at all as it sat there on my plate, daring me to take it seriously. I poked at it occasionally. Jane was only having a yoghurt, an apple, and a cup of coffee.

"How's Yani?" she asked.

"He's fine. He was asking after you."

"That's nice. Were you busy?"

"Not really. Yani reckons it's kind of dead at the moment."

"People are probably saving their pennies for Christmas."

"God, yeah. Christmas. I'd forgotten all about that." I must have pulled a face.

"Well, you know, it tends to come around every year, on December 25th. It's kind of traditional."

"Not if you're Jewish. Or Buddhist. Or a tree-worshipping pagan."

"I thought you loved Christmas," she said.

"Well, I do, usually. I'm not sure if I can face it this year, though."

She gave me a 'what the fuck' look.

"Mum and Dad have asked us over to theirs this year."

"Oh, have they?"

"Yes, they have. Emma, Geoff and the kids are coming too." Emma was Jane's sister. She was married to Geoff and they had three children.

"Oh, I don't know, Janie. I really fancy a quiet one. "

"We didn't go last year. They're kind expecting us."

"I know. But I'm..." My words trailed off.

"You're what?"

"I just... you know." English was quickly becoming my second language.

Janie had that look again. "I know it's been tough for you lately, Stephen, but you've got to pull out of it."

Her tone, as well as her expression, had now become harsh and alien.

"Right. And how am I supposed to do that?"

"I don't know, honey. But I really need you to come up with something quickly or we're going to hit a wall here."

I shook my head. I was beginning to feel pissed off.

"What's that supposed to mean?"

She sighed and gave a little shrug.

"I don't know," she said.

"Well, if you don't know, I certainly don't."

"Oh fuck. Are you going to finish that?"

I looked at her for a moment, not sure of what she meant. She nodded down at my plate.

"No. It's shit." I pushed the plate away.

"Well, I need a cigarette. Let's go."

We left the canteen and wandered downstairs and out of a door at the back. There was a paved area, with a couple of wooden benches, where the smokers and vapers gathered, though there were none out there just then. Jane lit a cigarette and we sat down.

"I'm sorry if I've been a pain in the arse lately," I said. "What happened to Frank knocked the stuffing out of me. I just feel as if I'm walking around in a fucking fog at the moment."

"I can see that, and I understand. But it's not just that."

"Well, what is it, then?"

She blew smoke up into the air, her eyes following it as it dissipated. She continued looking up, as if what she wanted to make out something that was written up there.

"I don't know," she said. "It's difficult to put into words. I just feel that we've kind of got stuck."

She looked over at me to see if I was going to respond. I didn't say anything.

"It's not about the stuff that's been happening lately, though of course that's hit me hard too. It's about where we were before that. Where we still are."

"Aren't you happy?" I said.

"I'm happy with you. I love you, honey, you know that. But I'm not happy with where we are."

I looked at her in silence, unsure of what to say. Did she want us to break up – is this what she was trying to tell me?

She took a drag of her cigarette, looked into space, and sighed.

"I want to have a baby," she said.

Now I really didn't know what to say. I opened my mouth anyway.

"We talked about this before."

"Yes, a long time ago."

"Even you weren't sure then."

"A long time ago, Stephen, as I said. Time's moving on."

"I don't feel ready, pet."

"Well, when are you likely to feel ready? You're nearly thirty-seven years old. I'm thirty-four. We've been together for a while now. If what happened to Frank told you anything, surely it must be that life is short and you never know what's going to happen today, let alone tomorrow, or next week. You don't always have the luxury of sitting around waiting for the right time."

"You know what I want to do, Jane. I still have that desire. Now more than ever."

"Of course I know. But I've been with you for three years, remember, known you even longer, and it's no closer to happening than when we first met."

"Oh, here we go."

"Look, before you lose your rag, please just listen. I'm not saying that it will never happen. I'm not saying you should give up – I never would. I'm just saying that we can't put everything else on hold in the meantime. Sure, you can carry on making music, but there will never be a right time, a point where the stars are in perfect alignment, when it all falls magically into place, and you can finally allow yourself to settle down."

"You've got me wrong, pet. I don't need everything to be perfect."

"Then what do you need? What has to change so that it's ok and you can move on?"

"Well, look at what's happening with St Ragnulf's. We don't even know where we'll be living in a few months' time."

"It's not going to happen that quickly. The last meeting with the rep from *Haven* pretty much proved that. You know, the one that you didn't feel like going to, that I went to by myself? I told you about it, though. You can't always trust those people, but I didn't get the impression that it was imminent. Anyway, they'd have to relocate us while the place was being renovated."

"It all sounds a bit precarious. How can you consider something as life-changing as parenthood, when everything is so up in the air?"

"You're talking as if we have any real control over anything. We may have an idea of how we would like our lives to pan out, but things can change in a second. I see it all the time. People have accidents or get ill. This wasn't something they had anticipated, but people are resilient, and they adapt."

"I see what you're saying, pet, but I'm still not sure."

"Well, I need you to sure, Stephen. I need you to let me know where we are and where we're going. This is something I really want. Something I really want to share with you. You have to work out what it is that you want."

She took another puff of her cigarette. I felt as if I'd been beaten up and I didn't like it.

"Well, you're gonna have to give those fucking things up for a start," I said, an ugly sarcasm in my voice.

She gave me a dirty look, leaned down, and stubbed it out on the ground. Then she got up.

"There, I just quit. Now I've got to get back to work."

She moved off, then turned around to face me again.

"You need to fucking grow up, Stephen. And soon!"

She pushed through the swing doors, which flapped against each other, as if washing their hands of me. I was on my own.

CHAPTER THIRTEEN

I rang Hal to see what he was up to. I was seething and looking to do something to let off some steam, have a crack with someone, mouth off, get hammered, I wasn't sure what. I just knew that I didn't want to go home.

My argument with Jane might not have been a particularly bad one. In fact, we'd often had worse, though they tended to be about things that were less important. This one, though, was too close to home and questioned aspects of our relationship that I thought we were really tight about. Things that we both agreed upon. I could take criticism from Janie – from her more than anybody else – but this felt like more than that. It felt like an attack on all I believed in. Everything that I was, maybe everything that we were about as a couple.

Hal said he was planning to head down to Hammersmith to have a night out with a bunch of his friends. They were mostly musicians, people from other bands and a couple of guys who busked regularly on the circuit. I knew a few of them. Not that well, but they were ok. I said I'd meet him down there.

We met in The Brook Green at around six. The place was reasonably lively, even at that time, with some suits from the local offices still around, having a few pints after work. Hal and a couple of the others had already arrived. There was a guy called Liam who I'd met before and knew very vaguely – a tall, gangly sort, a bit of a joker but basically a nice guy. He was the drummer in a band called The Angry Villagers, a very post-punk influenced outfit, kind of rough around the edges but quite tight and with some decent songs. It turned out that it was Liam's birthday, his twenty-seventh, and this was the excuse for a knees-up.

Once our party was fully assembled, we drank up and headed on to our next hostelry of choice, had one there and moved on again. It was obviously going to be a good old-fashioned pub crawl. Once you've drunk in two pubs then moved on to another, it can be nothing else. The idea becomes an organism with a gravitational pull of its own. A self-fulfilling prophecy. I let myself be dragged along by it. I was not feeling particularly sociable when I first turned up – I didn't want to be there, really, I just didn't want to be at home. However, the alcohol soon worked its dubious magic, as it will, and I found myself getting into the swing of it.

They were an entertaining bunch. Musicians mostly, of varying style and taste, and each with a doggedly irreverent take on the world. We talked about music. We talked about lots of other things too. Sometimes we talked shite. Sometimes the bar was too loud to hear anything, the group fragmenting into smaller units, the conversation too.

The night flew by. The Swan became The William Morris became The Hop Poles became The Hammersmith Ram – all merging into one pub with different rooms. None of them were a living room away from your own living room, just waiting rooms on the way to your destination, whatever that might turn out to be.

Liam suggested that we go back to his place, and we all agreed that this sounded like a great idea. We headed back down King Street and found an offie. Having stocked up with booze, we took a bus from the Broadway, heading down to Barnes, just a twenty-minute journey away. When we got off the bus, a chill had most definitely set in. There was snow in the air. You could feel it.

We made our way over Barnes Common. It was very cold now, but spirits were still high amongst our merry band of travellers – there may have been singing. We came to a little group of houses with a very old-fashioned feel. If you didn't know that it was a short bus ride from Hammersmith or hadn't passed the shops, pubs, bars and restaurants at the other end of the Common, you could have been forgiven for thinking that this was a tiny village in the middle of nowhere, about to be cut off by an impending blizzard. 'Straw Dogs' territory.

Liam's place was in darkness when we arrived. His parents had separated a few years back. He lived with his dad, but Liam told us that he was out and wouldn't be back that night. Once through the door, front or back – I couldn't quite figure out which – there was a cramped little hallway. You felt as if you should bend down to avoid hitting your head, but that wasn't the case. To the left was a narrow stairway leading up to the next floor and, to the right, a galley kitchen, which didn't have a door and so just seemed like another part of the hall. We took our plastic bags, filled with bottle and cans, and headed through into the front room.

It was huge, seeming even more so after the cramped space we'd just left. With its high ceiling and sparse furniture – there were only a couple of well-worn easy chairs and a sofa in there – the room was overwhelming. Heavy, dark curtains obscured the windows, and a large, open fireplace was set into the chimney breast. It was like being in the belly of the whale in the Disney film, *Pinocchio,* and we were all drawn deeper into the room, wandering around, as in a trance.

Despite the fact that we were now indoors, it was still cold, and nobody was taking their coats off just yet. There was a hi-fi in front of one of the windows and Liam put some music on – *The Best of Blur* – then went off to find some wood for a fire.

The place had a casual, restrained feel – as if the people living there weren't really bothered how it looked but kept it sparse, so it seemed cool anyway. I went to the kitchen and opened one of the bottles of Chilean Merlot that I'd bought in Hammersmith. The kitchen area was very cramped indeed, though it contained all that you might expect to find – sink, oven, dishwasher, cupboards, and drawers – but it would have seemed more natural to find such a space in a caravan or a canal boat, rather than in a large suburban house. Lord knows how it managed to accommodate two grown men – Liam was quite tall so I could only imagine how big his dad might be. I guessed that they were never in the kitchen at the same time.

It wasn't the cleanest of areas either. There were unwashed dishes in the sink and a few dirty cups and glasses on the draining board. I found a wine glass, gave it a good rinse under the tap and poured myself a large one.

"Here's to me. Sinbad," I said, and took a mouthful of wine.

I stepped back into the front room. Liam had managed to get a fire going, with flames licking around a massive log, producing a smoky though not unpleasant smell, that for the first time gave the impression that people actually lived here. It was then that I noticed her – sitting in one of the armchairs, wrapped in a black Crombie with her legs pulled up under her. She hadn't arrived with us, and I didn't see her come in afterwards.

She had dirty blonde hair and wore it in a way that suggested she didn't fuss with it too much. Her features were girlish, though there was a world-weariness about her that undercut this and made her look a lot older. I guessed that she was probably in her mid-twenties. I was drawn to her, intrigued by her, this attraction loaded with a feeling of protectiveness that I couldn't adequately explain.

Liam was talking to her now. He had to kneel down to do so, though his gangly frame still managed to dwarf her. It was only then that I noticed she had been crying – her mascara was smudged, and her eyes were puffy. Liam produced a packet of cigarettes, and she took one. When Liam lit it for her and she took a drag, it made her immediately older, as if she'd seen everything and was just taking a minute to contemplate the weight of it all.

Hal called me over to the hi-fi and the collection of records in a rack beside it. He drew my attention to vinyl copies of *Psychocandy, Hatful of Hollow* and *Bossanova,* and I soon got drawn into a conversation with some of the others, though I was still distracted by what was going on by the fire. Liam came over in a little while, quite drunk and with a little swagger, puffing on his cigarette. He said something to one of the others and there was loud laughter. Then he must have caught me looking over towards the fire.

"That's my sister, Sammy," he said.

"Oh, right. Is she ok?" I said.

"She's a little upset. Think she had a bust-up with her boyfriend or something, I don't know. Not sure what she gets up to these days."

"Does she live here?"

"Nah, she lives with Mum. Their place is just nearby. I'm guessing she wanted some time to herself." He pulled a face. "Bad luck, eh?" He went back to mucking around with the rest of the group.

Sammy was staring into the fire, still smoking her cigarette, lost in thought and totally unconnected to what was going on around her.

I walked over to where she was sitting, gazing at the flames.

"Hi," I said.

She turned and looked up at me. To her, I was probably just this odd-looking stranger, towering over her in my black great coat, a glass of wine in my hand. Probably swaying a little. I should have known better.

"Hello," she said.

"I'm Stephen." I offered her my hand.

"Sammy," she said, taking my hand and shaking it slightly.

"Short for Samantha?" I offered, for want of anything better to say.

She nodded, with a slightly suspicious look.

"But don't ever call me that."

"I promise I won't."

The wary look on her face was lightened with a slight smile.

"Would you like a drink?" I said.

"I don't drink alcohol."

"Oh, sorry. I do."

"I figured that one out for myself." The smile was one of amusement now.

The Universal was playing. Melancholy, resigned and defiant – all at the same time.

"You should sit down," she said.

"You could be right," I said.

I sat down on the floor beside her chair. As I did so, Sammy got up out of the chair and I thought that she'd sucker-punched me and was going to walk off.

"It's getting hot in here," she said, and took off her coat. She was wearing tight, faded, blue jeans and a grey, moleskin waistcoat, with a white blouse underneath. On the waistcoat, there was a brooch that caught my eye immediately. It was in a grey metal setting, shaped like a stylised hand, which clasped a dark purple stone.

"That's really unusual," I said, nodding towards it.

She glanced down at the brooch, then back at me.

"It's my soul," she said.

I laughed uncomfortably, not sure whether she was joking.

"That's not your soul," I said.

"Yes, it is," she said, firmly.

I was brought up as a Roman Catholic and, when I was a kid, I had a real faith, even during my teenage years. I thought about it a lot – it was not an unquestioning belief, but it was deeply held, nevertheless. I carried on practicing, attending Mass, and taking the sacraments, until my early twenties but, once I left home and moved to London, I soon stopped going. However, once a Catholic, always a Catholic, as they say – you can take the boy out of church, but you can never take the church out of the boy. I don't know whether there is a Higher Power and there is something in all of us – think of it as a spiritual ethernet port – which I've stopped using but it's there and I can get connected if I want. Let's call it 'plugging into the infinite'. Or maybe it's just habit, because the Church got me early enough and I'll always be their bitch. The bastards.

I remember, in infant school, there was this picture on the wall in one of the classrooms. It was an illustration of two children, a boy and girl – very Janet and John. They were in a forest. It was an Eden-like scene, colourful, friendly, and serene and, true to form, from behind a tree came the devil – green, scaly and lizard-like – offering the two innocents a shiny red apple. The picture was entitled 'Temptation'. That little scene scared the willies out of me at that age and, if I was ever walking through a park, particularly on my own, I'd half expect Old Nick to pop out of the foliage with a big red apple, like the one the wicked stepmother offers Snow White in the Disney movie. That feeling has never totally left me. The world still seems a place where devils can jump out at you, souls can be lost, and miracles can happen. I've always been of a fanciful disposition, with an overactive imagination. Call it temperament or conditioning, I don't know. Perhaps it's a bit of both. Whatever it is, I've still retained an interest in religion and matters spiritual, ready to ask questions or argue the toss, depending on the situation.

The mention of the 'soul' though, specifically brought to mind a visit to my junior school by Father Healey, the parish priest of St Jude's, the local Catholic church. He drew a chalk circle on the blackboard. Think of this as the soul, he said.

The children in my class all stared, taking this in, processing the concept, offered to them by an adult whom they both respected and feared. A soul, there on the blackboard before them. Father Healey filled the circle in with white, leaving one space black. Original Sin, he said. Indelible, unshakeable. Ours at birth. God makes the difference, he continued. Faith and the sacraments and the death and resurrection of our Lord Jesus are the instruments of our salvation, unworthy as we are. He then covered up the black spot with white until there was what seemed like a crude representation of a communion wafer on the blackboard now. But when you sin, Father Healey said, and took the board rubber – another black spot, which gets bigger and bigger until it fills and poisons the soul. The only thing separating it, and indeed distinguishing it, from the overwhelming darkness that surrounds it, is its white chalk outline and, once this is wiped out, the soul and the darkness are one. The soul is lost, and the void has won.

Of course, even at that age I was aware that this was only a symbol – a visual metaphor for something that, if it does exist, is an unseen and unquantifiable essence, which animates the body and connects us to the Divine. I was taught that each person's soul is created by God at birth and that it is immortal – it is incorporeal and does not perish with the body after death. It is the element of a person which is most especially in God's image, and which signifies the spiritual principle in human beings. Regardless of my spiritual beliefs and how substantial or otherwise they might be at any time, it was the concept of the soul, of that spiritual element in each of us, that I had never lost. All of this, combined with my advanced level of intoxication at that point, was what Sammy and her brooch had let out of the box.

"You mean that this is a symbol of your soul, or your spiritual life?" I said.

"No. It really is my soul."

I took a deep breath.

"The soul, if any of us has one, is an imperishable thing, invisible and intangible."

"Well, you may believe that. It's ok. A bit medieval but ok."

"Who gave it to you, then?"

"A good friend."

"Not God though?"

She gave me a sour look.

"No. Not God."

"So how was it his to give, this good friend of yours?"

"It was a gift. He knew that I was ready for it, that I'd reached a level of understanding and it was the right time. It was also to act as an inspiration for me."

Her face, as she was saying this, changed. Her expression, the tone of her voice, became quite different. Her voice deepened and each word was spoken deliberately, as though every syllable contained a revelation, and she expressed herself with a child's conviction that what she had been told was true.

"How could this person be qualified to decide all this?" I said.

"He's very insightful. He receives wisdom all the time. The depth of his knowledge, his understanding, is awesome. I've learnt so much from him."

I was drunk enough to see what was floating about in the air and sober enough to grasp it before it flew away. It doesn't happen very often but there is an insight that sometimes comes from inebriation, occasionally turning us into the alcoholic equivalent of idiot savants.

"Is this the guy you had the argument with?"

She registered some surprise, then narrowed her eyes, perhaps trying to figure out where I was coming from.

"Who told you that?"

"Your brother. He said you'd had an argument with your boyfriend and that you were upset."

She took a deep breath and looked at me again. She could have told me to fuck off, that it wasn't any of my business. She could have decided that I was being a pain in the arse, got up and walked off. Instead, she chose to explain it all to me. Very earnestly.

"It wasn't really an argument," she said. "More of a disagreement. I was misguided, thought I knew better. I can be wilful sometimes. He is just concerned about me. He wanted to get me back on the path."

I nodded. I couldn't come back from that.

"And he's not my boyfriend," she added.

"Right."

"Our relationship is on another level. It's very intense. He loves me, I know he does. But in a special way. You wouldn't understand."

"Probably not," I said, feeling I'd gone too far. "I'm sorry if I hurt your feelings."

She shook her head and looked into the fireplace again for a few moments. Then she turned to me again.

"So, you came over to talk to me because Liam said I was upset."

"Yes," I said.

"You wanted to cheer me up, then?"

I nodded.

"Very unorthodox way of doing it. Please tell me that you don't do counselling or work for the Samaritans or anything like that."

"No, I don't. Never thought of it before actually, but now you mention it…"

"You're funny," she said.

I nodded. "So, can I really not get you a drink?"

"No, I don't drink alcohol. Really. It's a religious thing. I don't eat meat either."

"Not even fish?"

"No. Not even fish."

"It's ok, you know," I said. "They don't have any feelings."

We carried on talking like that for a while, about a lot of other stuff too. Sometimes she was enthusiastic and engaged, eager to learn and to be involved. Other times, when that sadness became apparent again, she seemed world-weary and disheartened. Either way, she was getting under my skin.

Liam changed the CD. He put on a Madness greatest hits compilation and wandered around the room, getting everybody up to dance.

"Come on, you two," he said to Sammy and me.

We all got up and did a tipsy approximation of the Nutty Boy Walk around the room to *The Prince*. The dancing and chat continued for a while longer and, somewhere amongst it, Sammy left. There was little warning. She was just standing there, with her coat on again, lifting her hand in a wave and, with the slightest of smiles, said, "Bye" and was gone.

My enthusiasm must have left with her because I suddenly felt very down. The music and chat continued but I soon found myself wandering out of the room, ostensibly to get some more wine. I did pour myself another glass, then loitered in the cramped hall. There was a telephone table just to the left of the entrance to the kitchen. On the wall above it was a black and white framed photograph. It was of Sammy – aged nine or ten, I would guess. I stared at it for a long time, studying every detail. Her face – pretty and full of fun, with a mischievous smile just breaking through. It was so fresh and natural that I half expected it to speak or burst into laughter at any moment. There was a little stool, pushed under the table. I pulled it out and sat down, still looking at the photograph, waiting for it to say something to me. Then I thought of Jane.

She'd crossed my mind a few times that evening, earlier on while I was still mad at her. I'd pushed those thoughts away and then, as the night went on and I'd had more to drink, they didn't have any chance of coming back. Now, she was there in my head, and I felt ashamed, as if I'd forsaken her. What the fuck was I doing here? What had I been thinking? I reached into the pocket where I normally keep my mobile phone, but it wasn't there. I searched through the other pockets. Of course, I'd left it at home – when I'd called Jane on the way to meet her, I'd had to use a phone booth at the station. I picked up the phone on the table and dialled home. It rang for ages but no answer. I tried Jane's mobile but again she didn't pick up. She must still be mad at me – I wouldn't have blamed her if she was. I looked at my watch. It was two in the morning. I wouldn't be able to get a bus up to Hammersmith now. I looked out of the window – it was snowing heavily. I suddenly felt very tired and hopelessly lost. I went back to the table and sat for a while longer. There was a pencil by the phone. I picked it up. It had no point. I sat there, weary, and close to tears, as the music and laughter continued in the other room.

CHAPTER FOURTEEN

I woke up in the morning on the chair by the fireplace, my big coat draped over me. The fire had long gone out and it was pretty cold. Everyone else had gone, apart from Hal, who was sprawled out on the sofa. I assume that Liam was asleep in his own room upstairs. I got up and gave Hal a shake. The kitchen was a mess, but I managed to rustle up a cup of tea for each of us, while he was rousing himself. We drank our tea quickly and stepped outside. It was white all over and the snow was a couple of inches deep. We trudged over the Common. The duck pond had frozen over a little and the trees were glazed with ice. It was a beautiful scene, almost like a dream, though I suspect that both of us weren't as receptive to its wintry charm as we might otherwise have been.

We waited a while for a bus then sat in virtual silence as we travelled up to Hammersmith. We parted company there, Hal taking the Piccadilly Line North, while I took the District Line to Embankment. The train was pretty much empty – it was still quite early. I took my harmonica out of my pocket – I tend to carry one with me everywhere – and played a little. A mournful blues wail – just how I felt. Plenty more music to face when I get home, I thought to myself, though the irony did nothing to cheer me. I changed trains at Embankment, heading south on the Bakerloo.

There wasn't as much snow in Lambeth, but it was still bloody freezing. After the long walk down Kennington Road, I stopped off at Nellie's Cabin and bought a Guardian. Stepping out into the cold again, I was overcome by a serious attack of the munchies. I hadn't eaten for ages, it seemed. I knew that we didn't have much stuff in so, if I wanted to eat something nice, I'd have to buy it. As it was, I really fancied a proper fry-up – eggs, bacon, mushrooms, and baked beans – the Full English. With this tantalising thought in mind, it was my misfortune to be looking at a mini market over the road that called itself Round the Clock. My heart sank. If only I'd felt hungry a quarter an hour or so ago, I would have gone to Pinky's, near the tube station, and been more or less certain of getting what I wanted. I could have walked back up the road and done so, I know, but it was baltic, and I was really tired. I held my breath for a few moments, then crossed the road.

Despite its name, Round the Clock was not always open and its hours of business were never easy to determine. I could see that there were lights on now, giving off a friendly and reassuring message. I could also see the sign by the door which read: "Here for you, when you need us", but this was no guarantee that, when I got to the door and pushed, it would give way and I'd find myself inside. It could all be a diabolical trick.

If that sounds paranoid, it's probably because I am – you must have picked that up by now. In this case, though, such a feeling was not unjustified. When Round the Clock had opened, a few months before, I'd been quite pleased. As fond as I was of Pinky and his establishment, as much as I knew and liked what he stocked, and as consistent as his opening hours might be, having a store virtually around the corner where you could pick up staples when you ran out unexpectedly was not to be sniffed at. As it turned out, such promise faded into thin air once I actually tried to use the place.

My first visit had been to get some potatoes for tea. I had stepped inside and looked for any vegetables that might be in stock but could find none. There was nobody around to ask so I had a little browse, making a mental note of what they had on offer. It was just a small space but, apart from a chilled section, which contained the usual things like milk, cheese, butter, margarine and yoghurt, and a small fridge, stocked with cans of beer, there wasn't much else that jumped out at me. What else I could see seemed packed in shelves in one corner and wasn't arranged in any discernible order. Apart from that, there were some sweets, chocolate, and crisps on display near the till and shelves with bottles of wine and spirits behind the counter, mostly of a very cheap brand, yet still overpriced. After a few minutes, a man appeared from a door at the back. Tall and rangy, with a half-smile on his lips and a wary look in his eyes.

"Alright, mate?" he said.

"Not so bad," I said. "Don't you do vegetables?"

He seemed slightly taken aback by this question at first – as reasonable as it seemed to me – then swiftly regained his composure.

"No, not really," he said.

"Not really?" I responded.

"Well, we've got a few in the back but not much. What do

you want?"

"Potatoes."

"No sorry, don't have any potatoes."

"What do you have then, in the way of vegetables?"

"Depends on what you want."

"I want potatoes."

"We don't have any."

"Yeah, I know, but it might be nice to know what you do have, for future reference."

He squinted at me for a moment, probably working out if I was taking the piss, and whether or not it was worth telling me to get lost or maybe even giving me a slap.

"Look, mate, just give me the name of a vegetable and I'll tell you if we've got it."

It took a little while to focus my mind – it was like one of those quizzes where you have 60 seconds to name as many things as you can from a particular category – US states, British prime ministers, breeds of dog, whatever. This is always harder than you think.

"Carrots?" I offered.

"No," he said.

"Onions?"

"No."

"Broccoli?"

"No, mate."

"Mushrooms?"

"Sorry, no."

"Brussels sprouts."

"Don't have them."

"Cauliflower?"

"'Fraid not."

"Turnips?"

He shook his head. We stood there, looking at each other for a little while.

"So, what kind of vegetables do you have?" I said, somewhat exasperated.

"It's difficult to tell, mate. We get some in every now and then. The odd one, like. Hard to know what we've got in at any one time. I do know that we don't have the ones you mentioned, though."

I nodded slowly.

"Fair enough," I said, at last. "Thanks for your help, anyway."

I turned and headed for the door.

"No probs," I heard him say as I left.

I recounted this tale to Jane and the other residents of the Place, though I must admit with an increasing amount of embellishment each time it was retold. What exotic vegetables did they stock there, we asked ourselves? What could they possibly be? Chinese water spinach? Japanese bunching onion? Amaranth? Mung beans? Wax gourd? Or was it all just a front – a mundane façade for some kind of heinous enterprise being undertaken here, under our very noses, in sleepy Lambeth? The mind boggled and kept on doing so, indefinitely. I certainly had fun imagining what was going on in there, so I was drawn to the shop on further occasions, just to see if any more absurdity could be had. The next time I tried it, to get some milk, the man behind the counter (a different one) told me that they hadn't had a delivery that day. They'd been let down, he said. On another occasion they had no coffee or tea. And then there was the time that they didn't have any toilet rolls. The next time they were just shut, in the middle of a weekday and for no apparent reason. And so, we dubbed it 'The Inconvenience Store' – a place on which you could absolutely not depend, any time of the day or any day of the week.

On that cold and snowy morning though, and despite all of the aforementioned shenanigans, I found myself pushing open the door of Round the Clock and stepping inside. The place was empty, though there was music playing not very loudly from a speaker fixed high up on one wall – *Midnight at the Oasis* by Maria Muldaur, as it happens, which never fails to make me smile. I made my way to the chilled section and saw to my astonishment that there was bacon and sausages. There was even black pudding. The gods were looking down on me favourably and, on top of that, Maria was offering to be my belly dancer, if I would be her sheik, which sounded like a pretty good deal to me. I searched around the randomly arranged goods on the shelves in the corner and found a box of half a dozen eggs. There were a few cans of baked beans too – of an obscure brand and obscenely over-priced, but I took one anyway. The bread selection was fairly pitiful – I picked up a small white Weight Watchers loaf and counted myself extremely fortunate. Mushrooms were never really a starter, of course, but an (almost) Full English was a result beyond my wildest expectations.

There was, however, still no sign of anyone to take my money and complete the transaction. The door at the back of the shop was closed so I walked up to it and knocked. I waited for a while but nothing happened. I knocked again – still nothing. I reached for the knob and turned it. It was locked.

You can perhaps appreciate my dilemma. Whatever else I may be, I would consider myself an honest person. Although this was one of those occasions where that honesty was being sorely tested, my deep reserve of Roman Catholic guilt, combined with the very obvious security camera hanging from the ceiling in one corner, were enough to keep me on the straight and narrow. I knocked at the door again but, after a few minutes of waiting, I knew that the smiles on the faces of the gods were not as benevolent as they had seemed, and that good fortune had metamorphosed into some kind of sick cosmic joke. I considered leaving enough money on the counter along with a note explaining my actions, which I would make sure were slowly and clearly demonstrated for the security camera's benefit. I worked out that the stuff in my hands was going to cost four pounds and ninety-five pence then reached into my pocket. I had little or no change and a ten-pound note. *Hotel California*, by the Eagles, was now playing in the shop. I looked up at the camera and sighed.

"If I had any bacon, I'd have bacon and eggs." I said out loud. "If I had any eggs."

I put everything back where it had come from and left.

When I got home, the place was quiet. Banana and Louie came to greet me, both of them rubbing against my legs and getting under my feet. They were very hungry, I could tell. I popped my head around our bedroom door, but the bed was empty. It didn't look as if it had been slept in.

"Janie," I called, but there was no answer. As I was feeding the cats in the kitchen, there was a knock at the door. When I stepped back into the passageway to answer it, I saw a piece of paper, on the floor by the door, which I'd missed on the way in, most probably distracted by the cats' attention.

I picked it up and opened the door. It was Lydia, looking tired and anxious, her eyes a little wild.

"I saw you pass by our window. Where've you been, Stephen?"

"Sorry, I've..."

"Did you get my note?" she said, cutting me off.

"Just got it now." I showed her the crumpled paper in my hand that I hadn't yet had the chance to read. "What's going on? Has something happened to Grace?"

"No, it's Jane. She's had an accident, Stephen. She's in hospital."

As Lydia drove me up to St Mary's in her car, I was still struggling to fully take in what I'd been told.

When Jane had knocked off work the previous evening, she'd obviously had a similar idea to me and gone off with a couple of friends for a few drinks, at a pub near the hospital. Probably avoiding me as much as I was her. She'd left the bar, said goodbye to her mates, and headed for the tube station. It had been snowing and it was a little icy under foot. At that point, a car coming along Praed Street had skidded onto the pavement and hit her, sending her over the bonnet and a few feet up into the air. That shitty piece of luck was only balanced out by the fact that she was just a few yards away from the accident and emergency department, where she worked. I'll let you work out whether that was good fortune or poetic irony. I was too tired and numb to have an opinion one way or another at that moment. To tell you the truth, I'm still not sure.

Lydia had been quite short with me at first, probably just the nurse in her, very efficient and matter-of-fact, though it felt as if she was having a go at the time. Two policemen had turned up late the previous night, banging on our door and, when they'd got no response, they'd tried some of the neighbours. Lydia and Tom had been the first to answer. The police officers had filled them in on what had happened. They'd given the officers my mobile number but there was no response, so they'd asked Lydia and Tom to keep an eye out for me and let them know when I turned up.

Lydia asked me again where I'd been. I told her that Jane and I had argued, though not what it was about, and that I'd gone out with some friends and crashed at Hal's. Don't ask me why I bent the truth, it just seemed easier to tell it that way. She didn't push me any further on the matter. Neither of us had much else to say right then.

It was snowing heavily again. We got to the hospital and made our way up to the ward where Jane had been taken. Since Lydia worked there, she knew where to go and who to speak to. She was friendly with one of the nurses on duty.

Jane's parents had arrived. They'd driven in from St Alban's, where they lived, and were waiting in the visitors' room, having already had a chance to see Jane. Lydia said I should go and wait with them while she found out what was going on.

They were both sitting in silence when I stepped into the room. Jane's mother had been crying, I could see that, but she visibly pulled herself together when she saw me. It was not for my benefit.

"Hello, Stephen," said her husband.

"Hello John. Mary." I took a seat near them.

My relationship with Mr and Mrs Livingstone had never been exactly warm. Civil, perhaps, but never relaxed or spontaneous. They could never figure out what their precious daughter was doing with me. As far as they were concerned, I was a layabout, without a steady source of income or any prospects they could ascertain, and she could have done so much better. So, every time we were in the same room, the barriers went up, formality became a straitjacket and there was frost in the room, no matter how polite or stimulating the conversation might be. And it so often was. They were very intelligent people, with a wide range of interests and, believe it or not, I have my thoughtful and articulate moments too. But much as I might call them by their first names and eat dinner at their table, sharing a glass of (rather fine) wine with them in their lovely home, I still always thought of them as Mr and Mrs Livingstone.

They were both teachers, as I have mentioned – each of them retired now but what goes for Catholics goes for teachers too. They may have left the classroom, but the class-room had never left them. And if the police brought out the guilty person in me, you might guess that teachers brought out the stroppy schoolboy – maybe they weren't the only ones who hadn't managed to leave the classroom. I used to have a recurring dream where I would be back at my secondary school. I was as I am now, grown up, but I was still in my school uniform and wandered around, trying to find the room where my next lesson was to take place, but never quite making it. I'd encounter many strange things on the way, but I'd never find the room I was supposed to be in. There would also be rumours of an exam or test that I was to sit imminently and, of course, I hadn't revised for it. Then the day would end, and the school buses would come to take us home but, once again, I'd never find one that was going to where I lived. It always seemed to fade at that point and then it would be the start of a new day and school would begin again – my own personal Groundhog Day. I never got to go home. I stayed at school, but never learned anything. I once wrote a song, based on this dream, called *The School Bell Never Stops Ringing*. It wasn't a very good song – I never could capture that dream, the way it made me feel, in words or music.

"Where were you, Stephen?" Jane's mother asked.

People kept asking me that question. They really didn't need to – I was already asking it of myself, over and over again. I gave Mr Livingstone the same, half-false/half-true answer that I'd given Lydia. Maybe I was trying to make myself believe it had really happened that way. Maybe I wanted to convince myself that the Hammersmith pub crawl and the party back at Liam's house had been a dream. Sammy too.

"I'm sorry," I said.

"It wasn't your fault," said Jane's mother. I'm not sure if she really meant it, but it didn't matter. I didn't believe it myself anyway.

A doctor came in after a little while to talk about Jane's condition. She was lucky to be alive, he said, considering the force of the car when it hit her. In fact, the really amazing thing was that there had been no bones broken. There were some cuts and bruising but nothing serious, in that respect. She had suffered severe head trauma – how severe they could not currently determine; they would have to carry out further tests. She had not regained consciousness. She was stable and breathing on her own, without need of a respirator, but it was again difficult to say how long she would be in this comatose state. Jane's parents asked some questions to which he gave answers and offered some technical explanations that seemed to satisfy them. That new knowledge somehow managed to comfort them, to offer some floating wreckage that they could grab hold of and keep afloat, even though they were still in the middle of the ocean, far from land or help. I didn't really take much of it in and I cannot summarise it for you now. I'm sorry. Details again.

"Can I see her?" was my only question.

"That should be fine. Just for a little while, though."

He led me down a corridor to the Intensive Care Unit, which was more brightly lit and noisier than I would have expected. There was a nurse beside Jane's bed. She moved away to the nurse's station once I arrived, and the doctor joined her.

Jane seemed to be at peace, as if sleeping soundly. There was some bruising down the left side of her face and a cut above her right eyebrow but, despite this, the thing that impressed me was how normal she looked, how serene and in control of it all. It was strange to see her there, in that bed, being tended to rather than the other way around. It was still her natural environment, her patch. Janie in a hospital, not unusual at all. It was as if she'd had enough and decided to knock off for a while. To have a little rest, content that everything was being taken care of and she didn't need to worry.

They gave me ten minutes with her and then politely turfed me out, as Jane was off to have a CAT scan. I arrived back at the visitors' room, and the nurse brought in an extra chair. Mrs Livingstone started to cry, almost on cue, and her husband comforted her. Her parents talked to each other occasionally, almost in a whisper, but I couldn't make out what they were saying. I just kept thinking about the last time that Janie and I had been together, in this very building, and what we'd talked about, replaying our conversation again and again. You see, I had no problem remembering those particular details. Though, in another way, I did, since remembering them was in itself a problem, for these details hurt and tormented me. Jane and I rarely had arguments, so why did we have to have one then? Why couldn't we have made love the last time we'd been together, or had a nice meal or a jokey chat over a few glasses of wine? I tried to think of more positive things that had happened between us, but I couldn't, and all the while she was lying there, oblivious. She couldn't say anything to make it better. She couldn't say that she forgave me, tell me to forget it or make a Janie kind of comment, the sort of thing she'd say that would make me smile and realise that I was taking myself, and everything else, far too seriously.

She couldn't offer me that way out now.

The nurse came in and warned us that it might be a while before Jane was back on the ward so it might be a good idea to grab a coffee, get something to eat or some fresh air. We could come back later, we didn't need to worry about normal visiting hours for the time being, but we should give them an hour or so to do what they had to do.

Lydia was still waiting outside. She suggested that we go and get a cup of coffee or something, so I told Mr and Mrs Livingstone that I'd see them in a little while and left them in the visitor's room. I told Lydia that I'd rather not go to the hospital canteen. The place would just give me bad vibes and, besides, I needed to get some fresh air.

We went to a sandwich bar not too far from St Mary's. We both drank black coffee.

"How long is she going to be like that, Lydia?"

"It's difficult to tell. A coma can last anything from a few days to a few weeks, though they don't tend last to longer than that. There are exceptional cases where the patient remains in a coma for years. Sometimes the patient dies." She stopped and looked closely at me. "Sorry, Stephen, just tell me to shut up."

"It's ok. I want to know what we're dealing with," I said.

"It's the head trauma, that's the main problem, in Jane's case. But how long she's going to be unconscious depends on how serious the damage is, and they don't know that yet. It will also determine whether she'll have full physical and mental recovery. If she's had extensive neurological damage, that could complicate matters. She might still regain consciousness, but she may need therapy to get that functionality back. She may never get it back. She may go into a persistent vegetative state, where she could have some awareness and some basic body functions, but she won't be able to respond meaningfully to her environment." She paused for a moment, perhaps sensing that she was in serious danger of either losing me altogether or totally scaring the shit out of me. "We should wait and see what they say, though. For now, she's being well looked after, and they are monitoring her condition. The specialist who's dealing with her is one of the best in the field."

"Thanks, Lydia," I said. "Thanks for everything."

"You know that it's no bother."

"How's Gracie?" I asked.

"Oh, she's fine. She was a little shaky for a while after that day you found Frank, but she's pretty much back to normal. She plays that harmonica you gave her all the time."

"That's good. Perhaps it means she's thinking about me."

"Perhaps it does," she said quietly, taking a sip of her coffee.

I told Lydia to get herself home. She seemed reluctant but I insisted that I'd be alright. She said that she'd be on duty later on that day anyway, so she'd pop in and make sure I was ok, if I was still there.

I hung around the ward for the rest of the day, sitting with Jane for long stretches. Her parents and I had to take turns, as only two visitors could sit with her at one time. We were still pussyfooting around each other. As always, it felt as if they couldn't have their normal relationship with Jane when I was around, and vice versa. We were still competing for her attention, even though, right now, she didn't have any to give.

They left a little sooner than me since they had a bit of a drive to get home.

"I think we're alone now," I sang softly, once they'd gone. Then the tears started to come, lots of them – I felt free to let them out now. I lay my head on the bed, by Jane's side, and started to sob. It wasn't just for her, I knew that. It felt as if I'd been saving it up, carrying it around with me for a long time. I wondered how I'd managed to get by, talk and function, with all that inside. I was glad to be getting rid of some of it, though I knew that there'd still be some left over, to rattle around inside me.

I must have dozed off like that. A nurse gave me a little shake and told me that I really should go home and get some rest. They would be in touch if Jane's condition changed but, at the moment, she was stable.

I got the tube home. The cats needed feeding, but they didn't get much attention other than that. I was exhausted. I managed to get my coat and shoes off, found my bed and was soon dead to the world.

CHAPTER FIFTEEN

I slept until lunchtime the next day and woke up disorientated. It took a few moments before I realised that it had not all been a terrible dream and that Janie was very much in a coma, that I didn't know if she was still alive and that I'd wasted half the day sleeping. The cats had been fussing around me for a while and that had finally brought me around. The phone had obviously rung a few times too – there were messages on the answering machine – and I dreaded the possibility that I'd missed an important call from the hospital. As it was, the only recent messages were from neighbours – Michael and a couple of others, asking how Janie was and how I was doing. There was also one from the police, telling me to contact them as soon as I could. And there was one from Jane, at around nine o'clock the previous evening:

"Hi. Just ringing to tell you that I'm going for a drink with Liz and Debbie so I'll be late home. Guess you're out too or else you don't want to speak to me." There was a pause, and a slight sigh. "See you later."

She sounded tired. There was little emotion in her voice, certainly not enough to give anything away. I checked the call register. There'd been another call from Jane's mobile later on, but no message. I remembered my phone. Where the hell was it? I rang my number from the house phone and heard my ringtone.

It had managed to find its way under the sofa. I checked my messages. There was a missed call from Jane, around eleven o'clock:

"I'm on my way back. Don't know where you are but just come home. You don't need to avoid me. I'm too tired to fight anyway."

And that was it. I had one text message, but it was nothing. I flicked through some old ones, though, and found the one she'd sent me, God, what seemed a lifetime ago:

'Hi honey. Still sore? I'm not surprised :) x'

I sat there for a long time, unable to move. When I finally managed to get up, I fixed myself a cup of tea and made a few phone calls to let everyone know what was going on. When I took a shower, her lipstick kiss was there on the glass. It had been there for a while, of course, but I'd stopped noticing it. Not today, though. She was all around me, even in her absence.

I skipped breakfast – there wasn't much in to eat, and I doubted I could stomach any food just then. I got dressed quickly and headed out to visit Jane. When I turned onto Kennington Road, I saw him. He was sitting on his bike, in front of the Kool Kod Fish and Chip Shop. I made my way across the road towards him. He didn't have his helmet on – it was perched on one of the handgrips – and he was eating chips out of a polystyrene tray with his fingers. He ate them slowly, seemingly deep in thought, as if pondering on every bite. His radio was on, though music was playing this time rather than the usual weird messages. It sounded like a Buddy Holly record. Or, at least, it sounded like Buddy Holly singing, though the song was unfamiliar and contemporary in feel.

As I approached his bike, he looked at me, no longer lost in his thoughts.

"Alright?" he said.

"Yes," I said, not wanting to go into detail. "And you?"

"Never better. Would you like a chip?" He offered the tray to me.

"No thanks," I said.

He shrugged. "Your loss, my friend. There's nothing like a really good bag of chips and these are just about perfect."

He picked a chip up and held it in front of him, between his right thumb and index finger.

"Look at the colour. Golden brown."

He bit it in half.

"A slight crispness on the outside so you get just that touch of resistance when you bite into it."

He held it up again. Steam was coming from the now exposed inside.

"And yet, the inside needs to be white, soft and fluffy. Exactly like that."

He put it into his mouth.

"You know," he continued, "I get around a lot. I've stopped at loads of chippies all over London and the rest of the country – wherever – and this is one of the best, believe me. It's an art, my friend, and your man in there, by the fryer, is a true artist. Right on your doorstep, too. You're a lucky man."

"Really?" I said, with undiluted scepticism.

"Yes, mate. Really."

I was in a hurry and every fibre of my body was telling me to cut this conversation short, but Buddy Holly kept singing on the radio, transmitting from God-knows-where, and this strange biker and the mystery of his non-existent company were proving too intriguing to resist.

"How's business?" I asked.

"Ticking over nicely at the moment. Can't complain."

"That's pretty good, considering that your company isn't in the phone book and there's no trace of you on the internet," I said.

"And you looked, did you?"

"Yes, I did. It's almost as if you didn't exist."

"Well, obviously that's not the case, since I'm sitting here in front of you, enjoying these fine chips and shooting the breeze."

"You know that's not what I meant."

"Well, then, you'll just have to take my word for it, won't you? All I can say is that we're doing pretty well. We get a lot of business by word of mouth, and we've got a few big clients that keep us busy."

"You're a local firm?"

"No, we're pretty much a global concern."

"Global. And yet there's no trace of you?"

"Well, you keep saying that mate, but maybe you're not looking in the right places."

His radio was now playing another Buddy Holly track, though this time it seemed to be a cover of Dylan's *Subterranean Homesick Blues*, a slinky rockabilly version with a ghostly echo on the vocals – very similar in feel to his take on *Slippin' and Slidin'*. It was fabulous, though totally impossible. Holly died in 1959. Dylan's original wasn't recorded until 1965.

"What the fuck is this?" I asked, with barely concealed bewilderment.

"I'm not a big music fan but it sounds like Buddy Holly to me."

"Must be a hoax. Or a weird covers band, like that group that does Led Zeppelin songs with an Elvis impersonator singing the lead."

"If you say so, mate."

"What is this station, anyway?"

"A foreign channel, I think. It's the only one that this radio picks up. It's not really designed to get music stations, mind – must just be on a weird frequency that my set can tune into."

He switched channels and I heard the familiar croak of his controller:

"...lost in the forest with Red Riding Hood, not far from the Marzipan House."

He spoke into the radio. "What's that, boss?"

"You need to get moving. The crows are circling."

"Copy that. I'm on the road now."

He put on his helmet.

"What the hell is he talking about?" I said.

"We have our own code."

"Code?"

"You know, company jargon. Plus, he likes to mess around a little, you know. Deep down, I think the man has the soul of a poet. We kind of humour him."

He started the bike.

"See you, man."

As he pulled away, I caught a snatch of the voice on the radio again.

"...and give our regards to Sleeping Beauty."

I got a shiver down my spine. You know, the kind you get when people say that someone's walked over your grave, though this was an even weirder feeling than that. Like having your pocket picked while someone is giving you a blow job, and you're trying very hard not to sneeze.

Maybe I was just imagining things – my paranoia getting the best of me, not for the first time. The reception on that radio was so bad that the guy could have been saying anything. My ears were probably playing tricks. It was just the whole set-up. Who was that guy, and what was he delivering? What was he picking up?

CHAPTER SIXTEEN

I couldn't get up to Paddington quickly enough. My stomach churned all the way, my mind going round and round in circles, thoughts chasing their own tail. I don't know what I imagined was going to happen, just a general feeling of dread. That 'Sleeping Beauty' reference had well and truly spooked me.

It occurred to me then that I hadn't mentioned the despatch rider to the police after Frank's death. When they had asked me if there was anything I thought might be relevant, the biker had completely slipped my mind. I don't know why that had happened; it was certainly something that I should have told them. After all, he'd called at mine with a parcel for Frank, but he'd neglected to knock on his door, maybe because I was watching him at the time. But why would that make a difference to him if he really had something to deliver? That would be considered curious behaviour, even under normal circumstances but, given that the person he was supposed to be delivering to had died the next day, it must now surely qualify as nothing less than suspicious. Anyway, curious or suspicious, that's the sort of thing that the police like to know. Need to know. It might mean nothing, but you're still supposed to tell them stuff like that, and I had neglected to do so. See, I said it slipped my mind at first, now I'm talking about neglect. It may have been the shock, of course, but I think that I was a little embarrassed. I mean, what would I be implying? I found Frank. Whatever had happened to him – and I hadn't yet heard a satisfactory explanation for that from anyone – was some kind of horrible freak occurrence. I saw the aftermath, the terrible fucking mess. You couldn't plan that. Or actually execute it. Could you?

When I got to the hospital, Janie was in bed, where I'd left her, and remained stable, the duty nurse said. Still in a coma, of course, so any sense of relief was somewhat qualified. I had a word with the doctor. They were still not entirely sure about Jane's condition. It was proving to be difficult to ascertain her precise neurological status. There had been head trauma – the coma was the proof of that – but the nature of the possible damage was proving elusive. There would be more tests, including a further scan, which she was to have later that day.

I went and sat with her. The doctor had said that it was often a good idea to talk to someone who was comatose. I asked if she could hear me. He said that nobody knew for sure, but that it was reckoned to be beneficial. It could certainly do no harm.

So, I sat by Jane's bed, held her hand, and talked to her.

"Hi, Janie," I said. "I don't really know what to say to you, pet. I know you always tell me that I love the sound of my own voice – and you may be right – but you normally manage to stop me before I ramble on too long. Keep me on track, too. Now it's just my voice that I can hear, it's hard to find words that mean anything. I do want to say that I'm sorry though, that's for sure. Sorry that we argued. Sorry that you're here, like this. I'd give anything for you to be awake, for me to be able to take you home. I'd tell you that I want to have a child with you. Not just to be saying it, but because it's true. But saying it now makes me feel even more shitty because it seems like too little too late. I don't even know if you can hear me, or whether you would be able to respond to my words if you could hear them. I miss you, baby. I miss you very much. Nana and Louie miss you too. They didn't get much attention from me last night – poor little buggers must feel like orphans. Please come back. Please come back to me."

It was the closest I'd come to prayer for a long time. That was what it felt like though, and it seemed to require as much faith. Maybe even more.

My life took a new shape, determined by the lines of my journeys to and from the hospital, to see Jane. She had her own room now – the doctors had decided that the neurological damage was not pervasive, but they were still unsure of how she would be when she regained consciousness. All they could do was watch and wait. That's the thing with comas, you can't really treat them. Jane was breathing on her own, keeping herself going quite happily, on a certain level. She just could not, or would not, wake up and smell the coffee.

Her parents were often there, of course, and other friends and relatives called in too. However, because of what you might call my flexible lifestyle, I could get there more often and so I still managed to get time alone with her. I got better at talking to her. It became a conversation, I just had to imagine what her end of it might be. Fill in the gaps.

I also started bringing my acoustic guitar in with me. The ward sister said it was ok, as long as I didn't play too loud. Janie always liked to hear me play and sing, and it was a lot easier than talking, especially when the words dried up.

The first thing I thought to play was pretty unavoidable. Jane had always been a big Smiths fan. She was actually an even bigger Morrissey fan, to be honest. She adored the man. But, of course, *Girlfriend in a Coma*, however strangely appropriate, was way beyond the bounds of taste. Besides, if overheard by the ward sister, I'm sure it would have resulted in my guitar being confiscated, perhaps even in my ejection from the building and a possible lifetime ban.

All Apologies was another possibility, and closer to what I wanted to say, but I decided that it was too maudlin, too down. I wanted to make her feel better, after all. Trouble is, many of my favourite songs over the years have been sad ones. These are the songs I like to listen to and the ones that I like to play. Maybe I'd have to learn some new tunes.

I decided to stick with songs that Janie knew and liked. Actually, when you're playing in an enclosed space and you're concerned with not making too much noise, that kind of dictates your choice of material, even with an acoustic guitar. Oh yes, those things might not be plugged in, but they can still make one hell of a racket in the wrong hands (or the right ones, depending on what you're after). So, it had to be more low-key stuff, or subdued versions of more strident material. It was an interesting problem to have. Jane would have interjected at this point and told me that I was overthinking again and that I should just get the

123

fuck on with it. Then she would have smiled in that way she has.

All of this was going through my head when I first sat down beside her, with my guitar in my lap. I was a little self-conscious anyway because of the whole situation, not wanting to disturb the neighbours and all. I heard Janie in my head, telling me to get a move on, then smiling at me. It was real, or rather my own version of real, my own personal Memorex recording. But then I looked at Jane lying there, not talking or smiling, and I knew that it was an artist's impression. Like one of those court room sketches you see on the news, because they aren't allowed cameras in there. Is this all I had – all I'd ever have? It was made even worse by the fact that the real thing was still here, she just wasn't herself – maybe she never would be again. I had and I didn't have her. I'd lost her, only she was still here. I started to cry. Not sobbing uncontrollably, as I had done earlier on, but tears flowing, nevertheless. A nurse popped her head around the door. Her name was Amy, and she had just started at St Mary's recently. She was Chinese, I would think, in her early twenties and with a kind, open face.

"You alright?" she said.

"Yes, thanks. Just having a little wobble. This is beyond weird – this, you know, situation. It's taking some getting used to."

She nodded.

"You going to give us a tune, then?" she said.

"Might do." I said. "Having trouble figuring out what to play."

"Do you know that song, *Help Me Make It Through the Night*?"

"I do indeed."

"I really like that one," Amy said, smiling as she walked away.

I nodded to myself. I can do requests, I thought. I started to play the song. I'd never really played it before, but I could pretty much remember the words and the chords weren't too difficult to figure out. A Kris Kristofferson tune – big on emotion and lyrically poetic but simple in structure. I felt my way into it, gradually picking it up as I went along. Improvising. Filling in those bloody gaps once again. I had to customise it anyway. I usually play with a plectrum, but I figured that would be too loud, so I just strummed softly with my fingers, playing the chord but dampening the sound with the heel of my hand. And I had to sing it softly too, which makes you concentrate more on the words, their weight and meaning. It was a bit like making love in a room where other people are sleeping, or trying to sleep, and you don't want them to know what you're doing. You have to rethink the whole way you go about it and either just stick to the basics or be subtler and more intuitive.

That song liberated me. I realised then that I could adapt a lot of songs to that kind of treatment and just free associate, going where the mood took me. I also stopped agonising over whether a song was appropriate or not. I never worried about crossing the line and so, strangely enough, I never did. Which isn't generally the case in life. As I was heading off to get a coffee later on, I passed Amy in the corridor. She smiled and gave me the thumbs up. Sometimes that's all you need.

CHAPTER SEVENTEEN

The next couple of weeks flew by. I seemed to exist in a kind of artificial state. A parallel world. While the rest of London got on with their business, I appeared to move through a different space. Though it was nominally represented by the same map, the experience, the perspective, was very different. I had always felt apart from the normal run of things anyway, even in London. Even, to some extent, in my beloved Strangelove Place, my adopted home, my refuge. But now, I felt totally dislocated and adrift. Like that episode of *Star Trek*, where Captain Kirk is caught in a state of hyper-acceleration, and is moving so fast that the other members of the crew can't actually see him.

But I did have a purpose. I needed to be there for Janie. Truth is, I was still slightly spooked about that 'Sleeping Beauty' remark – the message from the despatch rider's crazy radio. That paranoia had never entirely left me, and I still had the vague feeling that something terrible was going to happen to her, even worse than had happened to her already. I knew that I couldn't be there all the time – I couldn't sit at the entrance with a shotgun – but I did feel that, if I was visibly there, even for a part of each day, that presence would be enough. And I prayed. My conversations with Jane, one-sided at first, then two-way, with me colouring in her part of the picture, had increasingly begun to resemble a kind of prayer, so I naturally fell back into the real thing. Maybe my world had become too precarious of late. I couldn't be awake all the time. I couldn't control everything, there was too much going on. Too many balls to juggle. Too many entrances to guard. I needed back-up, so I asked God to be my wingman. I spoke to Him, confiding my fears and my wishes. In many ways, what I said in my prayers was the sort of stuff that I used to share with Janie. The silly things that she understood about me. The things that most people, even those I knew fairly well, would consider odd, but that Jane knew were just me being me. I don't know if God heard me. I wasn't even sure that He, She, or They were there. I prayed anyway. It made me feel better. Maybe that's all it ever does.

Although the staff on the ward didn't want me hanging around all day, getting under their feet, Jane working there still carried some weight and I was allowed to see her outside strict visiting hours, so I could have private time with her.

It was a Wednesday. I'd arrived as usual, took my coat off and got my guitar out of its bag. I settled in a chair beside her and tuned the guitar. It was like preparing for a gig. I suppose it was really – an intimate performance, with an audience of one. I even used to learn new songs especially, ones I thought she'd like. To surprise her.

I strummed a few chords, not entirely sure what I'd play. I found a sequence that I liked, that sounded cool, and played it for a while. Then it segued into something more familiar, and I found my groove.

I started to sing:

"Sweet Jane...sweet Jane..."

Music often operates like a time machine. A song can become associated in your mind with a person, a place, a particular event, even an emotion, or a set of emotions. Then, when that song is played, sometimes only the introduction, the opening chord, you're back there, where you heard that tune for the first time, or where it first acquired that specific meaning for you. I closed my eyes, and, for a moment, Jane was dancing around the room, naked, slowly covering herself up as I played and sang. I felt myself getting aroused. I opened my eyes, then stopped playing, feeling embarrassed, foolish. I didn't want to play anymore. I brushed a hand against Jane's cheek and, bending over, gave her a kiss on the forehead. I decided that I needed some fresh air. I propped my guitar up against the wall in one corner and left the room. Amy was at the desk with another nurse.

"Are you off, then?" she asked.

"No, just stretching my legs. I'll be back in a little while."

"It's just that we need to..."

"I'll take my time then."

I wandered down the stairs, then along a corridor on the next floor, then down another set of stairs, then another, the way I usually go to get out, I thought. I wasn't really thinking where I was going, I suppose. I just assumed that I knew the way. I walked along the corridor at the bottom of the stairs, then took a left turn, before I realised that this part of the hospital was not familiar to me. I double-backed, turned right and walked back up the corridor, looking for the stairs, but I couldn't find any. The place seemed deserted – no nurses or porters around. It was all very quiet. Maybe I had taken a wrong turn and gone totally off track. I went back down the corridor, trying to retrace my steps. When I finally found a set of stairs, they also went down. I didn't know where in the building I was now but, as I was heading for the ground floor, down seemed like the right direction.

The corridor at the bottom of the stairs was quiet too. There was a set of double doors, so I went through them and walked for a little while longer. For the first time, I noticed that I could hear a kind of pulse – a heavy throb around me, coming from the walls, the floor, I wasn't sure. Was this the basement? Where the hell was I?

Then I heard the music. An acoustic guitar, coming from somewhere down the corridor. A steady strum, keeping time with the throbbing of the building itself. I moved towards the sound of the guitar. It seemed to be closer now and I recognised the chords. It was *Sweet Jane*. Not just that tune but my version of it, my style of strumming. It was just like in the tube station, that really weird sensation again. Of being somehow in two places at once, outside myself. Exiled from my own body and unable to get back. I felt cold and clammy. I moved on towards the music. I turned another corner. The music was louder still, then it changed. It was another Velvets' song now – *Sister Ray*, intense and hypnotic. An orgy of noise, transvestites, sailors, and knife-fights. A journey to the end of the night; a season in Hell. I came to the end of the corridor. There was a door to the right and, through it, another staircase, going up this time, with the music somewhere at the top. I took the stairs. One flight. The music had stopped, as had the heavy pulse beat. I felt dizzy and it was difficult to breathe. There was an exit door, with a push bar across it. I barged my way out into the air, close to a panic attack. Once outside, I squatted on the ground, my head down, and took deep breaths. I did this for a while and looked up, my eyes still getting used to the bright light outside.

I was in an enclosed concrete space, like a car park, but there were no cars there. The only vehicle was a familiar motorcycle with an equally familiar rider. I was still getting my breath back, but I felt a wave of anger sweep over me. I stood up and staggered towards him, my head still spinning. He had his helmet off and was reading a book.

"What the fuck are you doing here?" I said, my voice harsh and a little shaky.

"And a good afternoon to you too," he said calmly. "I was passing by and fancied a breather. No law against it, last time I looked."

"Are you dropping off or picking up?"

"Neither, mate. Just told you, I'm having a break. You alright?"

"Not really. My girlfriend's in there." I made a gesture towards the hospital.

"Sorry to hear it, mate. Understand why you might be a little upset."

"You just leave her alone, you hear. Just stay the fuck away from her." I was slurring my words now.

"Calm down, man. I'm sure she's very nice, but I'm not going anywhere near her."

"You sure about that?"

"Absolutely fucking positive. I have no business in that building whatsoever."

He paused, perhaps waiting for the penny to drop.

"Scout's honour," he eventually added, making the appropriate sign.

I was never in the Scouts, so this carried no weight with me at all. The truth of the matter was that I didn't know who the hell this guy was and every encounter with him only muddied the water further.

"You'll give yourself an aneurism, you know," he said. "You need to chill."

"You might be right there. There was a time when I used to resist the urge to shout at strangers in car parks."

"Perhaps meditation might help. Yoga's good too, I've been told." He gave a wry smile. "Look, let me buy you a cup of coffee."

"What?"

"You know, coffee. The drink. There's an awful lot of it in Brazil, apparently. I know a nice little place not far from here. Rumour has it that they sell the stuff – it comes in a number of varieties, apparently."

"A café?"

"No, an opium den. What do you fucking think?"

He went to the top box on his bike and took out another helmet.

"Here you go, hot shot. We'll try some of this fucking fancy coffee shit. I hear a lot of people like it. Sounds a bit iffy, if you ask me but, what the hell, you're only born once."

I took the helmet. He put his on and started up the bike.

"Come on, man. It's ok, I'll bring you back here after-wards. In one piece."

I stood looking at him for a few seconds.

"Pinkie swear."

He held up his right hand, with the little finger raised and crooked.

"In Japan, it's called *yubikiri,* which means 'finger cut-off'. You know how serious the Japanese take their promises."

I sighed, shook my head slowly and put the helmet on. The biker smiled and I got on the back of the motorcycle.

"Hold on tight, mate. Don't be coy," he said.

I put my hands on his waist and we moved off.

We headed east along Praed Street, across Edgware Road and then up until we were on Marylebone Road, heading towards Kings Cross. Once past the station, he took a left and started to take various back streets, until I wasn't sure where we were.

The area we were going through seemed bleak and run down. There were a lot of boarded-up buildings that looked as if they'd once been shops. There wasn't anyone to be seen. The streets were empty, and the smell of smoke was in the air. We came to an arched door with bars on it and a heavy padlock. He stopped the bike and turned off the engine. I got off, removed my helmet and I walked over to the door. Through the bars, I could see a little of what was inside. It seemed to be full of department store mannequins, naked and in various states of dismemberment. I could also see items of furniture, including a grandfather clock, old-fashioned hat stands and what looked like an ancient radiogram. The floor was strewn with pages from old newspapers, yellowing and irrelevant.

"You ready, mate?" he said, from behind me. I turned and we headed along the pavement. There was a dingy little cab firm next door – Thurnand Taxis – and, next to that, a cafe with garish red paint work on the door frame and around its big window. The windows were steamed up and a little paper card on the glass of the door declared that it was open. The sign above the door read 'Montana Café'.

Inside it was small and cosy. The tables had yellow plastic

tops, with wooden chairs and red lino on the floor. It reminded me of an ice cream shop in my hometown, where my Mam used to take me when I was a kid. That shop isn't there anymore.

We moved over to the counter, and I looked around the room. There were three other customers in the Montana Cafe, sitting in one corner by the window. The one whose face I could see was an ageing rocker, dressed from top to toe in crumpled black leather, his curly black hair heavily greased up into a bedraggled quiff. He wasn't a very big guy and he sat on the chair a little uncomfortably, tapping one foot occasionally as he talked and took sips from his coffee cup. A shiny black cane was leaning against his chair.

The man sitting opposite him was also his opposite in just about every possible way. Stocky and broad-shouldered, a little awkward with it, this man was wearing a smart, brown suit and black tie, and had on a pair of dark sunglasses. He seemed almost too big for the chair, the table, perhaps the whole room. He occasionally gnawed at his fingernails as he talked – it was he who seemed to be talking most, in a soft voice, while the greaser occasionally drawled a reply. They were both speaking so softly, almost conspiratorially, that I couldn't hear what they were saying. Beside the greased-up rocker in black leather, sitting by the window, was a young man, with an immaculate blond quiff, leaning his elbows on the table and reading a book – *The Observer's Book of British Birds*, a really old copy. He was slim, pale, with movie star good looks, and was wearing a gold lame jacket. He seemed engrossed in his book, only looking up from it and offering a brief remark when one of the other two spoke to him.

The guy behind the counter was plump and unsmiling.

He had jet-black hair and a moustache – the hair slicked back, and the moustache neatly trimmed.

"Hey, man, how you doin'?" said the despatch rider.

The guy behind the counter shrugged. "Oh, you know," he said, wiping a cup with a blue-checked tea-towel.

"Certainly do, mate. Bit quiet, isn't it?"

"Has been all day. What can I get you?"

"A couple of coffees would be great."

"Anything to eat?"

"Not for me, thanks," the biker said. He looked over at me. I shook my head.

"Just the coffees, mate."

"No problem."

He turned to the big chrome machine behind him and set it gurgling, swishing, and steaming. The three men in the corner got up and made their way to the door. The leather-clad man had a bad limp and steadied himself with his cane as he moved across the room. The man in the dark-brown suit walked in front of him and I could see now that he was a burly man – built like a labourer, though this impression was undercut by the smartness of his clothes and a slight feminine daintiness to his gestures. His head was long and impassive, with a large, jutting jaw. Picking up the rear was the young blonde man, and I could now see that his trousers matched his jacket and the ensemble glittered in the café's fluorescent lighting as he walked towards us.

"See you, bud," the man in black leather said to the guy behind the counter. He had an American accent, with a definite Southern twang.

"Yeah. You take care," said our patron.

"All the best," said the burly, well-dressed man, his voice soft and with more than a trace of the West Country in it.

Their young companion nodded and held up his right hand briefly, the other holding his book. They left and the door closed behind them, leaving me doubting what I had seen.

The man put two frothy coffees on the counter and the biker paid him. We moved over to a table near the door.

"Did you see those guys that just left?" I said.

"Got a bit of glimpse. What of it?"

"They looked like Gene Vincent, Joe Meek and Billy Fury."

"You think so?"

"Spitting image. Didn't you see them?"

"Wasn't paying much attention, mate." He yawned. "It's been a long day."

He took a sip of his coffee.

"Do you come here very often, then?" I said.

"Yeah, when I'm over this way. It's usually a bit busier, though. You get some interesting types dropping in..."

"I get that."

"...bikers, other despatch riders," he said, casually. "Maybe cabbies from the firm next door. Other individuals who just pop in, don't know where they come from. I get a bit of banter, but I don't really pry. Can't give you their names and addresses, or fucking shoe sizes, anything like that, but you get the picture."

"I think you're selling the place short."

"What, were you hoping the bloody Blue Caps got in here sometimes as well? Or maybe Screaming Lord Fucking Sutch?"

"I don't know," I said, with a shrug. I took a sip from my cup.

"As I told you, long day," he said, with a sigh. "Didn't mean to jump down your throat like that, mate."

"Don't worry about it."

"Ok, I won't. Cheers." He lifted up his cup and I clicked mine against it.

"Cheers," I said.

"Your girlfriend," he said.

"What about her?"

"You said that she was in the hospital. She ok?"

"Not really. She had a bad accident. Got knocked down by a car. She's still unconscious. Don't know when she's going to wake up, or if she ever will."

"Tough break, man."

"And the rest."

"Shit happens," he said. "Lots of it. All the time."

He stared out of the window.

"You know, I still don't know your name." I said.

"You can call me Ace," he said.

"I'm Stephen."

"Good to know you, Stephen."

"You know that day you knocked on my door," I said after we'd sat for a while in silence.

"Yeah?"

"Why didn't you deliver to the house that you were looking for? Number six?"

"Turned out I'd got myself mixed up. It was another estate I wanted. I'd taken the address down wrong."

"How did you know from just looking at the door?"

"Just clicked."

"The guy who lived there died the next day."

"No shit?"

"Yes shit. It was really bad. I found him. Not really sure how it happened."

He looked at me thoughtfully for a moment, then smiled. A strange kind of smile.

"I'm getting the idea now," Ace said. "You think that I'm some kind of wandering assassin who arranges weird mishaps, extravagant deaths. I killed your neighbour. I tried to get your girlfriend and failed. Now, I'm hanging around the hospital, looking for an opportunity to finish the job."

I couldn't really think of an answer to that. I don't think I was going to be able to say either 'no' or 'not at all' with anything approaching conviction, so I didn't say anything.

"Why didn't you tell the police about me?" he said.

"How do you know I didn't?"

"Just guessing. But I'm pretty sure of it now."

I stayed quiet again.

"You done?" he said, pointing at my coffee cup.

I nodded. "Yeah, guess so."

"Fancy going for a ride?"

"Like where?"

"Like out of town. Open road. Fresh air. Blow the cobwebs away."

"I don't know," I said. "I should be getting back to the hospital."

"Well, I can see where you're coming from, but I would say by looking at you that maybe you're spending too much time in the hospital. I can understand that you want to be there for your girl, but I think she's in good hands, man, and you look like you need some kind of break. Respite, I think they call it."

I searched for a response for him, but it didn't come. I began to feel weary, and the words were too heavy. The thoughts and resolve got stuck inside and then faded away.

"Look, I've got a job out of town," he said. "It's not too far but it'll be a nice spot and a decent run. I'd really like you to come with me. A couple of hours and I'll bring you back and drop you off at the hospital."

"I don't know," I said. "I just don't know." The words came out of my mouth but seemed distant and foreign to me.

"Come on," he said. "Let's go."

We got up and made for the door.

"Thanks, man," said Ace to the man behind the counter.

"Cheers," I said.

"See you, boys," the man said.

Outside, he handed me the spare helmet and I put it on. We got on the bike, he started it up and we were away. I did not know if I really wanted to go with him, but I had not said 'no' and didn't have the energy to resist. I just seemed to be pulled along, caught in his slipstream.

The next half hour or so seemed to pass by in a blur, my thoughts jumbled and my head fuzzy. The streets of the city slipped away and the motorway sucked us forward towards our own personal vanishing point. I began to feel a little sick and held onto Ace tighter.

After a while, we left the motorway and instead took winding, leisurely country roads until we passed a sign that said 'Cookham'. Soon we were in a beautiful village that, apart from a few parked cars, seemed much as it must have been decades before. I could hear church bells from nearby but otherwise the place was quiet and the streets deserted. The bike passed along neat streets with neat cottages and neat little shops. It was all very quaint and picturesque – like a full-scale interactive version of Camberwick Green or one of those sleepy and seemingly benevolent villages in episodes of *The Avengers* which are a front for something more sinister, though always so terribly English. Funnily enough, I'd always wanted to come to Cookham, mainly due to my affection for the paintings of Stanley Spencer, particularly the biblical scenes set among the graves by Holy Trinity Church. But now, adrift, and light-headed, almost seasick, the whole place felt unreal and oddly threatening to me.

We pulled up by the churchyard. I got off the bike and removed my helmet.

"Why here?" I said.

"Thought you might like it," said Ace.

"I do."

"There you go then. Everyone's a winner."

Ace headed off to make his delivery and I went into the churchyard. The bells had stopped ringing, but the church was as grand as I had imagined it, with its striking Norman tower, though the main body of the church – red-tiled roof and pale walls – looked almost Mediterranean in the afternoon light. I walked down narrow paths, past the stone angel at prayer, the tombstones leaning, as if disturbed by subsidence centuries ago, and the vaults with heavy railings, to keep their inmates secure. This was where Spencer had arranged people of the village in tableaux depicting war and resurrection and the business of supernatural ebb and flow. Perhaps he wanted to involve his neighbours, make them his tools and materials, or maybe he wanted to warn them of the Day of Judgement that was both to come but also here and now. Or perhaps, for him, the End of Days was an endlessly occurring event, like a loop of film in his head that he constantly tried to capture on canvas.

I longed for rumblings in the ground, the earth ready to spew up its dead. I wanted the serenity – the formality, precision, and good taste – to explode into bustle and vividness. I longed to see angels in the architecture and trees around me

– not stone ones, but creatures of colour and vitality. But the ground did not tremble underfoot, and the air remained undisturbed as the churchyard kept its peace and all its secrets.

I wandered around for a little longer then made my way back, finding Ace, sitting on a bench, and smoking a cigarette, listening to the irritable and inevitable buzzing of his radio.

"You had enough?" he said, getting up.

"Yeah."

He flicked his cigarette away and we headed down the path and out of the gate.

"Done the business then?" I said.

"Cancelled. Party not at home."

"I wouldn't mind going to the Stanley Spencer gallery."

"It'll be shut," said Ace.

"Ok, then how about a pint in the pub we passed before – *The Kings Arms*, was it?"

"Shut too. Everything's shut, apart from the graveyard. That never closes."

He put on his helmet and got on the bike. I did the same and we set off again. Soon we were back on the motorway, my head buzzing along with the engine of the bike. My skull felt big and hollow.

It didn't seem long until we were back in the city, as if the metropolis had felt the loss of us and sucked us back in forcibly, returning us to the noise and complication to which we somehow belonged, whether we liked it or not.

Ace took me back to the hospital, as he had promised, and dropped me off by the main entrance.

"Well, thanks," I said.

"You're ok, man."

There was a bit of an awkward silence. It was time to say goodbye, but all my questions hadn't been answered. As it was, he spoke first.

"I really didn't come here for your girlfriend, you know."

"Right."

"I came for you."

"Sorry?" I said, blankly.

"I thought it was time we talked properly."

He smiled and put down the visor of his helmet. He started up the bike.

"Be seeing you," he said, and then was off, down the street and soon out of sight.

CHAPTER EIGHTEEN

I kept myself busy during the next few days. I don't quite know why, but I was feeling a lot more positive. It wasn't that life had got any less weird – the opposite, in fact, as I'm sure you'll agree. There were more questions than ever hanging in the air, but I wasn't going to get any of them answered by moping around the house or lazing in bed, feeling sorry for myself. I also wasn't going to get anywhere sitting in the hospital all day. That didn't mean that I was going to stop visiting Jane. It just meant that I would cut the visits down a bit, fit them into my life, rather than the other way round. That might sound harsh and unfeeling, but I knew Janie. If she were well and I performed the kind of useless routine around her that I'd settled into since her accident, she'd be the first to tell me to sort myself out and be quick about it. Besides, I felt deep down inside that, if I was going to be any good to Jane or myself, I needed to be sharp and focussed. I needed to get myself together.

It seemed that Ace and I had become acquaintances, for want of a better word. Our paths kept crossing and there was something familiar about him, as if we'd met before but I couldn't place where or when. I didn't trust him though, not for a minute – I didn't even know if Ace was his real name – so I needed to be on the ball. He was showing me stuff, letting me in. I didn't quite know what any of it meant, but I was being given an insight into something. Not everything (I wasn't kidding myself there) – it was more a glimpse, or at least as much as he wanted to show me for the time being. He may have been toying with me, I don't know. I got the distinct feeling, as strange as it might sound, that he didn't really have anyone else to talk to.

I began to formulate something approaching a plan of action. I tidied the flat and gave it a bit of a clean. I got myself tidied up too. I had begun to look like one of the walking wounded.

Spruced up and relatively clear-headed, I sat in the front room with a big mug of tea and played my ukulele. I hadn't touched it for ages – I'd forgotten about it, to tell you the truth, and only came across it, in its lovely, hard, black leather case, when I was tidying up. I'd bought it in Brighton, a couple of years before. Janie and I had spent a weekend there, in early January, just after my birthday. We'd had a great time. I love British seaside resorts in Winter – to me they are at their most melancholy and romantic (and most British) when it's off season, most of the attractions are closed down and the weather is bad. And I've always loved Brighton, in particular – if I wasn't living in London, I'd love to live there. I'd talked about it to Jane on many occasions, but she had never been too keen. We had a good time that weekend, though. On the Saturday, we'd taken a walk along the pier. It was freezing and we were wearing big coats, gloves, and scarves. We'd had hot Bovril to keep us warm, rather than the usual candy floss or toffee apples. Drinking Bovril on the pier – that pleased me beyond words. Then it had snowed, and we walked along the beach, hand in hand.

In town, we passed a music shop and there was a ukulele in the window. I had always been fascinated by the instrument – there was something both exotic and slightly ridiculous about it – and I had wanted to own one for ages. There was also a poster of a Hawaiian girl on the wall behind it. She was wearing a grass skirt, a garland on her head and one around her bust. She had a lovely smile too. It was so deliciously absurd – snowing on our side of the window and Hawaii on the other – that it could not be resisted. I dragged Jane into the shop. She was very sceptical, couldn't understand what I was doing but, when I strummed the ukulele, basically just adapting normal guitar chords, she liked the sound I made and let me get on with it. It was only twenty quid – I think that was mostly for the case that came with it, rather than the uke itself.

The ukulele is a wonderful instrument. I picked it up quite quickly, from a chord book – *J.J. Handy's Ukulele Jamboree* – that I bought in a second-hand book shop on the Charing Cross Road. This particular morning, I took it out of its case. "My dog has fleas," I sang, using the notes – G, C, E and A – to see if it needed tuning. When I first bought it, I translated the chords to *Honey Pie* by the Beatles for the uke. I figured that was a perfect ukulele tune – it's as if McCartney wrote it especially for the thing. It sounded good but these days I felt that the instrument better suited more bluesy or country numbers. I tended to play a lot of Jimmie Rodgers,

Hank Williams, and Johnny Cash songs on it, as well as early Elvis tunes, especially stuff from the *Sun* sessions.

The cats tended to come in and crawl all over me when I played the uke. The harmonica also seemed to drive them wild. Only Nana came in today. I realised that I hadn't seen Louie for a couple of days. This was not like him. I went out into the back garden but there was no sign of him there either. I decided that I would ask around the neighbours to find out if any of them had seen him recently. This was part of my new plan too. Not just to find my wayward cat, but also to renew contact with the people of Strangelove Place. The folks around me had been kind and supportive after Jane's accident, but I had pretty much withdrawn from them. It was time to come out of my self-imposed exile.

I knocked on a few doors and said hello to those who were in. When I got to Michael's door, he gave me a big hug and asked me in. He made me a coffee and we sat in his kitchen and talked. It had been a long time since we'd done that. As I said earlier, Michael had been the one who'd brought me to St Ragnulf's in the first place. It was he who had created the scene that I'd so wanted to be part of. I'd slept on his couch for a period – sometimes I'd slept on the floor. He'd fed me and looked out for me. He had also educated me, particularly in film. He was a big movie buff, with a great collection of movies on tape, recorded from the telly over a period of many years – even after everybody had moved to DVD, Michael held onto his VHS collection. Some afternoons, we'd have double, sometimes triple bills, of movies, selected by him – westerns and films noir mostly. Anthony Mann westerns with Jimmy Stewart, like *The Far Country* and *The Man from Laramie*. Budd Boetticher's *The Tall T* and *Ride Lonesome* starring Randy Scott. And gorgeous paranoid noir fantasies – *The Dark Corner*, *Phantom Lady*, *Detour*, *Raw Deal*, *The Big Combo*, *Gun Crazy*, *They Made Me A Fugitive*. And there were other films that defied genres – *Pandora and the Flying Dutchman* and Nick Ray's *Wind Across the Everglades*. Musicals and melodramas. Douglas Sirk and Vincente Minnelli. Even after I moved into my own place, our afternoon sessions continued. Those films became ever associated in my mind with Michael. He usually made me something to eat, and there'd be beer and wine. Then we'd go to the pub afterwards and discuss what we'd watched, as well as life in general. I owed him a lot, even though recently we seemed to have drifted apart.

Michael was gay, openly, and unapologetically so. It was not always the case – the open and unapologetic bit. He was married until his late thirties – indeed, he has a son and daughter, who live in other parts of the country, though he keeps in contact with them. Once out of his marriage and the closet, he made up for lost time. In his mid-fifties now, Michael enjoyed his new life. There was a string of brief affairs (a couple of which were 'gloriously hopeless', as he himself put it) and two long-term relationships, both of which went up 'in flames' (again Michael's words). I'd been around for the tail end of the last serious one and it was a fairly rocky ride, even at safe a distance. Michael loved melodrama and, when his relationships headed for the final credits, you got the full-on Douglas Sirk experience, though sometimes it felt more like Fassbinder, crossed with John Waters.

So that day, there we were – me and Michael – talking in his kitchen.

"How is Janie doing?" he said.

"She's not doing much, Michael," I said. "I'm not sure if she's ever going to again."

"You can't allow yourself to think like that."

"I know but...you've seen her, man. She's lying there but she's somewhere else. I can't help feeling that I've lost her."

"She's a tough cookie, Stevie – you know that – and she'd be the first to give you a kick up the keister for that kind of talk."

"Yeah, you're right. She'd dish out some serious abuse. Which is why I've decided to pull myself together. Get myself going again. Things have just gone by the wayside."

"You been working?"

"No, couldn't be arsed. But money's getting too tight to mention and I'm going to have to get to it."

"I can always lend you money, Stephen. You don't have to worry about that."

"Thanks, but no. I'll be fine. I sign on tomorrow and I'm going to get in touch with Yani and do some work on the stall. I'm going to start busking again too."

"You haven't been in The Ship for a while. Eric's been asking after you."

"I couldn't face it, these last weeks. I'll pop in and show my face soon though."

"Look, you remember that party I planned a while ago, before all this crazy shit started? The multi-media thing – films and performance art?"

"Very vaguely," I said.

"Well, it was scheduled for the Saturday after next. I'd forgotten about it, with everything that's been going on, but a couple of people have mentioned it to me lately. I'm not sure about it though."

I thought for a moment and then said, "What do you mean?"

"I don't know if now's the time for such things," he said. "You know, with Jane the way she is."

"Look, Michael, I know that you're concerned about me, and I appreciate it. To tell you the truth, I decided to come out of my shell today. I wanted to see if I could track down Louie, but I also wanted to reconnect with people."

"That's good, Stephen."

"It's a start at least. Anyway, I think you should go ahead with the party."

"Are you sure?" said Michael.

"Yes, I am. I think, if she could, Janie would tell us to get our arses in gear and get on with it."

"Well, I tell you what," he said, "I'll go ahead with it if you'll do an acoustic set: your own songs."

"Oh, I don't know, man. Not sure if I'll be up to it. I'm out of practice."

"You'll be fine. It doesn't have to be polished. It can be as spontaneous as you like. The Two Daves were going to film the whole thing."

"Is that supposed to make me say 'yes'?"

"Come on. It'll be an excuse to let our hair down."

"I really don't know, Michael. I'm pretty rusty."

"It doesn't matter."

"I'm not sure I'm ready for it."

"You're out of your shell, remember?"

"Alright, but I'll just do a couple."

"Good man. It's a deal."

We shook hands and that was that. I'd gone looking for my cat and found myself a happening instead.

When I got back to my place, I went on the computer. I

wanted to see if I could find some trace of the music I'd heard on Ace's radio. I googled "Buddy Holly bootlegs" but found nothing remotely resembling the music I'd heard. Similarly, "Buddy Holly Bob Dylan" merely told me that Dylan had acknowledged Holly as a big influence, and it was observed that Bob's vocal style owed much to Buddy's. "Buddy Holly Subterranean Homesick Blues" was likewise a mishmash of sites that listed the greatest singles of all time, but Holly and the song were never more than passing strangers.

I headed down to the market behind St Martin's to see Yani. I wanted to find out if he needed any help on the stall soon. I also asked him if he had any idea where this impossible music might have come from.

"It's got to be a hoax. Can't be anything else," he said.

"Yeah, I know. It just sounded so real, and it made sense, in a weird kind of way."

Then I told him about the guys at the Montana Café who looked like Gene Vincent, Billy Fury and Joe Meek.

"This biker guy is really stitching you up, chief. He probably arranged the whole thing. He's fucking with your head. Stay away from him."

So, was this whole thing some bizarre practical joke? It was looking more and more that way, though why he'd want to do it, I couldn't figure out.

"I know a guy, name of Zak, I think I might have introduced him to you before. He's more of a bootleg junkie than me. He knows all about that kind of shit. He has a shop in Camden. You might remember the guy – about six foot four, huge spiky black hair, real goggle eyes. Mad on Hendrix, Hawkwind and Jap Rock."

"No, I don't think I do," I said.

"He's your man, chief. If you're looking for the Holy Grail, the Maltese Falcon, the Rosebud of bootleg material, even if you've only ever heard about it in fairy stories, or some urban myth, he'll tell you if it really exists, and how to get it. He might even have it himself."

Yani gave me the details of how to find the man. We gave each other a hug and said our goodbyes and I headed across the marketplace, on my way to Charing Cross Station. Down at the far end, there was a stall with a sign beside it saying:

'Come the day, come the dawn,
Free your mind, travel on.
Towards the light, to set you free,
Towards the end of mystery.'

There was another sign on the front of the stall saying:

'The Blood of the Lamb –
Everything You Think You Know Is Wrong.'

I've already given you a little bit of information about my religious upbringing and my attitude to all things spiritual. Although my own faith had waxed and waned over the years, I was still fascinated by the subject of religion and spirituality. When I was living in that tower block in Westbourne Grove that I was talking about – you know, the one where they held impromptu police conventions outside my flat – you'd often get a knock on the door by someone other than a witty policeman. Occasionally, you'd get a group of smiling, friendly people who'd come to set you free, to sell the most precious thing they had. In short, to save your soul. They'd picked you specially, I don't quite know how. Perhaps they too had a big computer or a set of numbered balls. Perhaps they had a list, written in a big, dusty book. Perhaps they didn't need any of these things, I don't know but, whosoever they might be, whether Jehovah's Witnesses, Mormons, or evangelical types of a different stripe, I would generally tend to ask them in. I don't know whether I did this out of an openness of mind, a questing nature that yearned for meaning in this seemingly meaningless existence. I don't know if it was because I was feeling lonely at these times and just wanted the company. I don't know whether it was due to the argumentative side of my personality or maybe it was out of sheer devilment. Maybe I had my own agenda – maybe I was trying to convert them to my own belief system, whatever that might be. Whatever the reason, or combination of the above, I invariably invited them into my home, offered them tea, coffee, or whichever drink did not undermine their particular belief system, and we'd lock horns on the tenets of whatever spiritual path they might be advocating.

Perhaps a similar impetus made me notice the Blood of the Lamb's stall, but it was more likely that, standing by this stall, was a young woman I recognised. I'd seen her only once before and in an entirely different context, so it took me a few moments to be sure, but it was most certainly the girl from the party – Liam's sister, Sammy.

She was talking and smiling, engaged in conversation with a couple of other young women in the group. After a little while, she excused herself and headed over towards the main church building, so I followed her. She came to a door at the back of the church and went down some steps. The way she did so, and her flustered demeanour, might have called to mind the White Rabbit, going down his hole into Wonderland, but actually it was just Sammy going down the stairs to St Martin's coffee shop. That's where fanciful thinking gets you. I don't recommend it.

I followed her down the stairway, cramped and a little slippery under foot. Downstairs it was like a catacomb – warm and cosy, but a catacomb, nevertheless. At the bottom of the stairs stood a table, piled up with pamphlets and flyers, the wall behind it covered with posters advertising events at the church and tourist attractions. There were three doors, one marked 'Café'. I took a look inside – the place was bustling but I couldn't see Sammy. Then I chose one of the other doors and moved tentatively down the corridor leading from it, passing little rooms, office areas, some doors open, and others closed. She didn't seem to be in any of them, though it was difficult to tell. I moved back up the corridor to the bottom of the stairs and there she was.

I saw a flash of recognition in her face, then just plain surprise.

"Hello," I said, "remember me?"

"Yes, of course I do," she said. "Hi, how are you?"

She offered her hand, and I took it.

"What are you doing around here?" she said.

"You know, just looking for the truth."

She pulled face.

"It sets you free, apparently," I said.

She nodded slowly, a tentative smile on her face.

"Actually, I just dropped by for a chat with a mate of mine who runs a stall on the market, and I saw you coming in here."

"Well, there you go," she said. "The truth certainly set *you* free. A real get-out-of-jail card."

"Fancy a coffee?" I said.

"I don't drink tea or coffee," she said. "Stimulants."

"Stimulants. Right." I said. "God forbid."

"I'll let you buy me a mineral water, though."

"Would that be still or sparkling?"

"Sparkling, please."

"Sparkling, eh? A bit radical but I reckon I could probably square it with my general principles."

"Well, if it's not too much to ask," she said.

"No, it's fine by me. As long as it's not too stimulating. All those bubbles and all."

"Bubbles are fine," she said.

We went inside and she took a seat. I went to the counter and got the drinks – a black coffee for me, a mineral water for her.

"Thanks," she said, with the same slightly bemused smile I remembered from that night at Liam's place.

"You're very welcome," I said. "Good to see you again."

"You've really got a friend who works on the market?"

"You don't believe me?"

"Yes, I do actually. I thought I'd see you again sometime anyway. How it was going to happen is immaterial."

"That's a tad spooky, if I may say so, but we'll let it go, for now. You really thought that though?"

"Yes. I came around the next morning, after the party. I thought I might bump into you then, but you were gone."

"You came around to see me?"

She narrowed her eyes a little, the same odd smile on her lips.

"I came around to tidy up, wash a few dishes – you know,

153

that kind of stuff. Liam and my dad are a pretty shit at that kind of thing, as you probably noticed. I was just surprised that there was nobody left around after the party, that's all."

"So, you didn't hope that maybe I'd still be around."

"What makes you think that?"

"I don't know. We were getting on really well, I thought."

"You were very drunk," she said.

"I suppose you're right. Can't say that I wasn't."

At this point, a man approached our table.

"Oh, there you are, Samantha," he said. "We wondered where you'd got to."

"Sorry, I got talking. We haven't seen each other for a while."

The man was dressed casually – in fact, his whole demeanour was casual, his actions and speech relaxed and open. He was smiling, a very charming smile, but his gaze was searching and somewhat unnerving.

"This is Stephen – he's a friend of my brother's," Sammy said.

"Pleased to meet you, Stephen," he said, offering his hand. "I'm Jason."

I shook his hand. "Pleased to meet you, too."

He was a very good-looking bloke – tall, slim, and dark-haired, with a winning smile. His manner and the tone of his voice were very polite and friendly too, though there was nevertheless an unsettling quality about him. Perhaps it was the pair of striking blue eyes that he possessed and the way he had of fixing them on you, like heat-seeking missiles.

"Do you mind if I join you?"

"Not at all," I said, though when I glanced over at Sammy, her face had lost its warmth and looked a little nervous and strained.

He smiled again and sat down.

"Were you visiting the church?" he asked.

"No, I was just browsing around the market and fancied a coffee. Bumped into Sammy and, there you go."

"There you go indeed," he said.

His accent was strange, hard to pin down. When he first spoke, I was convinced that he was American but, each time he opened his mouth, this seemed less certain. A little Irish seemed to creep in here, a little Scots there, perhaps a trace of somewhere vaguely Eastern European, though settling more often than not into something maddeningly Mid-Atlantic, forever in transit, but never arriving at any place you might recognise.

He looked at me, then Sammy, then back to me, his expression remaining genial, and his manner relaxed, though his eyes were still active and probing.

"So, you believe in chance then, Stephen?" he continued.

"Yeah, or fate, whatever you want to call it."

"You consider them to be the same thing?"

"I don't know, maybe. Depends on which way you look at it."

"And which way do you look at it, Stephen?" he said, with a smile.

"Well, you know, maybe fate is just chance with a purpose, designated as such with hindsight."

He laughed – a short grunt that was both grudging and patronising, as if to say 'touché', rather than signifying any real amusement.

"Maybe we're always convinced we're doing one thing," he said, "for our own particular, conscious reasons, while we're actually doing something else, the nature and motive of which we are unaware."

"Seems fair to me," I said. "Like a hidden text that we can't actually see or hear but it's there and determining what we're doing and where we're going anyway."

"It's interesting that you should call it a text rather than a higher power."

"It could be a higher power – I wouldn't dismiss that – but maybe there isn't much difference either way."

"Though one seems to be internal while the other is external."

"Perhaps they're linked."

"So, let's say you came here looking for some kind of truth while a higher power made sure it was waiting for you."

"Maybe. Haven't recognised any truth so far though, I just bumped into Sammy and now I've met you."

"Well, it could be that Samantha and I are agents of fate and instruments of the truth."

I looked over at Sammy. Her expression hadn't really changed during this exchange – she still looked ill at ease and not likely to join in the conversation, whether because she didn't wish to contribute or that she felt it wasn't appropriate to do so.

"Could well be," I said. "After all, the Lord does work in mysterious ways, his woodwork to perform."

"Just so," he said, with a smile and a glint in those eyes. "You really are a strange mix, Stephen, if you don't mind me saying so."

"How do you mean?"

"Well, you seem to operate on a combination of idealism and cynicism, thoughtfulness and glibness. You think and feel deeply, I would say, but you cover it up by laughing it off."

"You've obviously got me sussed," I said, trying hard to

keep the irritation out of my voice, though I would guess that I probably failed.

"Oh, I wouldn't say that," he said, trying not to sound smug, at which he most definitely failed.

"You should come along to our group some time," he continued. "You might find some answers there."

"I'm not much of a joiner," I said.

"You don't have to join. Just come along to find out for yourself what we're about."

"I might just do that, though I'm not sure if I'm ready to be affiliated."

"Oh, but we're all affiliated, Stephen, to one thing or another. Whether we know it or not."

He started to get up.

"Well, I must be getting back. See you in a little while, Samantha."

He turned to me, again offering his hand.

"Once again, good to meet you, Stephen."

I shook his hand. He looked into my eyes.

"See you," he said, and left.

I turned to her. She looked very thoughtful.

"Not one for small talk, is he?" I said.

She shook her head. "No, not really."

"And don't ever call you Samantha, right?"

"He does. I don't encourage it."

"Is that the guy, then?"

She made a face as if she didn't know what I meant and gave a little shake of her head.

"The guy you'd had an argument with that night?" I said. Realisation flickered in her eyes, and she looked down at the table for a few seconds.

157

"Yes," she said finally, looking a little uncomfortable. "I'd better get back."

"Look, I'm sorry," I said. "I didn't mean to pry. Or offend you"

"No..." she shook her head, "...no, it's ok. I do have to get back, though."

She got up, seeming somewhat flustered.

"It was good to see you again," she said, rather shakily.

"You too," I said.

She turned and walked away.

I decided to head up to Camden to check out this guy Zak, the bootleg guru Yani had mentioned. Charing Cross Station was unusually quiet. I found myself wandering through various corridors for a while before I realised that I didn't seem to be getting anywhere. What was it with me and tube stations these days? I know this station well, I thought to myself, how could I not know where I was going?

I could hear a guitar playing and a lone voice singing, cracked and plaintive. It was the Hank Williams song, *I'm So Lonesome, I Could Cry,* though it sounded like Kurt Cobain's voice singing it, as incongruous as that might be. But it wasn't at all, that was the thing. It was totally natural. Slower and more racked with pain than the original, but a beautiful version, nevertheless. I moved to the end of the corridor and turned left, towards the music. It led, rather predictably, to another corridor, which stretched off into the distance, the music echoing from further down the tunnel – eerie, forlorn but enticing, though somehow incredibly far away. I wanted to follow it. To see if it was old Kurt, strumming away. I'd have given anything to have stood in front of him and said hello, passed the time of day, anything really. Hell, I'd have been glad to have simply dropped a few coins in his guitar case and moved on, just to get a look at him. As it was, I had the funny feeling that I would never get to him. I turned and began to retrace my steps. I could hear that he had started to sing another song, *See That My Grave Is Kept Clean*, the old Blind Lemon Jefferson number that Dylan covered on his first album, then later again during *The Basement Tapes* sessions. It was sharp and clean and true. It made my heart ache. But I continued back up the corridor, took a left turn, then another. There was a set of stairs and I walked down them.

Soon, I could hear the rumble of a train. I followed it until I came onto a platform where there were a few other people. It was the Southbound Bakerloo Line train, going in the opposite direction from Zak and his treasure trove of bootlegs. I don't know whether this was fate or coincidence, whether I was being gently impelled to go home or what. Whatever it was, I was too tired to fight it just now. I decided that I would leave Camden until another day. I got on and the train pulled away. As it did, I looked out of the window and caught a glimpse of a young man with straggly, bleached blonde hair and big dark glasses with thick white frames, sitting on a seat at the very end of the platform, a guitar case leaning against his legs and smoking a cigarette.

CHAPTER NINETEEN

The day of Michael's arty party arrived – far too soon, for my liking. The festivities were to start around six o'clock that evening. I was feeling out of sorts, and a shindig was the last thing I needed. I'd had a terrible night's sleep and my head felt fuzzy. Everything was a little abstract and my stomach was playing up too, a burning sensation in my gut that was making me restless and irritable. On top of that, my gums were bleeding badly, so I constantly had the taste of blood in my mouth. Maybe even on my mind.

I'd woken up late, got myself together and made my way up to the hospital to see Jane. There was nobody at the reception desk when I arrived on the ward, so I went straight to her room.

Except Jane wasn't there. Instead, a complete stranger was occupying her bed. Had I gone into the wrong room? I looked up and down the corridor – no, this was definitely the right one. So where was she? Was I going crazy? My head started to spin and the pain in my stomach was even more intense now. Ace said he had no business with her. How could I have been so gullible? So stupid.

"Stephen?"

I turned around. It was Amy.

"We've moved her to another room," she said. "Just down the hall."

"Is there anything wrong? Has her condition changed?"

"No. She's fine. Just a bit of reorganisation."

"Why didn't you let me know?"

"We don't usually. Of course, we'd have rung you if there was any kind of change in her condition."

"Yes...sorry, Amy. It just really threw me, that's all. I'm not having a good day."

"Do you want to have a sit down? Can I get you a cuppa?"

"No, I'll be fine. Where is she?"

She led me to Jane's new room. It was odd, after she had been in the same place, the same position, for so long, to see her somewhere else. She was still lying in a bed, eyes closed, motionless, but the change was amazing. The room was a lot brighter and the sun coming from the window caught her face and lit it up. She looked beautiful.

"You been gallivanting again?" I said to her quietly. "Can't keep track of you, can I?"

I started to cry. I leaned my head on her stomach. I felt ridiculous, reacting like that, so close to panic, so quickly. But I also felt relief. And the sense that she was in good hands. I should have known that already, but I felt it profoundly now.

I calmed down and started to talk to her. The usual one-sided chat with me imagining what she was thinking and what her response might be. I told her about how shitty I was feeling. About how I was worrying about Louie. That Nana was missing him, missing her too. I talked about Michael's soirée and my misgivings about it. It was nice. I even thought I noticed a change in Janie's expression. The slightest of smiles perhaps? I don't know, maybe it was just the change of location. After all, it's as good as a rest, so they say. After a good while, I kissed her gently, on the lips, and stroked her hair.

"See you soon, Pet."

I got back home around four o'clock. I figured I'd practice for a couple of hours, so I headed to the front room with a sandwich and about a third of a bottle of Scotch that I'd forgotten about and found underneath the kitchen sink (not sure what it was doing there). I put on a DVD – *Pandora and the Flying Dutchman* – and set it going with the sound down, while I ran through the four or five songs that I was planning to perform later. 'Pandora' is one of the great British movies, though not particularly well known. It was made around 1950 and is very reminiscent of the films of Powell and Pressburger in its visual style and its blend of fantasy and melodrama. Ava Gardner is gorgeous as the free-spirited heroine, trailing broken hearts, scandal, and death in her wake, until she meets her match in a brooding James Mason, who is in fact the Flying Dutchman of legend, doomed to wander the earth until he finds someone who loves him enough to give up their life for him. Only then can he be freed from his curse, free to die. The movie achieves an intensity and a kind of loopy grandeur that is all its own. Once more, love and death walk hand in hand along the beach towards a Technicolor sunset of sublime oblivion.

The film's karma imbued my own music with something

of that intensity of feeling as I ran through the songs. Nana came in and rubbed herself up against my legs – she also knew that feeling. She was missing her soul mate, just like me, and had no idea when he'd be back. We could sympathise with each other, that's for sure, and even offer some kind of solace, but we could neither of us make up for that absence, that loss, that the other felt.

Around six o'clock, I stopped playing and got changed to go out. The songs were as ready as they'd ever be. I finished my latest glass of Scotch – there was not much left in the bottle now – and headed out.

Everyone was meeting in The Ship, as was usually the case, though tonight didn't feel usual at all. It was the first time I'd been in the place since Frank's wake – Jane was with me then of course, and so much had happened since.

There were quite a few people in, the usual crew mostly. Eric spotted me straightaway and gave me a warm smile as I approached the bar.

"Good to see you, lad. How are you doing?" he said. He was already pouring me a Guinness.

"Not so bad, Eric. Good to see you too."

"How's the princess?"

"No change. She's well looked after but there's no sign of recovery yet. We'll just have to be patient."

He put the glass of Guinness on the bar in front of me.

"There you are. On the house."

"Cheers, Eric. Your health." I raised the glass and took a sip.

"And yours, lad."

The television was on, high up on the wall, at the far side of the room.

There was a boxing match in progress. Strange time of the day to be showing it, I know, but Eric was a real fight fan. He had loads of DVDs of that stuff. An East Ender and a natural battler, the fight game appealed to his sensibilities. The purest of sports, he always maintained. All the paraphernalia stripped away – no bats, balls, protective headgear, body armour, goalposts, or nets – just two guys going at each other, the victory signalled by one of them going down and staying down, as simple as that.

"Good fight, Eric?"

"One of the best, son. Rocky Marciano versus Jersey Joe Walcott – Philadelphia, September 23, 1952, for the World Heavyweight title."

Michael was holding court at a table in one corner, surrounded by familiar faces, including Maddy and Yani.

"Hello, Stephen," he shouted to me. "Come join us."

I went over and sat down.

"Hi everybody," I said. People responded. The usual pleasantries.

"How's it going, Floyd?" asked Maddy.

"Not so bad," I said with a shrug. "You know how it is."

"Yeah, I do" she said. I thought I detected a trace of concern in her voice, but that was so unusual for Maddy that I shrugged it off.

At a table nearby, next to the jukebox, there was some kind of time warp in operation. In that spot, and that spot only, with the music machine flashing brightly and *That's Entertainment!* by The Jam blasting out, it was the fourteenth century, and the Age of Chivalry was alive and well, though not in particularly high spirits. The six people sitting there, four men and two women, were dressed in medieval finery – doublets and hose, shoes with curled toes, the women with flowing garments, one actually wearing a tall, pointed hat with a trail of organza spiralling from its tip. The other woman was hatless and wore a long white dress. Her hair was jet black, her face deathly pale with dark eye shadow accentuating that paleness. The others were talking quietly but she did not join in their conversation. Her eyes were instead fixed at some point across the room. She was grimly beautiful and her presence was unnerving. At the other end of the table sat a dumpy, pie-faced individual, moping under an unfortunate hat, which sprouted a sorry-looking feather whose flying days were long gone. Whenever I found myself looking in this man's direction, his eyes were always fixed on me. I took an instant dislike to him.

I couldn't get into the conversation – Michael and Yani tried to include me, but I felt detached and uncomfortable. *When I Dream* by The Teardrop Explodes was playing on the jukebox now, dumpy medieval man continued to glare at me and, on the television, the two big, sweaty men were still beating the shit out of each other. I wished that Jane was with me. I wished I was far away from this pub and these people. I wished I could just disappear.

Michael left a little before the others to finish preparing stuff and I went with him – the whole scene in The Ship was getting me down. When we got back, Michael went to check on the food that he'd left cooking. He asked me to set the DVD player up for a showing in his bedroom of some short movies by the Two Daves. The musical performances would take place in Michael's spacious living room – a space in the corner would be the stage. There was also a projector set up on a table – Yani's movie and some others would be projected on the wall at some point in the evening.

I joined Michael in the kitchen. He opened a bottle of red wine and poured us both out a large glass.

"Fasten your seatbelts," he said, doing his best Bette Davis impersonation, "it's going to be a bumpy night."

The place soon filled up as the carousers from The Ship arrived. This was the kind of night that I had grown to love, the sort of event that thrilled me and made me feel that I had arrived at some long wished-for destination – a destination that I had dreamed of while I festered in Redtown in my teens. American music, film and literature had fuelled this dream, conjuring up a specifically American poetry to distract me from my essentially prosaic north-east England existence. Whether it was the films of Scorsese, Altman, Peckinpah and others of the so-called American 'New Wave' of the 1970s, movies of the eighties and nineties by the likes of Jim Jarmusch, The Coen Brothers, or Gus van Sant, the music of Dylan, the Velvet Underground, Patti Smith, R.E.M. and the Pixies, or the books of Hammett, Chandler, Kerouac, Vonnegut and Pynchon, it had all woven a powerful and evocative tapestry, which suggested to me that there was another world out there, where different kinds of creatures existed and more exciting lives were lived. I knew that I was really one of those creatures and that this was the kind of life I wanted for myself.

Strangelove Place, when I had arrived there, seemed to be

part of that life, that dream. And parties like this seemed to be an intense expression of the whole ideal that I'd been moving towards. But not tonight. No, though I walked through this scene and observed it, I felt strangely removed from it all. My mood and my state of inebriation meant that the sensory stimuli that bombarded me and that would normally have made me feel elated now only pushed me further towards a sort of despair. A kind of darkness.

It was soon my turn to get up and perform my songs. I stood, with my guitar and my harmonica holder, looking out at the people in the room, who were all looking back at me, expecting something. I knew many of the faces in that crowd, most of them really, but I was not sure if the house was sympathetic or hostile. Or rather, it was only the strange faces that I could really focus upon. I could discern the super-8 lenses of the Two Daves but, though I liked them as people, these artificial eyes were cold and unforgiving, two snipers poised to take me down at any moment. At one side of the performing area, Dumpy Medieval Man glared at me, as might be expected, while the pale, dark-haired woman stood near the back, her gaze on me, but also somewhere else.

I started with a song called *Country Hoodoo*, which I had written relatively recently. It was perhaps not the best of ideas, given that I'd only just learned the words and was playing it live for the first time, but it was an opportunity to test out new material in front of an audience, so it was worth a try. The song had a bluesy feel and lyrics based on a book I'd read about folk magic.

Hoodoo – not to be confused with Voodoo, which is a different animal altogether – was put together by African slaves in the Deep South, mixing various spiritual beliefs derived from traditional African religious practices, and kept secret from slave-owners and white people in general. It was a way of keeping sacred traditions alive, as well as being a covert act of rebellion and survival for an enslaved people in an alien land. These beliefs evolved over time and drew from old wisdom, magic, and medicine, and they became a way of looking at and negotiating with the world and nature, incorporating folk tales, songs, and festivals. At the heart of these rituals is a reverence for the spirits of dead ancestors and the conviction that these can provide guidance, protection, and good fortune to the living.

> All these things are written in the book.
> Conjure magic finds you when you look.
> The sun hangs high, the sun hangs low,
> The four winds cry, and the four winds blow.
> The spirits of the dead will have their song.

My voice was a little shaky at first and my playing lacked confidence, the rhythm unsteady, but I eased my way into it, enjoying the sound and feel of the lyrics, though I had to concentrate hard as they hadn't become second nature to me yet.

> Meet me at the crossroads after dark,
> Where two realms touch and we shall see them spark.
> Conjuration in the hills,
> Bottle tree will cure your ills.
> Bon Dieu must abide past right or wrong.

I must admit that I had originally written the song as a bit of an exercise, though the subject matter interested me, and it seemed like good material to play around with. I'm not sure if I felt, at the time, that I was indulging in any kind of cultural appropriation or that I was running the risk of upsetting any spirits by singing about these things but nevertheless the song was a conceit, and I was little more than a tourist in the world that the lyrics described. However, given the sort of experiences I'd been having lately, the words seemed to take on a new significance as I sang them at this moment. There was something else going on in between and around these words – something I couldn't account for. Maybe I really did live in this world now.

Shaky spirits stalk the land,
Feed and fix a mojo hand.
Get me some of that country hoodoo.

Close your eyes and cast a spell,
Shadows come with tales to tell –
Lord I love that thing that you do.

The idea of the crossroads as a place where this world and the world beyond might meet and interact – this is where the legend of Robert Johnson selling his soul to the Devil for the secret of the Blues comes from – seemed to me less fanciful than it might have before. Too many strange things were happening around me to dismiss the idea that our lives could be acted on and influenced by powers outside our knowledge and reason. I saw the pale, dark-haired woman, standing in one corner. She was swaying, her eyes closed, and I could have sworn she was smiling.

I did three more songs, with little patter between them, then my fingers started to tremble, so that I had trouble playing chords. Maybe I'd had too much whiskey earlier – or maybe not enough to eat – so I decided to cut my set short. I finished, as usual, with *Elvis on the Moon,* which is, as you might guess, about meeting the King on the lunar surface (as you do). It was wishful thinking, of course – a fan's fantasy of spending time with your hero, just you and him, in a rarefied, almost magical space. Once the title had come to me, the song practically wrote itself.

> Elvis on the moon.
> I'll be talking to him soon,
> In a rhinestone-studded spacesuit on Mons Agnes.
>
> We'll sing some gospel songs
> And work out what went wrong
> And the Earth will sure look good through our
>   sunglasses.

I'd performed this song live so many times that I thought it would never be able to surprise or affect me in the way that it used to but, once again, something I had written seemed to take on a new life, and the words, the feeling of loss, regret and maybe redemption, that flow through the song, along-side its fanciful imagery, hit me in a way they never had before.

> Well, the Jungle Room is quiet now,
> And the Colonel's dead and gone,
> But what was lost is less than what was won.

Elvis on the moon.
The time is coming soon,
When we'll be with Sam Phillips in the sun.
Yes, that big, bright, yellow label
That means sun.

I came to the end of the song and left the makeshift stage, accompanied by some polite applause. As I headed towards the kitchen, I bumped into Michael, who put his arm around me.

"Steady there, fella. You ok?" asked Michael,

"Yeah, yeah, I'm fine, man. Sorry my set was a bit brief – it was all I could manage."

"Not at all. You did really well, Stephen."

"Glad somebody liked it anyway."

"Don't be daft. They all enjoyed it. Rest easy, young Padawan."

They showed Yani's film – a scratchy, surrealist road movie called *Octopus* – while I hung around in the background and tried to calm down. I kept bumping into Dumpy Medieval Man, who seemed to be forever under my feet, I could only imagine intentionally. He would glare at me, then seem to feign insouciance and move on. I was not the only one whose back he got up that night. He seemed to upset a good many of the others as he skulked about the place with his air of lackadaisical arrogance.

It was soon the time for his troupe of players to perform. They called themselves the Nevermore Collective and their performance resolved itself into a sequence of staged scenes, dances, and songs. There may have been a loose narrative thread that held these separate pieces together, but it was difficult to discern what it might be. One of the men declaimed a poem. Another man and the woman with the pointed hat danced together to a tune played by the dumpy one on a lute. There was more declaiming in an acted scene between this same man and woman, on the subject of courtly love. Two of the men then indulged in a mock duel, in which one of them met his death, resurrecting himself soon afterwards to a smattering of applause. There was verse that hinted at a quest and a promise to the eternal spirits and there was an evocation of the Great Goddess. Then, the ghostly woman in the white robe stepped alone into the performance area and sang unaccompanied, her eyes closed, hands by her side. The song, so far as I could tell, was called *The Raven's Wing*. She sang in a low, mellifluous voice, like an English Nico, perfectly pronouncing every word:

As I walked out into the hills,
My soul most heavy laden,
The blackest of birds, he quoth to me,
'Where goest thou, fairest maiden?'

'I go to the deep cold river, sir,
To cast myself in the water.'
The raven he asked, 'What saddens thee so
As to take thine own life, sweet daughter.'

'My Love, sayeth I, is the dearest of souls,
A youth for whom I yearneth.
But he is to take another maid's hand,
And my love can never returneth.'

The narrative unfolded into a pact between the maiden and the black bird in which he was to secure for her the love

172

of her sweet youth in return for her devotion. Of course, her devotion would not be enough. This was a Faustian pact, with a soul as the price, seemingly the maiden's own. Death followed, as the pale woman continued to sing, her eyes still shut, enunciating the words of her tale as if serenely possessed, her very life depending on it. The young man's intended met a sorry fate and he was released to be joined with the heroine of the song but, at the moment that they were to be reconciled and united forever, the trickster bird took him away. It was his soul that the raven had wanted all along, as well as the sublime heartache of the maiden to feed on for all eternity.

As the raven's cruel laughter did echo and ring,
There falleth to earth a feather,
The blackest, most dreadful, from the tip of his wing,
My only remembrance forever.

She came to the end of her sad tale, the last note hanging in the air like a warning, or a curse. Everyone stirred, as if from a troubled sleep, with a slightly dazed ripple of applause. The pale girl opened her eyes, her lips parted slightly, then turned, almost imperceptibly, and left the space that she had owned for what had seemed the longest time. Dumpy Medieval Man left his place by the performance area too and, while moving across the room, bumped into me, and walked on. I looked back after him, my hands forming fists.

I took a couple of deep breaths and went into the kitchen. I found a bottle of red wine, about three quarters full. I filled my glass and stepped out of the kitchen door, into the garden. The Moon was out, partially obscured by thick cloud, unable to totally escape from its shackles, but still able to cast a ghostly light. I could see her, standing over near the back wall, her white gown caught by the moonlight, lending it a bluish glow.

"Hello," I said, but she gave no answer. She seemed lost in thought, staring over at the far side of the garden. I moved towards her.

"Hello," I said again. This time she turned to look at me and, as she did so, the moonlight caught her face, giving it a terrible aspect, the pallor of her features transforming into an intense white flame, her eyes black hollows, her mouth, slightly open, a chasm ready to break open and swallow everything, me included. Perhaps especially me. I felt the pull of her gaze, heard the silent call of her monstrous mouth. I knew deep inside that I could not trust what I was seeing but that faint knowledge gave me no comfort. I took a few steps backward, trying to distance myself from this alarming, hypnotic figure, while she remained inert, continuing to stare at me, that terrible mask burning in the cold, night air.

I closed my eyes, and, with some effort, I was able to wrench myself from the grip she had exerted on me and turn myself towards the house. When I opened my eyes again, my vision was blurred. I could see Michael's kitchen – the light on in the window and the door still open – but, though I knew it was only a few yards away, it felt somehow as if it would take me hours to get back there.

With some effort, I reached the kitchen door, tripping slightly over the step but managing to stay on my feet, only to find him there – as dumpy and incongruous, and perhaps as inevitable, as ever. His usual sneer in place, he seemed rooted in the middle of the room, as if he owned it now and nobody else was welcome there. At that moment, it seemed to me that this room had become his kingdom and that, if I did not escape from it as quickly as possible, I would be trapped there, with him, forever. I moved towards him unsteadily but, as I reached him, he remained resolutely in place and glared at me.

"Excuse me," I said.

"No," he said, his voice cold and certain.

"No what?" I said.

"No, you're not excused," he said. "Go ahead and ask me why."

Instead of asking why, I punched him. He fell back against the table, spilling food onto the floor. Blood was streaming from his nose, though his expression was one of defiance.

"Go on, ask me, and I'll tell you why you'll never be excused," he said.

I hit him again, and he went down onto the floor. I felt arms tugging me back.

"Come on, Stephen." It was Michael's voice, trying to calm and reassure me, but with a distinct tremor of fear in his tone. I was led into the big living room, through a crowd of people who had gathered at the door to see what was going on. As I was steered across the room, I noticed Posh Dave, filming my rescue, or ejection, I wasn't sure which way it was going to pan out. Whatever it might be, though, it was being recorded, ready to be incorporated into a future work of art – cinéma vérité, the cinema of cruelty, the cinema of the absurd.

I pulled free from the hands that held me, pushing them away, moving towards the front door.

"You need to calm down," said Michael, though I could not see his face.

"And you need to fuck off," I found myself saying.

"Stephen, please."

I got to the front door and opened it.

"Just keep your hands off me and leave me alone."

A hand pushed the door closed again.

"Please, Stephen. Just wait a minute."

I could see Michael's face clearly now. I felt the tension in my shoulders ease a little and leaned back against the wall. My breathing calmed down. I closed my eyes, squeezing out tears. I felt very weary. Michael led me into the spare room. There were two beds in there, with a sleeping body on one of them. Michael lay me down on the other bed and sat beside me. He spoke to me gently but, in my tired, drunken haze, with the stale smell of dope in the room and the dull thud of music from the bedroom next door, words soon lost all meaning and I drifted off to sleep.

I woke up later – I don't know how long I'd slept. There was a dim light in the room, coming from one small lamp on a desk by the window. The other sleeping body was snoring loudly. My head was pounding, and I ached all over, but I managed to sit up on the bed. I stayed like that for a few minutes, getting my bearings, allowing the fuzziness in my head to clear. I got up, not without difficulty, staggered to the bedroom door and opened it – the party was still going strong, from the sound of things. I let myself out.

I looked up at the roof, my mind working out strange equations. They seemed to add up. I could see the paper with all the working out, the numbers and symbols making a daft kind of sense. I walked along the path towards the archway that led to the road. Passing the stairwell inside the archway, I stopped, took a deep breath, and climbed the stairs. My head was still spinning, and the going was not easy. Nevertheless, I got to the very top and opened the door that led on to the roof.

It was very cold now. The wind was piercing and, as I moved across the asphalt towards the middle of the block, round about Frank's old place, I stopped and looked up at the sky. No moon. No stars. The ink-blackened clouds owned the sky and the obscurity of night seemed to have triumphed. I looked around and off to the front of the building. I walked towards it, stopping a few feet from the edge. I thought for a little while, but not at all clearly. Too much interference. A head full of white noise.

I stepped to the edge now, my toes pointing over it slightly. I could feel the cold wind massaging my face, troubling my hair, squeezing tears from my eyes. I looked over into the wasteland – that God-forsaken plot of ground. It had stood there, like that, for years. All hope of renewal must have rusted by now, like the crane and the diggers that stood inert, no longer deserving of their names.

I looked down over edge. How hard can it be, I asked myself? Just close your eyes, take a deep breath, and lean forward. Let yourself go. Imagine you're at the swimming baths. High board. Come on in, the water's lovely.

"It's at this point that you have to ask yourself, is my journey really necessary?" A voice said, somewhere behind me. I turned around. A few yards further back on the roof, a man stood, smoking a cigarette. It was very dark now and I could only see his silhouette.

"I mean, you'll probably only break a few bones. 'Course, you might break your fuckin' neck and die, but you're more likely to end up in a wheel-chair." It was a nasal drawl, its Liverpudlian sarcasm diluted only a little by transatlantic interference. There was warmth there too, though not without irony. I knew that voice very well, though I never expected to hear it on the rooftop of St Ragnulf's – the roof of the Apple offices maybe, but that was a long time ago, before I was born.

I walked closer to him. I could make out his long, lean frame, his gaunt features, the round dark glasses, the hair longish and swept back. He was wearing a dark leather jacket, with the collar up, jeans and cowboy boots.

"Well, when you put it like that," I said, at this point believing that I was talking to myself.

"You're not talking to yourself, you know," he said.

"I've only got your word for that."

"Clever little bastard, aren't you?"

"I don't feel so clever at the moment."

"Well, we all have our lost weekends, son. Times when we go a bit fuckin' crazy."

"It's funny, I thought I saw Gene Vincent the other day."

"It's quite possible," he said. "The little bugger gets around a hell of a lot, for a cripple."

"Do you ever see Elvis?"

"Mr Parsley? Yeah, every now and then. He gets about too much, I would say. Still loves the publicity you know. All the adulation. He'd turn up for the opening of a fuckin' envelope, that one. I love the guy to bits, but he could be a little more discreet. No wonder all those nuts think he's still alive. He never really did leave the building. Must have shares in the National Fuckin' Enquirer or something. Got to have a scam going down somewhere. Still, it's a lot better than fuckin' Vegas. Anything is."

"The way things are going, Vegas doesn't sound too bad."

"You're delirious, son. Been up on the roof too long. I'd get back indoors if I were you. Out of the wind."

"Thanks. Think I will. I'm in a place I never thought I would be. Figured I had other stuff on the cards."

"Life is what happens to you when you're busy making other plans. Death too. Believe me."

He took a drag from his cigarette.

"I better be making tracks," he said.

"Where are you off to now?"

"I'm not sure. I really fancy a drink to be honest. I could murder a Scotch and Coke – haven't had one of those for a long, long time. I think I'll try and find the Pelvis though, see what he's up to. It's not gonna be easy, mind. So many fuckin' impersonators around these days – some of them very good too. Needle in a bloody haystack."

"Nice to meet you," I said, which was, you'll agree, a bit of an understatement.

"Likewise, I'm sure. And you take care of yourself, son. There are some crazy fuckers out there."

He wandered off towards the wall and disappeared into the shadows. I headed for the stairs and got down from the roof the more sensible way. The party was still going at Michael's. I walked past his front door and found my own. I made myself a cup of tea, went into the front room and put on The Beatles' *Anthology 3*. Banana came and sat in my lap.

I began to think about my life and the point it had reached. What had passed before, particularly of recent, was confusing, sometimes downright bewildering. What lay ahead was foggy and uncertain. All I had was me. All I had was now. I couldn't take anything else for granted. The world was wrong, that was for sure. I couldn't depend on life to work out right and I could only guess at where things were going, and why. Either the universe was operating in a random fashion, and I couldn't plan for that, or there was some governing force – whether you call it God, or some other name is up to you. But if such a force, such a being, should exist, how can you negotiate with it? How could you? If you wanted something from such a power, what could you offer in return, what would your bargaining chips be? And, then again, looking around, what sort of force were we dealing with, that was either responsible for, or else at least countenanced, such wanton madness and destruction? And if it was not responsible, was it therefore powerless to change the rules of the universe it had made? Did it have to abide by those rules itself and, if able to act on our behalf, only be able to do so by finding loopholes that it had left there in the first place, eons ago? I was left with a choice between nothing or a mercurial, potentially cruel, possibly powerless God. This was what I had to work with – something perilously close to the rock/hard place interface though, the more I thought about it, the less equal these two options seemed to be. In the end, I decided that I couldn't negotiate with nothing, so I chose to take my chance with God. In that moment, I made a pact with whatever was out there – my bargaining chip being myself.

John sang *Cry Baby Cry* in the background. I yawned, Nana purred, and we both drifted gradually and gratefully into sleep.

CHAPTER TWENTY

I could not escape them. I was lost amidst scenes of medieval pageantry and crow black cruelty. It was a dumb show, a morality play – though the moral was not too clear, and not easily discerned as being particularly moral. There was a ritual and a sacrifice. Dumpy Medieval Man presided over it, moving awkwardly to the tune of his own lute, with a movement that was a combination of dancing and sulking. He wore his habitual scowl, made even more unpleasant by the fact that his nose was knocked out of shape and both his eyes were blackened. It was a barren landscape – rendered monochrome by the severity of the time, like Ingmar Bergman's *The Seventh Seal* or *The Virgin Spring*. I looked for the gaunt, haunted features of Max von Sydow, but I looked in vain.

It was all sickeningly inevitable. God was far away – His colour and warmth absent, almost faded completely from memory. I was gagged and bound, led across the bleached wasteland, a rope around my neck. Holding the other end was the pale-faced, dark-eyed, black-haired woman. A sole tree reminded the landscape of ancient fertility, though it was a cruelly mocking reminder since the tree was bare and desiccated, fecundity an old belief that no-one shared anymore. A raven was perched on one of its branches, croaking loudly, either offering mockery or giving orders. There was a crude altar beneath the tree – a mess of knotty wood planks that formed trestles and table-top, with thorny branches growing from them. On this altar lay Janie, draped in white, her face nearly as pale, her eyes closed, her breathing almost impossible to detect. I was pushed to my knees. The pale, dark lady began to sing – a wordless, murky tune that made me terribly certain that all was lost, and things could not be made well or whole again. A figure appeared from behind the wasted tree and moved towards me, all in sinuous black, from head to foot, with his head a shiny helmet that reflected the waste and wantonness around him. He produced a huge pair of shears and spoke in a language I didn't recognise – it sounded like an incantation. The others bowed their heads. Janie opened her eyes abruptly and stared at me, cold and accusing. The shears opened and closed. My head left my body, and the black and white was suddenly scorched with red.

The phone woke me up abruptly, with a terrible sense of dread and an even worse hangover.

"Hello," I growled into the receiver.

"God, you sound terrible." It was Michael.

"I feel worse," I said. "Sorry about last night. I dimly recall behaving like a total arse."

"Don't worry about it, Stephen. That little twat was getting up everyone's noses. If you hadn't hit him, there was a not-so-orderly queue forming behind you for the privilege. I was more concerned about you, we all were. I looked in on you a few times and you were sleeping soundly, then later on you'd disappeared. I rang you at home and there was no answer."

"Oh, I just got home and flaked out. I was dead to the world until you called just now."

"How are you feeling?"

"Pretty shitty but I'm alive and a few pots of tea will probably bring me around eventually."

"Well, when you've got yourself together, pop around here, right?"

"Why? Do you want me to help you clean up the mess?"

"No, you cheeky sod. I've already done that. Just come over for a chat. OK?"

"Yeah, alright. It may be a while though."

"That's fine. See you later."

It was good to hear his voice. The events of last night were starting to come back to me. The fact that Michael was still speaking to me meant a lot.

I had a shower, brushed my teeth, and got dressed. I went into the kitchen and put the kettle on. Banana was soon in there, brushing against my legs, making pitiful little noises.

"Is lover boy still not back, my little Nana?" I picked her up and gave her a kiss on the head, stroking under her chin. "Is my little pussens a sad little pussens? I'm sorry, darlin'. I can't bring him back. I can't bring Mummy back either."

A little later, I stepped out of my front door and closed it behind me. I could see Maddy coming along the path, a plastic shopping bag hanging from one hand, a cigarette in the other, which found its way frequently to her lips.

"So, the dead really do rise again. It must be the Day of Judgement," she said, with a smile.

"If you're going to tell me what a fool I made of myself last night, you really don't have to. I'm well aware of my sins."

"I'm sure you are, Floyd. But it's always so nice to remind you of them every now and then. It's one of my guilty pleasures."

"You're up bright and early."

"I ran out of fags. My head hurts like hell but there was nothing else for it but to drag my sorry carcass out to Nellie's."

"You had a good time, then?"

"At the party? Nah, it was shit. Pretentious twats and boring conversation. You beating up that fucking minstrel was the definite high spot of the evening."

She took another drag of her cigarette, and her expression became thoughtful.

"Look, do you fancy a coffee?" she said, as if she'd surprised herself by suggesting it.

"Yeah. That would be fine," I said.

I must admit I was fairly surprised too. I mentioned earlier that Maddy and I had been involved a few years ago, before Janie and I got together. We had remained friends, it was true, but it was a spiky kind of friendship, conducted somewhat at arm's length, with plenty of verbal sparring and liberal amounts of sarcasm, of which Maddy was the reigning champion. When we did see each other, it was likely to be at The Ship or at one of Michael's soirées, but neither of us had set foot over the other's threshold for an awfully long time, though our flats were only a few doors apart. To tell you the truth, Jane and Maddy didn't get on. They were always very civil, spoke to each other in company when they needed to, but I'd always suspected that there was no love lost between them.

As I stepped into Maddy's hallway now, it occurred to me that the last time I had done so, the two of us were probably still in a relationship. I followed her into the front room. It had not changed much – still messy, plates with the remnants of recent meals on the floor and ashtrays stuffed with butts, pictures in varying states of completeness (or incompleteness), either tacked to the walls or strewn about the room.

"You must have been expecting me," I said, "but, you know, you really shouldn't have gone to any trouble."

"Give it a rest, Floyd. Remember, you're on a special dispensation from the Pope, so you'd better tread very fucking carefully."

"I'll fucking have to," I said, stepping, in a rather exaggerated fashion, over an empty wine bottle, a bowl caked with days old muesli and a piece of paper with a sketch of angry male genitalia, realised in bold black pencil.

"I'll get the coffee. Milk, one sugar, right?"

"I'll take it black, thanks." I do actually take milk in my coffee, but I resented her presumption that I hadn't moved on since our relationship.

She picked up a couple of the soiled plates and headed out of the room.

I wandered around, looking at her pictures – sketches mostly, wild and intense, whether of strange scenarios, some surreal and others vaguely pornographic, or the occasional portrait, some of people I knew. She was as prolific as ever, I could see, restlessly putting her weird visions down on paper. Never still, never at peace.

One picture on the wall particularly caught my eye. It showed an angelic figure, though dark and with oversized,

185

ragged wings, in a landscape of broken guitars, shattered vinyl LPs and reels of film unravelling all over the place. The angel wore a crown of thorns on its head and there were bloody holes in its feet and hands. Its face looked remarkably like my own. It was smiling.

"I call it The Angel of the Ersatz."

Maddy had come back into the room, with two steaming mugs in her hand. She came over and handed me one.

"Michael dubbed you that once. I couldn't resist it."

"Very flattering," I said.

"Too fucking right, Floyd. You finally made the grade. The Madelaine Marrs Hall of Infamy."

"And this is how you see me?"

"The guardian angel of popular culture. The Messiah of Trash. Yeah, if you like. You take all that stuff so seriously and your head is filled with so much trivia I'm surprised you're able to remember important things, like where you live or what year it is."

"God, you're on fine form."

"You just bring out the beast in me, Floyd. You always have."

"Is that because I'm such an easy target?"

"Maybe so. But if it was that easy, it wouldn't be so much fun, would it?"

"How did we ever manage to get together, Maddy? What the fuck was that about?"

"Don't ask me. We were drunk most of the time. Then we sobered up and realised we just didn't fit together."

"You dumped me, though, I seem to remember."

She looked at me for a moment, almost sadly, and shook her head.

"No, you'd pretty much lost interest. I could see it in your eyes. You'd gone missing."

"Missing? What the fuck's that supposed to mean?"

"Lost in your own world, sweetheart. The Wonderful World of Floyd, with you at its centre, caught up in your music and your dreams. You didn't have much room for me."

"But you finished it."

"Yeah, I did. I'm funny that way – I won't stand being second best. I like my man to be in the same room as me and pay me some attention. You can be great company, Floyd, but you tend to move through this world as if you're not really in it."

"I sound like a hopeless case."

She lit a cigarette and smiled.

"No, you're not. As long as you have Jane."

"I always got the idea that you didn't think much of her."

"Not true. She's never going to be my best buddy, for sure, but she's totally right for you. You're a lucky bastard, I can tell you."

"It doesn't feel like that at the moment though, Maddy."

"Don't give up on her just yet, Floyd. She loves you and she's bloody strong. Strong enough for both of you. Fuck knows, she's had to be. Now it's your turn to take up some of the slack. It's time for you to man the fuck up."

"You know, Maddy, I can never figure out whether you like me or not."

"Everybody likes you, Floyd, you should know that by now. Not that it really matters, mind you. Being liked is not the point. There are things that matter much more than that."

She studied my face for a moment.

"Hey, I was just wondering," her voice was gentler, more

187

vulnerable, than I'd heard it for a long time, possibly ever, "would you mind sitting for me – for a drawing?"

"Now?"

"Yes, now, dummy."

"Well, since you ask so nicely."

"I don't do nice, Floyd. You know that."

"But you've already drawn a picture of me. Surely you've exhausted that particular subject."

"Oh, that?" she said, nodding over at the Angel of the Ersatz. "That was just a joke really. A whimsical notion. A cartoon. I'm talking about a proper portrait."

"Ok, sure. If you like."

"I wouldn't be asking otherwise."

"Go ahead then."

She got up and disappeared out of the door. As I sat, finishing my coffee, I could hear her ruffling around in the next room – her usual smash and grab method of finding things. I'm not the most tidy or organised person in the world, I'd be the first to admit, but I need my immediate living space – the personal area of my life in which I operate – to be reasonably ordered, otherwise I'm lost. My head seems so packed with activity and my thoughts so haphazard most of the time, that my external reality can't be the same if I have any chance of functioning in any meaningful fashion. Maddy's way of going about her life was so different – her inner and outer chaos feverishly chasing each other's tails. It had been one of the things about her that had most driven me crazy while we were together – if we ever really were.

She returned with an A4 sketchpad in one hand and an overflowing pencil case in the other. She put the pad on her knee, rifled through the pencil case until she pulled out a thick black pencil, then put the case on the floor, bits and pieces tumbling out of it as she did so. She opened the pad and turned to a fresh page, then looked over at my face.

"Is this going to take long?" I said.

"Why? You have some place better to be?"

"I promised I'd call on Michael."

"Well, the Queen of Strangelove Place will have to put off holding court for a just a little while. I'll be half an hour, tops. Just want to get your face down, to give me something to work with."

"You just want me to sit like this?"

"Any way you like, as long as you stay fucking still."

I started to get restless pretty much straightaway. My mind began to wander, and I sorely needed to keep myself engaged. This was all very strange and not at all comfortable. Although I was very fond of Maddy, being here alone with her was awkward. I decided that the only thing to settle me was to go on the offensive.

"How's your love life, Maddy?"

She stopped drawing for a moment, looked over at me and smiled.

"In stasis. Suspended animation, like Walt Disney. Until they find a cure and it can be revived and released into the community again."

"That's an urban myth, you know. The Disney thing."

"So is my love life. They tell it on cold Winter nights, as a cautionary tale for the foolish and impressionable."

"Are you're off men, then?"

"There you go, Floyd, mixing up love with sex again. They are so not the same thing. Men I can have anytime. Sex is easy, it's the love part that's tough. Anyway, stop gabbing now and let me get this down."

As she drew and I tried my best to keep quiet, I thought

back on my affair with Maddy. It was blurry at best, most of it, but I could remember that there was a lot of laughter. I could also remember the sex. There was a lot of that too. Maddy was pretty insatiable and very adventurous.

I remembered the first time we'd met. I was sleeping on Michael's floor after a heavy night out with him and had got up in the morning to fix myself some tea and toast in the kitchen. I was sitting in there, half asleep and hung over, when Maddy walked in, wearing only a white bath robe that was quite short and hugged her figure in a way that left the imagination with not much work to do. She was staying with Michael for a while, in his spare room, while she was looking for a flat. Michael had mentioned her to me, but she was out the previous night, so I hadn't seen her. We got on pretty much straightaway and the attraction was immediate too. We met for a drink soon after that and that was it. I got to thinking about some of the nights we'd spent together, the ones I could remember anyway.

"What are you smiling at, Floyd? I can't be doing with that. You'll spoil the picture."

"Terribly sorry."

"And you're blushing now."

"Am I?"

"Yes, you are. If you're thinking about me naked, please stop."

"Can't we put some music on, while we're doing this? I'm getting restless."

"No we can't. I have to concentrate. Stop whining and relax for fuck's sake."

I tried my best while she continued to draw for what seemed like an age. I hate sitting still and doing nothing, so I started my usual strategy for when I'm walking somewhere

or trying to get to sleep and made some lists in my head –
essential films noirs, road movies or American science fiction
movies of the 50s, perhaps, or a perfect compilation of a band
I liked. Maybe even the running order of a favourite album,
track by track. I had just finished compiling a killer Bobbie
Gentry sampler and had turned my mind to listing all thirty-
three Elvis movies in chronological order when Maddy
stopped drawing, put the pad face down on her lap and lit
another cigarette.

"That's enough for me to work with. You're free to go."

"Can I have a look at it?"

She shook her head and blew some smoke up towards
the ceiling.

"No fucking way. You'll have to wait until it's finished."

I eventually made it to Michael's place. His flat was remarkably clean and tidy, for a morning after the party before. The
man himself was very chipper too – bright-eyed, bushy-tailed
and with a mischievous glint in his eye.

"You have no right to look so goddamn suave and svelte
this morning, man," I said.

"The sleep of the just, Stevie Boy," he said. "Anyway, what
kept you?"

"Oh, I bumped into Maddy. She wanted to draw a picture
of me."

"An honour indeed."

We sat and talked for a good while. He was very attentive,
gently quizzing me on my state of mind and then just letting
me talk, listening closely, giving me time to open up. He'd

seen how shaky I was the night before and wanted to sound me out. See where I was and how I was doing.

"What do you want, Stephen? What is it you're looking for?"

"Oh, I don't know. I used to think it was making my own music and doing it full-time, for a living – be that great song-writer, produce timeless classics. That seemed to be all I ever wanted. That and to be with Jane."

"And has that changed?"

"Of course. It had to. The music was still important until recently, but it doesn't really seem to matter now. I just want Janie back. I would give anything for that to happen. Just to have her sitting with us now, having a good crack."

"Me too, Stevie. Christ knows we need to figure out what's important to us, especially with so much change in the air. Whether it's those fuckers at *Haven*, looking to line their pockets, or what's happened with Frank and Janie. We just seem to be getting blown in another direction. Maybe it's time to move on."

"You mean move away from St Ragnulf's? You?" I said. That was something I wasn't expecting.

"Don't sound so surprised. Things change, you know."

"Such as?"

Michael's face grew more thoughtful.

"I got a scare recently," he said. "I was starting to have certain problems and went to see my GP. He was worried enough to send me for tests. There was something there. It turned out to be benign and I'm having treatment. But it made me look at where I am and where I want to be. Even at my age, Stephen, you have to make those choices."

"You're ok, though?" I said.

"Yes, for now. But I do feel that maybe it is the time for

doing something different. Not growing old gracefully, as you put it. I'm too much of a dirty old queen for that. But growing old would be nice. I'd hang around for a slice of that."

He smiled. A very affectionate smile.

"I can't imagine this place without you." I said. "It wouldn't be the same."

"It's not going to be the same, though, is it? It's already changed, just over the last few weeks, and it'll change even more, if those fucking wankers have their way. Wouldn't piss on them, even if they spontaneously combusted in front of me and I was really dying for one."

"God, I love that community spirit," I said.

"We had that spirit, Stephen, whatever you want to call it. We really did. Had it for a good while. That's the sort of thing that scares those fuckers. This was the place. Our place. Maybe it's time to leave it. Before it leaves us."

We gave each other a big hug and I left him. As I was passing Tom and Lydia's, I remembered that I wanted to have a word with Lydia about this *Haven* business – she was secretary of our resident's association. I stopped at their door and knocked. Tom answered.

"Hi, Stephen. What's up?"

"I was looking for Lydia. Is she in?"

"No, mate, she's at work and won't be back until late. Do you want to come in anyway?"

I hesitated. It was really Lydia I wanted to see. Besides, it occurred to me that Tom and I had never actually been alone together – the two of us, in a room, without the buffer of our other halves, whether it was at their flat or ours, or in The Ship. Even if we were involved in our own particular conversation, there was always a chaperone at hand.

"I've got a few cans of Guinness in the fridge," Tom said. "I was just listening to some music and chilling out." For some reason, he seemed really pleased to see me.

"Yeah, ok. That would be great," I said.

We stepped into his front room.

"Just take a seat, mate, and I'll get us a drink."

A CD was playing quietly in the background – *Future Days* by Can, the title track. Weird German alchemy, incantation and invocation, the music pulsing and poised, the lyrics profound gibberish, neither giving too much away – at least not on the surface – just letting themselves unfold, speaking volumes without really saying anything. Tom was a big Pink Floyd fan, but he occasionally took more interesting byroads. I was beginning to feel better already.

He came back with a couple of cans of draught Guinness and two glasses.

"Cheers, mate," I said. My Guinness was cold, and those first few gulps were very good indeed. My body didn't recoil. I obviously needed it.

"God bless you, son," I said, raising my glass.

"Cheers," he said, taking a drink himself.

We made a little small talk, though it didn't stay small for long and we soon moved on to the Kennedy assassination. All roads lead to JFK, sooner or later.

"Did you know," said Tom, "that on the day that Kennedy was killed, his family were at home when they got the news. JFK's father, Joe, was wheelchair-bound and there was a nurse looking after him. Any idea what the name of that nurse might have been?"

I thought for a moment, trying to figure out where he was going with this.

"Mrs Oswald," I said.

"Not a bad guess, but wrong," he said. "Her name was Mrs Dallas."

"That is a pretty odd coincidence, I have to admit."

"If it is a coincidence. The more you look into the whole affair, the coincidences pile up and, let's face it, how many coincidences do you have to come across before you concede that there is some design, some plan, there."

We were talking about details again, and you know what I'm like about those. Remember what I was saying earlier about how it all depends on who was looking at the details, which ones they chose to take notice of and what their particular agenda might be. This is exactly what I was talking about. Textbook stuff.

"Of course, there's the whole Lincoln-Kennedy thing," said Tom. "The coincidences between those two guys and the circumstances of their deaths. Like Abraham Lincoln was elected in 1860, John Fitzgerald Kennedy in 1960, 100 years apart."

"Yeah," I said, "and both men were assassinated on a Friday, with their wives by their side."

"Both were killed by a bullet that entered the head from behind."

"Lincoln was killed in Ford's Theater. Kennedy was assassinated while riding in a Lincoln convertible..."

"... made by the Ford Motor Company," Tom chipped in.

"Interruption. I get another one for that," I said. "Let me see, both Lincoln and JFK were succeeded by vice-presidents named Johnson, who were both southern Democrats and former senators. Also, I believe that Andrew Johnson was born in 1808 while Lyndon Johnson was born in 1908, exactly one hundred years later."

"That's technically two coincidences, you know," said Tom.

"Sorry," I said.

"How about this? The first name of Lincoln's private secretary was John, the last name of Kennedy's private secretary was Lincoln."

"Getting into Twilight Zone territory now," I said. "And I think we'll stay there. Booth shot Lincoln in a theatre and fled to a warehouse. Oswald shot Kennedy from a warehouse and fled to a theatre."

"A member of the Lincoln staff called Miss Kennedy told Honest Abe not to go to the theatre that night, while a Kennedy employee called Miss Lincoln told JFK not to go to Dallas."

"I don't believe that one," I said.

Yes, folks, we were playing the paranoid conspiracy theorist's version of Top Trumps. We hadn't even exhausted all the coincidences – there are more, believe me, but you can look them up yourself.

"It does get silly after a while, though," said Tom. "But it's all there. It's just a case of digging out the details and making the connections."

"Yeah, but when you have that many coincidences, it gets to the point where it could mean something, or it could actually mean nothing at all."

"Point taken," said Tom. "You know, something occurred to me recently. What if Oswald was approached, at different occasions, by the Mafia, the FBI, the CIA, the White Supremacists and all the other various powerful cartels that wanted Kennedy out of the way. Unbeknownst to each other, they all paid him to take JFK out. He took their money, banked it, then went ahead and did the deed. And the twist is, he was going to do it anyway, for his own reasons. So, it was a massive conspiracy, involving all the usual suspects, but he also acted alone. There you have it – the conspiracy theory that pleases everybody."

"Yeah, that's pretty neat. Everyone did it, like in *Murder on The Orient Express*."

"Oh, I haven't seen that one. Thanks, Stephen."

"Sorry, Tom."

Grace came through. She may have heard us talking and come down to see what was going on, I don't know. I'm not sure if curiosity and Grace were even on nodding terms. It was good to see her, though.

"Hi, Gracie," I said.

She looked over in my direction, but there was no response, verbally or facially. She had blue dungarees on today and a big book under her arm. She sat down, cross-legged on the floor in front of us, and looked at the book. It appeared to be a collection of fairy tales, quite lavishly illustrated. After a little while, she reached into a pocket and pulled out the harmonica I had given her. She played it softly, while she slowly turned the pages of her book.

Tom asked me why I'd wanted to see Lydia, and this led to some speculation as to what *Haven*'s motives were and what action they were likely to take. Grace got up at this point and wandered out of the room, the book of fairy tales left open on the floor, just as Snow White had taken a bite from the poisoned apple.

With Grace out of the room, our conversation turned to Frank – the strange circumstances of his death and how the police hadn't really been able to come up with a totally convincing explanation. Tom was keen on the idea of spontaneous explosion – spontaneous combustion is accepted, though rare, so this would only be a more extreme form of that phenomenon, he reasoned.

"Let's face it, Stephen, we don't really know what's in the water that we drink or most of the food we eat – additives, preservatives, E numbers, the rest of it. And routine treatment, whether it's at your GP, your dentist, or the hospital – you go in for one thing, a filling, an injection, whatever, who knows what you're getting into, or what's getting into you, for that matter? Plus, you take the atmosphere, all the shit in the environment, God alone knows what we're breathing in or absorbing through our skin all the time. I'm not saying that this is planned – part of some grand design or experiment – though I'm also not saying that it isn't. All I'm getting at is that we may have absorbed all this diverse stuff over the years and all these elements might interact harmlessly most of the time but just maybe, once in a while, they might come together in a particular way and – BOOM! We might all be ticking time bombs, just waiting to go off."

"Wow," I said. "You've obviously given this some thought."

"You have no idea, Stephen," Tom said. I'd always known that he had this way of looking at the world. I kind of looked at it in the same way and we'd talked along these lines before, for sure, but I suppose we'd never explored all the possibilities, or the implications, so intensely. Maybe because Lydia wasn't there, he felt free to be more effusive in his fears and speculations.

I mentioned Ace and Swift Despatches. Tom's ears pricked up immediately. The expression on his face was priceless.

"Come on," he said. "We're going to the Den."

The Den was a small room towards the back of the flat, which I had not seen before. On the door was a sign that read: 'The Truth is in Here'. He took a key out of his pocket and unlocked the door. The room beyond it was small and cluttered, with a PC on a desk at the far side, and the other walls of the room pretty much taken up with bookcases stuffed with books, magazines, and periodicals. The room was windowless.

"Oh, hang on a second," he said, and went out again. I had a look at some of his books. There was stuff on religion, politics, espionage, nuclear power, space travel, economics, electronics, history, astronomy, astrology, crime, and the environment, as well as a collection of science fiction novels – lots of Philip K. Dick – and comic books. He returned with another chair.

"I only have the one in here. Don't usually have visitors," he said cheerfully. He put the chair down and closed the door. Then he sat down in the swivel chair by the desk. He switched on an anglepoise lamp by the computer monitor.

"What do you think?" he said.

"Well, it's certainly a den, Tom."

"It is that. A little refuge from the madness of the world."

"To give you more time to analyse the madness of the world," I said.

"Got it in one," he said, with a smile.

"I knew that you were into this kind of stuff," I said, "but I had no idea how much."

He switched on the computer.

"Right, how do we find out about this 'ghost rider' guy and his supposed employers?"

He started searching, putting in a variety of words and getting much the same as I had at first, which was not much at all. Then his search-words became more esoteric and tenuous, so that I couldn't really figure out what the connection was or what he was getting at. It was a game of free association that got freer and more disassociated as it went on. Tom knew some forums that were worth checking out – ones with names like 'Disinformation', 'Misinformation', 'The Watch', 'Silent Sentinels', 'Invisible Threads', and, strangely enough, 'Shit Happens'.

We learned that there was a despatch company in England, in the Eighteenth Century, run by a gentleman called Orlando Swift – said to be possibly a distant relative of the author of *Gulliver's Travels* and *A Modest Proposal*. The company was outwardly respectable but was later the subject of government attention when it became known that it was trafficking in illegal substances and highly confidential information, sometimes of a scandalous or incendiary nature. It also transported outlaws and dissidents, finding safe houses for these people. There were links to similar organisations abroad. The company was eventually disbanded and Swift himself disappeared.

Tom also searched for various meanings of the word 'Swiftus', that led to, amongst other things, a natural language processor, used in speech relay systems, and a rap artist. Most interesting, however, was a heretical sect that was mentioned in texts dating from Dark Age Britain and also resurfaced in the Twelfth Century, causing much consternation for the Church over a number of years until it was stamped out, though there seemed to be links to later cults such as the Seven Keys and the Locano Dieus Group.

I also mentioned Sammy and her involvement with the Blood of the Lamb to Tom. His face lit up – he must have thought that his birthday, Christmas and the Roswell incident had arrived all at once. This led us through a rather predictable set of sites about various churches and groups around the world, pretty much standard Christian stuff, along with points of theology, biblical quotations, and predictions, plus a couple of death metal bands. Tom then played around with the name a bit, translating it into other languages, then translating it back, using the result as our search phrase. The sites we found this way were inevitably either very pious, earnest, and boring or totally apocalyptic and quite frankly bonkers. It must be added that, at various points, Tom would bring in another couple of cans of Guinness.

We visited a site called 'The Whisperers'. Tom logged in and introduced himself, asking whether anyone out there had heard anything about either Swift Despatches or the Blood of the Lamb. We drank our Guinness and waited.

The place began to buzz, with various posters offering suggestions, some quite interesting but right off track, some asking for a bit more clarification of what we were talking about. Swift Despatches sightings and anecdotes were surprisingly common. PlayfulAlien saw a van bearing the name make a delivery to a chemical factory in Seattle. Later that day, there was a horrible accident involving toxic material that had the area cordoned off for weeks – the factory was finally closed down. Hornet739 caught sight of a 'Swift Deliveries' truck parked outside a hotel in Alberta – there was a fire that wiped out the place later that day. Crazy_Pete from Boulogne saw a school bus full of kids crash into a river after a motorcyclist with Expéditions Rapides cut them up and rode away. Charlie-the-Monkey saw a messenger from Swiftus Ltd leave a house in a Berlin suburb where the police discovered a multiple suicide the next day. There was more stuff like this. Sometimes it was a sighting or a visit, then a neighbour, often elderly and living alone, would be found dead the next day or a few days later. A student of Renaissance art gave us a list of references to Swiftus, a minor demon and messenger of the underworld in works by Bosch, Baldung and Cranach the Younger, as well as in some of the more obscure Italians. It was all very strange and disturbing, like a blurred picture that had now become razor-sharp and rather chilling.

Oh, and among the responses to the Blood of the Lamb was this one:

"Shit, man, are they still on the go? Stay away from that bunch, compadre – they're fucking poison."

This was from Baby_Manolito in Juarez, Mexico.

We looked at each other in silence. Tom shook his head and took a sip of his Guinness.

"I have to give it to you, Stephen. You keep some really interesting company."

CHAPTER TWENTY-ONE

I popped into the local police station next morning and asked for PC Swann, who had been on the scene after Frank's death. Given the information I had now, I was ready to tell her about Ace. She wasn't there, so I left my name and number and asked her to call me when she got the chance.

I took the tube up to Camden. It was time to see a man about some bootlegs and I was determined to be more successful this time. While on the train, I read the book that Tom had leant me, about religious cults, prophecies, and the end of days. I don't know where he'd got his hands on the book. It was written by a guy called Jeremiah Moss (I figured this might not be his real name) and published by a company called Jonah Limited. It was a real home-made job, almost like a fanzine. It appeared to be well-researched, though some of this research may have been conducted under the influence of powerful hallucinogens. When he'd handed me the book, Tom had told me, almost in a whisper, that it was 'good shit', but definitely not for 'the masses'.

The Blood of the Lamb were mentioned a few times,

though not in any particular detail. It seemed that they were a group who had popped up in various parts of the world over the last twenty-odd years. These different branches were often short-lived, but the name and a similar set of philosophies seemed to resurface every now and then, usually headed by a charming charlatan who figured it was a good way to gather people around him. They had links with another sect called The Last Chapter, who had a whole section of Mr Moss's book devoted to them. They were an apocalyptic cult, though their modus operandi seemed to involve a touchy-feely kind of evangelism, with the usual precepts of love, mercy, and redemption, as symbolised by the ultimate sacrifice of Christ's blood, to cleanse and heal. The cleansing and healing were definitely a big deal. This was sexed up with a bit of Eastern mysticism and some New Age platitudes thrown in to make it seem vague and unthreatening. It was all very jolly and self-affirming but, though the sheep's clothing might suggest the stuff of those best-selling self-help manuals, inside the wolf was reading the Book of Revelation and getting ready for dinner.

I got to the station and wandered up towards Camden Lock. Just before the Magus bookshop, there was a clothes market with some steps at one side leading down to a basement where there were a few other little shops and stalls. Here I found it – Zak's Aural Artefacts, or 'Bootleg Heaven', as Yani described it – the place where all the really juicy and obscure pirate material goes when it dies.

It wasn't a big space, but there was plenty of stuff in there. Not packed – Yani said that Zak was very discerning. He stocked the kind of stuff you couldn't get, for sure, but also generally artists and music that he himself liked or that interested him in some way.

There were a couple of guys looking through the CDs. Zak was behind the counter at the back of the shop, listening to something through a substantial pair of Sennheiser headphones that were plugged into a beatbox at one side of the counter. He was very tall indeed and not just tall, but bulky, a mountain of a man, with a shock of dyed black hair, like some dark age berserker, or a figure from a Scandinavian folk tale. He was wearing a torn black T-shirt with the words "Burn It Now" slashed across his chest in jagged white writing. His face was big too, almost like a papier mâché head on a carnival float, pale and slightly pock-marked, as if the glue hadn't quite dried yet.

I moved to the counter and nodded to him. He grimaced and took off his headphones.

"Och, that's really shite. Supposedly some ultra-rare Joy Division. Some demos made just before Ian popped his clogs. I don't believe a word or a note of it. Some cunt trying to put one over. I'll have the bastard."

I don't think he was speaking to me, or anybody really – he was just responding immediately to what he was listening to, and it had obviously riled him somewhat. It was then that he noticed me, standing there.

"What can I do you for?" he said. His voice was much calmer now, though he still sounded as if he might be up for a fight, if the slightest opportunity presented itself.

"I'm a mate of Yani's. He said that you might be able to help me track some stuff down."

"Yani, eh? How is the old frog?"

"He's fine. Sends his regards."

"Oh, does he now? Well, tell him he should maybe drag his smarmy French arse up here some time and buy me a drink. Fuckin' regards."

One of the browsers came to the counter with a CD in his hand – a Pavement gig from 1991. One of their first, apparently.

"That's very good," said Zak. "A bit ramshackle, wi' that fuckin' hippie drummer, but you can still see the greatness there."

The guy nodded timidly, an implied smile failing to light up his features.

"Did you see the Frankfurt gig from 1994? That's really worth a listen."

"I've got that one," said the man.

"Oh yeah, and where'd you get that from, then?"

"Billy's Boots in Soho."

"Ah, so why didn't you buy this there?" He waved the 1991 Pavement gig in front of the man's face.

"They didn't have it."

"Too fuckin' right they didn't."

Zak put the CD in a little plastic bag with ZAA on it. The guy paid him and was off before his judgement could be called into question any further.

"Billy's Boots, he says. I'll fill his fuckin' boots," Zak said, with disdain. "I've been in this game for years. I take care and I do it right. Fuckin' fly-by-nights."

He looked down at me, almost as an afterthought.

"What do you want, son?"

"Have you got any Buddy Holly stuff?"

"Not much. A lot of the stuff around is poor quality and most of it you can already get on official releases. I like the man, but it's not the sort of thing I sell. Is it something specific you were after?"

I told him about the songs I'd heard on Ace's magic radio. He scowled.

"You taking the piss? I just sell bootlegs, son, I'm not a fuckin' medium in touch wi' the fuckin' dead. And I don't deal in fakes or piss-takes."

I took a deep breath and steeled myself.

"Sorry, I'm not taking the piss. I appreciate that it might sound a bit weird, but I know what I heard. I'm a musician myself and I've got a good ear. It sounded like Holly, but I know that it couldn't be him doing the Dylan song and the other one was just too contemporary in sound and style. It sounded wrong. Buddy was a pioneer, for sure, but he wasn't that far ahead of his time. I didn't think that it was bona fide, I just wanted to know if you were aware of stuff like that and how I could track it down."

"Did you ask the biker bloke?"

"He said it was some foreign radio station."

"Aye, from the land of fuckin' Nod, son."

He looked at me for a moment, then sighed.

"Sounds like a Valhalla Rag job. Come on."

He took me into a little room to one side. There were a few cardboard boxes lying around, full of CDs. He picked one up and put it on a small table.

"This is the stuff I keep out of sight. I can't vouch for any of it, whether it's authentic or anything. But some of this stuff is really good and it kind of interests me. I won't sell it in the shop, but I hang onto it until I get more info about it. If I can verify it, I'll put it out front. If people come asking for anything like this and I've got it, I'll let them take it, but I take no responsibility for it being what it says it is. You can have a look through them. I'll be back out there if you need me."

It was a weird collection of discs – all by dead artists. On paper, it looked like a treasure trove, to be sure, a goldmine. But was it fool's gold, that was the question?

Sometimes it felt as if this stuff was made to order for me – bespoke from one of my own musical pipe dreams. There was an album by Kurt Cobain – mainly cover versions. *I'm So Lonesome I Could Cry* was on there, as were a couple more Hank Williams songs, some other blues, folk and country tunes and a couple of titles – *Been Dead So Long* and *Hurt Won't Go Away* – which I didn't recognise, but which were both credited as "written by K. Cobain". This was a feasible collection – Nirvana's *Unplugged in New York* album suggested that a more acoustic-based approach might be on the cards for the band and there was a soulful, folky feel in the material by other artists that they tackled in that concert, miles away from the Led Zeppelin and punk covers of yore.

There were other tantalising prospects too – stuff by Bob Marley, Nick Drake, Sandy Denny, and Marc Bolan – but there was one CD that really stopped me in my tracks. I'd often had fantasies about Elvis and Dylan getting together to make music. Though they seemed to walk quite different paths, occasionally there were weird overlaps. Dylan had recorded songs also done by Elvis – *A Fool Such as I* during the Basement Sessions, *Blue Moon* on *Self Portrait* and *Tomorrow Night* on *Good as I Been to You*. The song, *Went to See the Gypsy*, on *New Morning*, is allegedly based on a meeting between the two of them. Also, in 1996, when he'd recovered after a very serious illness, Dylan remarked that he'd "almost went to see Elvis."

The King, for his part, was keeping an eye on Dylan too. He recorded *Tomorrow Is a Long Time* in 1966, which popped up on the soundtrack album of an otherwise forgettable movie, *Spinout*, before Dylan had even released his own version. Elvis had heard it on *Odetta Sings Dylan*, a favourite album of his which he apparently listened to obsessively and his reading of the song is certainly based on Odetta's. Greil Marcus also writes of seeing Elvis perform at Vegas and the King mentioning at one point that he felt as if "Bob Dylan had been sleeping in his mouth". This collision of two seemingly distant worlds had a big impact on Marcus. He also describes, in *Invisible Republic*, Elvis's attempted version of *I Shall Be Released*, which sounds promising but unfortunately breaks down before it really gets going. It ends with Presley intoning the name 'Dylan', maybe as totem or invocation, or an admittance that the other had travelled down a road he himself would have liked to, if he hadn't been shackled to Colonel Tom.

These tantalising hints and references worked on my imagination too. *Nashville Skyline* is a Dylan album I love, and, on that record, Dylan is playing with a lot of Nashville musicians who also appear on Elvis sessions of the late sixties – you can hear similarities to the playing on something like *A Little Less Conversation*. There are a few songs on the Dylan record – like *To Be Alone with You*, *I Threw It All Away* and *Tonight I'll be Staying Here with You* – that just cry out for the King to sing them, and I had often hoped in my heart that I would read somewhere that this was the case and that they might be sitting on some out-takes album somewhere.

Well, here in this box, and now in my hand, was such a thing. It was a CD called *The King Sings the Zim* – eighteen tracks, all Bob Dylan songs from different periods and albums, allegedly performed by Elvis Aaron Presley. The three songs from *Nashville Skyline* I've mentioned were there, along with *Lay Lady Lay*. I started to shake. I got goosebumps. And there was more – *Baby, I'm In the Mood for You* and *Long Ago, Far Away* (both on *Odetta Sings Dylan*);

Knocking on Heaven's Door; *The Man in Me*; *Tangled Up in Blue*; *Shelter from The Storm*; and *You're a Big Girl Now*. This was all great stuff, and though it was pretty hard to believe it existed, it could have – Elvis didn't die until 1977 and all of these tracks had been released by that time. Then I read the remaining titles – *Gotta Serve Somebody* from 1979's *Slow Train Coming*; *Every Grain of Sand* from *Shot of Love*, which came out in 1981; *Angelina*, an outtake from the same album; *Everything Is Broken* from 1989; *Tryin' to Get to Heaven* from 1997 and *Mississippi*, from 2001; and *Workingman Blues No.2* from *Modern Times*, which was released in 2006. This music really couldn't exist, and I realised now why Zak didn't have it on display. It was definitely not for public consumption. It never could be.

I went out front, with the Elvis and Cobain discs in my hand. I waved the Presley CD at him.

"What the fuck is this?" I said.

"You tell me."

"Have you listened to it?"

"Yeah, it's great. But it's so fucking wrong."

"Can I hear it?" I said.

"Sure," he said. He took it from me, got out the CD and put it in the beatbox. He passed the headphones to me.

Like the man said, it was great. Better than you'd even imagine. Much, much better. It was as you'd guess those songs would sound if Elvis did them, the arrangements playing to his strengths, but they just had an extra something, and his voice had a different quality, deeper and more mature, resonant of something beyond Tupelo, Memphis, Hollywood, Las Vegas or Hawaii. He was reaching somewhere, like that great arm gesture he did on stage in the seventies, but he was also digging deeper than he ever had before. I had tears running down my face. It may not have been right, but it felt so fucking good.

I took off the earphones, removed the CD from the machine and put it back in its box.

"You alright, son?" Zak said.

"Yeah. Sort of. Where do you get this stuff?"

"Well, most of it is issued by a label called Valhalla Rag. I'd never heard of them before, but they seem to specialise in that kind of material – fuck knows where they get it from. It creeps me out, kind of like the musical equivalent of a snuff movie, but some of it is so good that I have to hang on to it. Can't let it go. I get it from a guy called Oscar Champ, a chubby little fucker who's my only contact wi' that lot."

"Where do I find this guy?" I said.

"You want to find him?" He sounded totally baffled by this.

"Well, I want to find out where this stuff is coming from. Aren't you curious?"

"Curious maybe, but I don't really want to go there. Got better things to do, son."

"Well, maybe I haven't. There's been so much shit happening to me lately, this just seems like another piece in the puzzle that I need to put in place."

He studied my face and scratched his stubbly chin.

"The number he gave me is a pub called The Saints and Sinners, up past King's Cross, somewhere around Holloway Road, I think. He takes all his calls there – he doesn't use a mobile for some fucking reason. Other than that, I only see him when he comes in here, pestering me wi' more freak-show stuff."

He scribbled the pub's address down on a piece of paper and handed it to me.

211

"Thanks for that. I'd like to buy these, if it's ok." I held up the Elvis and Kurt CDs.

He shook his head. "I told you, son – they're not for sale."

"Oh," I said. My heart sank.

"I mean that they're yours, if you want them," he said. "I don't want to take your money. If they're not bona fide, I'm not sure that they're worth anything. If they *are* for real, I wouldn't know what to charge you for them."

I went to a newsagent and had a look in an A-Z to see exactly where this pub was. Then I took a number 214 bus down towards King's Cross. I got off a little while before the station and headed up into the Pentonville area.

I soon found myself in a dilapidated part of town, with the buildings run down and people and cars fairly scarce. This was the same area where the Montana Café stood. Every day was like Sunday here, but like a good old-fashioned Sunday, in the times when everything closed down and there was nothing to do. A Sunday where nothing was forgiven, and nobody was saved. Where everything was so dead, you could hear the sound of all those lives lived in quiet desperation, no matter how pin-drop quiet that desperation might be.

The pub was on a corner, where two roads converged, almost in a V-shape. It was old and grand, in a run-down sort of way. The Saints and Sinners, it said above the door, in chipped, gilded letters. The painted sign depicted an angelic figure and a demonic one, strangely at peace on the same faded board, pretending not to be bugged by each other for eternity, or at least until they pulled the pub down or changed its name.

I got to the other side of the road and pushed the saloon door open. It was empty of customers, as far as I could tell – a large bar, dimly lit and seasoned with dust. There was a dark red carpet down on the floor, and little faux gas-lamps on the walls, giving the place a sepia tint. I walked up to the bar. The barman could easily have doubled as the pub's bouncer. He was thickset, solid, with tattoos on his arm and a beaten-up face.

"Good afternoon," I said.

The barman looked up from the glass he was wiping but said nothing.

"Do you know where I can find Oscar Champ?"

"Who's looking for him?"

"I'm a singer-songwriter, into weird and rare music. A guy in Camden who buys and sells bootleg CDs sent me. He said I could find Oscar here. I might be able to throw a little business his way."

He looked at me as if he hadn't understood a word I'd said.

"Do you want a drink?"

"Yeah, ok," I said, a little rattled. "Do you have draught Guinness?"

"No," he said, like he would punch me out if I asked him why not.

"Right. What bitter would you recommend, then?"

That threw him. He pondered it for a while, as if he'd never been asked such an impertinent question before.

"The Pale Rider is a good ale," he said, already pulling the pump and filling a glass.

"I'll have a pint of that, then," I said, unnecessarily.

He stared at me as he pumped the bubbling liquid in, as if we were arm wrestling across the bar and he was winning. When the contest was over, he plonked the foaming glass onto the counter.

"Four pounds," he said. I paid him.

"Can you tell me if this Oscar bloke will be around anytime today?"

"Might be. He's not here now."

"Right. Thanks." I took a sip of his brew. It was fruity and full-bodied. Not bad at all.

I looked around for somewhere to sit, though I was fairly spoilt for choice. It was then that I noticed the faint strumming of an acoustic guitar. By a window at the far end of the bar, a guy sat by himself at a table, leaning over the guitar in his lap. I moved across the room towards him. The man was wearing a white felt cowboy hat, a dark blue suit – thick material with a ridged, corduroy look – a white shirt with black musical notes printed on it and a black tie, the top button of the shirt unfastened, and the tie loosened. There was a hard guitar case leaning against the wall and a white overcoat folded up on the seat beside him. On the table in front of him, there was a bottle of Old Grand-Dad and a glass with some liquor in it.

"Take a load off, son," he said, without looking up. His voice was Deep South, low and bluff, with a friendly twang to it.

I sat down at the table.

"How y'all doin'?" He looked up from his guitar, his fingers still picking at the strings. He had a smile on his face, both sly and generous, with a keen intelligence etched deep into his features. "You look as if you got the blues."

"It's been a weird few weeks. I don't know quite where I am at the moment."

"Why, you're right here, son. Having a drink with me."

"Well, that kind of proves my point, if you don't mind me saying so."

His smile widened.

"Get your drift, hoss. It's a might confusin' to me sometimes too. I once thought that I'd never get out of this world alive. Looks like it wasn't quite that simple. Sometimes it's kinda difficult to tell one from t'other."

"So, what brings you here?"

"What, you mean here in this barroom?"

I nodded.

"I'm here to have a drink with you, son. No other reason."

"What if I didn't come in this afternoon?"

"You did, though. Didn't you?"

He looked me straight in the eye for a moment, then went back to his playing. He started to sing *(I Heard That) Lonesome Whistle*.

I'd listened to that song many times before, of course – on CD, blasting from my stereo. I'd sung it myself too, sometimes at the top of my voice, to a guitar or ukulele accompaniment. Hank's songs are so great to sing; they are songs that can make you feel happy and melancholy, both at the same time. Songs that make you glad to be alive, even when they touch on despair. Brian Wilson is the only other songwriter I can think of that can do that, with the same combination of pop savvy and spiritual power.

As much as I might know the song, though, to hear the man actually singing it, in the same room, just a couple of feet away from me, was something else. He sang it quite softly, since I was so close, but he gave the words their due emphasis and meaning. It was a beautiful, intimate performance, as if he'd just written the song and was playing it to me for the first time.

When he finished, I applauded.

"Well, bless your heart, son. Much obliged."

"I always loved that one," I said.

"Yeah, didn't turn out too bad."

"Can I ask you a favour?" I said.

"Sure, you can. Fire away."

"Will you sing *My Bucket's Got A Hole in It*?"

"That old thing? Reckon I might be able to remember it."

"And...can I sing along with you?"

He smiled. That sweet, foxy smile.

"Glad of the help, son. Just take a swig of that beer of yours, first off. Clear the pipes."

He started to play, jauntier now, tapping his foot, as we sang along together, trading lines. God, I wish I'd had my guitar there too. It was a version that went on quite a while, with verses repeated many times – there are only three anyway. By the time we'd finished, we were both laughing. It was a hoot.

"We just about got there, boy," he said.

That was when something struck me – him calling me 'son' and 'boy'. When he died, Hank Williams was a few months short of his thirtieth birthday, nearly eight years younger than me. Time had passed since then but, under the circumstances, I'm not sure if that strictly counts. Anyway, he looked pretty much the same as he had in the few photographs and film clips that I'd seen of him. And he still seemed older than me. I was a boy, and he was a man.

"I reckon I got to go now, son," he said, laying the hard

case on the floor and putting his guitar to bed. He pulled on his overcoat.

"It was really great to meet you," I said.

"Well, I enjoyed your company too. You take it easy, you hear?"

"I'll try."

He headed towards the door, then stopped and turned.

"And that girl of yours. She's not going anywhere in a hurry."

"Um, yeah. Fair enough." I wasn't quite sure what he was getting at. It seemed pretty obvious that she wasn't going anywhere. She couldn't.

"I mean it's not her time. Not for a good long while. Keep on in there, son."

"Yessir," I said, smiling.

"Maybe I'll be seeing you again sometime. Farther along," he said, tugging at the brim of his hat with one hand, and giving me a slight nod.

I sat there for a while after he left, not knowing what to think. This was getting to be the weirdest ride. You could have sold tickets – you'd have made a fortune. I was surprised that Disney hadn't thought of it already. But I couldn't work out what the fuck it all meant. Or if it was really happening to me. Had I lost it completely, after all the shit that had been happening – Frank and Janie, the whole thing? When I spoke to Tom about what had been going on, I mentioned nothing about the rooftop interlude with my favourite Beatle. Was that because I didn't really believe it myself? I was totally pissed, after all. Maybe I was afraid that Tom would think I'd cracked.

Do you think I'm cracked? You've come a pretty long way

with me now – do these seem like the ramblings of a mad man? Or a liar? What do you reckon?

After a while, I finished my drink and got up to leave.

The barman shouted over to me. "Aren't you going to hang around for that guy you were asking after?"

"No," I said. "I don't think I will."

When I stepped outside, Ace was waiting. Sitting on his bike, eating a sandwich.

"Oh, there you are. You certainly get around," he said.

"You too."

"Well, it is my job, you know. To get around."

"You keep telling me that," I said, "but I still haven't quite figured out yet what your job is, exactly."

I walked away from him, heading back the way I'd come.

"Hey," he shouted after me. "Let me give you a lift."

"No, you're ok. I can walk."

I heard the bike rev up behind me and move along the road in my direction. It seemed to slow down as it came close to me, then gathered up speed and roared ahead. Once it had gone, the air cleared and the area was, once more, silent and empty, with me the only one out on the streets, walking alone through a ghost town.

CHAPTER TWENTY-TWO

The next day, I went down to St Martin's early on, to cover for Yani until midday. I'd put my new purchases onto my iPod and listened to Elvis singing Dylan on the tube up to Charing Cross. To tell you the truth, I'd been listening to that and the Kurt Cobain CD ever since I'd got home the previous day. It was the Elvis set that I found most irresistible though. Something that perfect, that right. And yes, it was right, despite any reservations I might have. I had no idea if it was the result of some kind of strange technical jiggery-pokery or whether it had been conjured up by witchcraft – wherever it had come from, it seemed natural and fitting. It was as if the Cosmos had decided to issue its own director's cut, to put the record straight, with all the possible controversy over artistic integrity that this might entail.

Listening to it made me think of something that happened at the beginning of Elvis' career, just after he had made those first records at *Sun* and had quickly become a phenomenon. This process started at a local level, with the word spreading outwards, beyond Tennessee, until this strange punk kid who didn't look or sound like anybody else became so talked about that *RCA Victor*, one of the world's biggest record companies, came calling and signed him up for a heap of money. He made that leap in 1956 but, later that year, on the fourth of December – a Tuesday afternoon – Elvis is back in Memphis for the holidays and calls by the storefront studio of *Sun Records* at 706, Union Avenue with a girlfriend called Marilyn Evans, a dancer he'd met in Las Vegas. Just to say hello. To catch up. Sam Phillips, the head of *Sun* and the man who'd discovered Elvis, is there, overseeing a Carl Perkins session. Perkins had made a splash earlier in the year with *Blue Suede Shoes* and he's in the studio, looking for a follow-up. His band includes his brothers Jay and Clayton, a drummer called 'Fluke' Holland and Phillip's newest discovery – a cocky, young, blond-haired guy from Ferriday, Louisiana, called Jerry Lee Lewis – at the piano. They've run through a few numbers, including *Matchbox* and a cracking version of *Put Your Cat Clothes On* and the session has pretty much finished but, once Elvis has turned up and after a few pleasantries, a very loose jam session kicks off. There are a couple of Christmas tunes to begin with – instrumental versions of *Jingle Bells* and *White Christmas* – before Elvis runs through a couple of his own hits.

Then comes the real meat of the session. The boys move naturally into gospel songs, and this is when the whole thing starts to swing, with the band providing a rockabilly backing while Elvis and Jerry Lee duet over the top to winning effect – the King sermonising and the Killer whipping up the congregation as they go. These young Southern guys, who pretty much invented the early sound of rock and roll, fall so easily into the sacred music that they have grown up with and use the distinctive *Sun* sound, that bewildered and outraged so many, to praise the Lord. They are certainly taken by the Holy Spirit here and it is wonderful to behold. And you can hear it because Sam Phillips was canny enough to get the tape rolling to catch whatever might happen. He also called Johnny Cash – *Sun's* biggest star at the time – and told him to come over. And Cash is certainly in the pictures taken that afternoon, of what was quickly dubbed the 'Million Dollar Quartet', though you can't really hear him on the tapes. He always said he was singing along, though he reckoned you couldn't make him out too well, as he wasn't near the mike and was singing in a higher register than he normally would to keep in with Elvis. Well, I wouldn't want to question the Man in Black and anyway you can make up your own mind because it's available on CD and it's worth it, believe me. The sound is shaky in parts, for sure. The boys chat along between songs, with Elvis calling out the chords and others talking in the background.

Yes folks, it's another one of rock's lost documents that's been found, like *Smile, The Basement Tapes,* and the recordings that Buddy Holly made, in his New York apartment, just before he died – rough demos of new songs that he laid down and which were given overdubs and released after his death. These are things that weren't meant to be heard but are nonetheless available, here and now, to buy on CD or download. Yet, somehow, despite being officially released, they still seem like mirages, like we're dreaming them as we listen.

And now, here on my iPod, was another strange artefact, from the other end of the King's apparently ongoing career. Another document that's like a dream, something unreal, not to mention impossible. Sure, Elvis's death hadn't really affected his power, popularity, or influence – it had only enhanced it, both consolidating his mythic status and contin-

uing to generate the sales of records, allowing new genera-
tions to discover his work again and again. This posthumous
phase of his career was the strangest yet but, as far as the
record company was concerned, it was business as usual. In
the light of that, with any number of home movie clips and
previously unreleased performances seeing the light of day –
whether live, in the studio or at home in Graceland – this
weird CD somehow wasn't as insane or improbable as it
might have been.

And it did sound like Elvis. You can fake anything these
days, I suppose, and there are so many Elvis impersonators
out there, but this was uncanny. The songs were well chosen
for him and impeccably arranged – stripped down on some
songs, like *To Be Alone With You*, a punchy *Gotta Serve Somebody* and *Everything Is Broken*, sinuous and rocky, while
many of the others had the fuller arrangements of his post-
comeback period, with female backing vocalists and horns,
the kind of sound that Dylan himself appropriated in the
late seventies and early eighties, on albums like *Street Legal*
and some of the Christian stuff. And the voice was that of a
natural, a pro, who understood his art and was relishing the
chance to tackle something meaty and meaningful, to
stretch himself, travelling to the sort of lyrical areas that
would not normally be his territory. There were some fluffs
too, at times it almost sounded live, or early versions,
outtakes. God knows what the finished article would sound
like.

Even when I took the earphones off, this stuff continued
to play in my head – it would not let me go. I was in a
different zone now. I think I may have been there for a little
while. Maybe I had crossed over the border some time before
and had got so far in I was lost and couldn't get back. I didn't

know the name of this zone, but the music in my head was its soundtrack. The static and crackle in the air around me.

I arrived at Yanni's stall, but he wasn't around. He'd set up but had to go somewhere. Lily, a girl on a jewellery stall next to his, was watching it for him until I arrived. I took over, sat down, and continued to listen to the Elvis bootleg from who-knows-where.

The morning dragged on, with very little action. A few browsers but no buyers. I was lost in Elvis's aching rendition of *Every Grain of Sand,* when a young woman stopped by the stall. It was Sammy. She gave me a little wave and smiled. I pulled out my earphones and stood up.

"Hi," she said. "So, this is how you occupy yourself during the day."

"Yes indeed. Can I interest you in anything? Some Algerian rap, perhaps? A fine example of lush French electronica? Or how about some really heavy dub, so heavy I'd probably have to help you carry it home?"

"No," she said. "I'm sure that won't be necessary."

"Well, can I interest you in a cup of tea and a sandwich instead. It's got to be nearly lunchtime."

"It's around eleven."

"Near enough. How about it?"

She thought about it and shrugged.

"Ok, but I can't be too long."

"Great," I said. I asked Lily if she'd watch the stall and we headed off.

There was a nice little café near the market, called Benny's, on Chandos Place. We went in and took a seat.

"What do you fancy?" I asked her.

"I don't know."

"Are you hungry?"

"A little," she said.

"Well, I'm going to have a toasted fried egg sandwich with tomato ketchup. Would you care to join me?"

She pulled a face.

"You don't like the sound of that?"

"I don't know," she said. "Never had one."

"You've never had one?"

"No. Never."

"Then let me introduce you to the experience. You've got to try it. It's the best."

"I don't know."

"Are eggs not kosher?"

She smiled.

"Eggs are fine," she said.

"What about bread and ketchup – the partaking of either of these substances wouldn't be regarded as sinful, would it?"

"Don't push it," she said.

"I apologise. Can I buy you a fried egg sandwich with tomato ketchup? Please."

"You can."

"A beverage with that?"

"An orange juice would be fine, thanks."

"Hallelujah," I said.

I went to the counter to order and came back to our table with a big mug of tea in one hand and a glass of orange juice in the other.

"Thanks," she said.

"Here's mud in your eye," I said, lifting my mug in a toasting gesture.

"Yours too." She lifted her glass.

"So, do you come down here every day with your lot?" I asked her.

"My lot?"

"The Blood of the Lamb."

She wrinkled up her nose in a curious manner.

"We kind of take turns. I normally do two or three days a week here."

"And what do you do the rest of the time? With your group?"

"There are other places where we have stalls and there are always things to organise. We have prayer meetings and meditation sessions too. Why do you want to know?"

"I'm just interested. You obviously want to share this stuff with people. Why else would you have a stall?"

"I don't get the sense that you're ready to be converted."

"You might be right there. But I'm interested, nevertheless."

Our sandwiches arrived. I tucked into mine straightaway.

"Just divine." I said. "You know, one of these and a bottle of Lucozade is the best hangover cure in the world."

"Not something I would need, of course, but thanks for sharing."

She studied my face as we ate. Her own had a more thoughtful look now.

"You've got to come with an open mind," she said. "And an open heart and soul. There shouldn't be any other agenda."

"And what do I get in return?"

"You get salvation. What else is there?"

"Oh, I don't know – love, companionship, music, fun, the warmth of the sun?"

She looked at me, without smiling, for a few moments, then picked up her sandwich and took a bite. Egg yolk spurted from the bottom and onto her plate, some finding its way to the side of her mouth and onto her chin too.

"You've got a gusher there," I said. "The best kind."

She smiled, then worked her tongue around her mouth, trying to catch the stuff. She dabbed her chin with a paper napkin to take care of the rest.

"This is good," she said.

"Not at all sinful, then?"

"Just good. I'm not going to admit to anything more."

"Fair enough," I said.

We both attended to our sandwiches and finished them off. I sucked my fingers to get the remaining yolk and sauce off them. She did the same.

"That was lovely," she said, taking a drink of juice.

"I'm glad you enjoyed it."

"So, you really do work on a friend's stall," she said.

"Yeah. Of course, I do. Why else would I be freezing my ass off on a bitter winter's morning?"

"I don't know," she said.

"I haven't seen your group around much before though."

"We've witnessed at other places, as I said. We've only had the stall here for a short while. We're starting to expand."

"Oh, why's that?"

"Are you really interested?"

"I'm interested in why you're interested."

"That's not the same thing."

She took another drink.

"So, why are you expanding?" I said.

"Because there isn't much time left."

"Can you be a little more specific?"

"Are you making fun of me?"

"No, I really want to know."

She frowned. I don't know if she thought I was winding her up or if she was figuring out whether I was worthy of salvation, a suitable receptacle for the sacred truths that she had to impart. After a minute or so, her face settled into a serious expression. She started to 'witness'.

The world was in a terrible mess, she said. You just had to turn on the television – powerful viruses and widespread diseases, regional wars, genocide, earthquakes, hurricanes, and famines. The Middle East and Asia were ticking time-bombs. The United States was arrogant and short-sighted – blighted by racial division, scandal, and escalating gun crime. Britain was weak and accommodating. In fact, you didn't need to even turn on your telly – you just had to take a walk outside. There was crime in the streets. Lawlessness and unrest in our towns and cities. And climate change – a buzz word for governments and world leaders now for sure but used in the usual blind and uncomprehending way, with most people missing the point. The freak weather, the way that nature was misbehaving, as she put it, was a warning – a sign that mankind had strayed and that things were out of joint, past the point where they could be put right. The time had come for intervention. The world needed a cleansing.

She said this quietly, in that tiny voice of hers, but with such conviction that I did not doubt that she believed every word. She nearly had me believing it too. Let's face it, the world *was* in a mess – she was not wrong about that, and I myself had experienced enough recently to know that things were certainly out of joint. There was so much stuff going around me that I could not fully figure out. Me being here with her, sharing tea and an egg sandwich, the most mundane, natural thing in the world, was part of that process of figuring it out, of putting the pieces together. But as we sat in this café – just two people talking – outside the sky was falling, with enough Chicken Lickens around to raise the alarm and many more reasonable Turkey Lurkeys and Ducky Luckies to tell them that they were being silly, that everything was alright and that they were overreacting.

What worried me, though, what made her words, and the way she said them, chill me, was that her particular bunch of Chicken Lickens were relishing the chaos and impending doom. They were waiting for it to happen and planning their parts in detail so that they would be ready when it all kicked off. They were cheerleaders for the Apocalypse. Sure, people like Tom, the paranoid conspiracy theorists of this world, were looking out for signs and wonders, trying to read them, and figuring out that there was something up, something that we weren't being told by the media or the government. But the Blood of the Lamb and outfits like them were not just prophets of doom – they fancied themselves as agents of it. What this agency would entail, one could only guess at, but I didn't figure that it was going to involve kind words and prayer books. I had read in Tom's book that groups like these often resorted to violence, psychological or otherwise, to keep members in line and that physical intimidation was also part of their methodology, if not their message. I wondered how much Sammy knew about this. She told me about her beliefs with conviction. There was a light in her eyes as she spoke, even though she was sharing all this, all that she believed most dearly, with an unbeliever.

"Do Liam and your mum and dad know about all this? About your beliefs?"

"Not really. It's my own business. They wouldn't be bothered anyway. Liam's got his music, Dad's always busy and my mother is usually drunk. That's why my parents split up. They never really lived in the same house, even when they were together. I don't even think they lived in the same world. Talking about spiritual matters to them would be a waste of time anyway. They're too tied to the material world and all that goes with it."

"That's a bit harsh and uncharitable. Judgmental even."

"And you're not judging me?" she said, her eyes burning now.

"No," I said, "I'm not."

"Think what you want. I've got to go now."

She got up. I stood up too.

"Please don't go," I said.

"I've got to get back. I've been away too long."

She headed for the door, and I started after her.

"Hey there," the woman behind the counter shouted. "Your bill."

I went over to the counter and gave her a tenner. I didn't wait for my change.

I caught up with Sammy a little way down Chandos Place. I took her arm, hoping she would slow down. She winced, pulling the arm away with a jerk.

"Sorry, I didn't mean to hurt you," I said, alarmed by her reaction. "I just didn't want us to leave it like that. I'm sorry."

She stood there, rubbing her arm. There were tears in her eyes.

"What's the matter, Sammy?"

"Oh, I fell over a little while ago and bruised my arm. It's still a bit tender. It's nothing though."

"You fell over?" I said.

"That's what I said. Look, I really do have to go."

"Hang on a minute," I said, reaching into my coat. I took out my notebook and pen, which I always carry around with me, to jot down lyrics and song ideas. I scribbled my name, address, and mobile number onto a page, ripped it out and offered it to her.

"Please take this. If you want to see me or, you know, just have a chat, give me a ring. Any time you feel like it."

She looked at me for a moment.

"Please," I said again.

She took the piece of paper, glanced at what I'd written down and then put it in a coat pocket.

"Thanks for the sandwich," she said.

"You're very welcome," I said and watched as she turned and walked down the street, towards the market.

When I got back to the stall, it was still slow going. Yani's wares remained untouched, but I was not. I couldn't stop thinking about Sammy. There was something up and I wanted to find out what it was. I wanted to help her. I felt somehow that I was meant to, maybe that she felt it too and that she was looking to me to do something about it. It seemed as if I had some kind of purpose, as silly as that might sound. What's more, that this purpose, this thing that was calling me, was tied in with everything that had been going on in my life recently. I remembered my drunken deal with God, with myself as a bargaining chip. Maybe it was time for me to honour my side of the bargain.

My mobile phone rang.

"Hello, Stephen?" It was Lydia.

"Yes, it's me. You ok?"

"Yeah, fine." She sounded excited. "Stephen. It's Jane."

"What about Jane?" I blurted out. "What's happened?" My heart started to thump loudly in my chest.

"You've got to get over to the hospital now. She's regained consciousness."

CHAPTER TWENTY-THREE

I got to the hospital as quickly as I could. To say that my head was spinning would be something of an understatement. It was a whirligig, with flashing, coloured lights, and carnival music blaring inside my skull. The tube train couldn't get me up to Paddington soon enough. I was dying to see her, to hear her voice, to see the colour of her eyes again. Lydia hadn't said too much on the phone, but she'd assured me that Jane was responsive and aware, though obviously pretty confused about where she was and what had happened to her. She was going to need loads of physio, but she was awake and able to speak.

I had tears in my eyes as I sat on the train, my thoughts jumbled and conflicting. I had Janie back – something I was convinced would never happen – but I could also not shake a nagging sense of dread. It seemed, these days, that the carpet was always being pulled from under my feet when I least expected it. Maybe there would come a point when there were no more carpets to be pulled away, where I could feel a bare floor under my feet and know that I was safe, though I suspected, at that moment, the floor would probably give way as well. God knows where I'd end up.

When I got to St Mary's and arrived on Jane's ward, there was a kind of buzz around the place. There was definite excitement, though muted and cautious. What had happened was extremely encouraging but it was also provisional. You had to keep an eye on it. After all, every recovery is only temporary, because every recovery is just one closer to the condition from which none of us ever recover.

But Janie had recovered. This time. When I stepped into her room, I could see that she had been raised up slightly in bed. Lydia was sitting beside her. She was in uniform, on duty, and was talking gently to Jane, who was conscious and looking up intently at Lydia. I stood there for a little while, feeling awkward. Lydia looked over at me standing in the doorway.

"Here he is," she said to Jane.

I moved over to the bed. She looked up at me, with a dazed smile. I looked into her eyes. It felt as if we hadn't been properly introduced.

"Hello, baby," she said, her voice croaky and slight.

"Hello, pet. It's good to see you."

"You too."

"You overslept, just a tad."

"Yeah. Think I need a better alarm clock."

Lydia got up.

"I'll be outside if you need me," she said, and left.

We looked at each other for a few moments, then I leant over and kissed her gently on the lips.

233

"I missed you, pet," I said.

"I think I missed me too."

I sat down and took her hand.

"How are you feeling?"

"My head hurts. Can't really think straight. Feeling really tired."

"That's what lying in bed for weeks does for you."

"I know. Aren't I a lazy cow?"

"Maybe. You'll do for me though."

She smiled sleepily. Her eyes were a little moist.

"How are you?" she said.

"Me? I'm fine."

"You been keeping out of mischief?"

"Yeah, you know. Rattling around."

She studied my face for a moment. The expression on her own was thoughtful, maybe a little sceptical.

"It's the weirdest feeling," she said. "It's like I've just spoken to you recently. I remember us having lunch, getting into an argument about having a baby. I can remember being pretty mad at you for a while and then just wanting to have you with me, really missing you. And that's it."

She paused for breath.

"Could you pass me that glass of water, hun'?" she said. I handed the glass to her and she took a few sips before continuing.

"Next thing, I wake up in a hospital bed, with this sense of dread. Can't put my finger on it at first – I'm still a bit confused – but I can feel, in my gut, that something has happened to you. That I've lost you."

"I think that it was the other way around, pet."

"Yeah. Maybe. But I still can't shake that feeling."

"You're bound to feel weird, darling. You've been through a hell of a lot."

She reached up a hand, with some effort, and touched my face.

"You'd tell me if something was wrong, wouldn't you?"

"Janie darling, at this moment, I could not be better. I've got my baby back and nothing else matters."

She let her hand drop to the bed and sighed, as if having laid down a great weight and exhausted by the effort.

"You tired, pet?" I said.

"Yeah, really whacked, "she said, her words slightly slurred. "Like really bad jet lag, and a stinking hangover, rolled into one."

She smiled wearily, then closed her eyes. I took her hand and kissed it gently.

"You get some rest, darling."

"Yeah," she said, her eyes still closed, though it was more an exhalation of breath than a proper word. I watched her for what seemed like a long time, watched her chest rise and fall and her eyelids flicker gently, every now and then. She was unconscious, for sure, as she had been for the past few weeks, but it was different now. Her face was alive, the muscles loose and on standby, her complexion showing bloom and blush, capable of excitement, anger, and embarrassment – far from the stasis that had frozen her features for so long. She might well be dormant, but she was no longer in suspended animation. She had been defrosted, revived, and was once more full of promise.

I closed my eyes and inwardly gave thanks, though I'm not sure who or what to. The air in the room seemed to crackle with static, faint but still palpable.

I opened my eyes. Janie was still there, still sleeping, as

beautiful as ever. I watched her for a while longer, then leant down and kissed her on the forehead.

"See you later, pet," I whispered, close to her. "Sweet dreams."

I stood in the corridor outside her door for a while, trying to take it all in. My feelings were all over the place. I felt elated. I felt tired. I also felt a little sad. My mind was trying to assimilate so much information while my body tried to contain all these emotions.

A scene that I had written in my head so many times over the past few weeks had now happened for real, or at least I thought that it had. I opened her door a little, just to make sure. She turned onto her side, as if on cue, and made a little sigh. She was no longer comatose. She was sleeping, a restless and purposeful sleep, not too far from waking and closer to me than she had been for what seemed like an age.

I looked down the corridor and saw a figure approaching. The lights were dim now and I couldn't make out who it was at first. The figure was white-clad and its progress towards me was steady and purposeful. I blinked my eyes and braced myself, as if waiting to receive a blow. The figure moved closer until I could finally see that it was Lydia. I felt both a little unnerved and faintly embarrassed.

"How did it go?" she said, examining my face.

"It's lovely to have her back – to be able to speak to her," I said, as Lydia continued to study me. "She's a little groggy and obviously exhausted but she's stringing words together and still has her sense of humour. She's Janie."

"It is early days," said Lydia. "There's always a possibility of relapse but, at the moment, she's coming along well, and the signs are good. She'll have to stay here for a while longer, of course. If she continues to improve, she'll be moved to the Rehabilitation Unit. The doctors will do more tests – we're still not sure what damage she's sustained – but, nevertheless, she's doing remarkably well."

She checked herself. She was even blushing slightly.

"There I go again, babbling away in nurse-speak."

"It's ok. You're fine."

"You look as if you could do with some rest too."

"Oh hell, I'm buzzing at the moment. I certainly don't feel like resting. Don't know if I'd be able to."

"Nevertheless, you do look weary."

"Well, it's been a weird old time, one way or another. Takes it out of a body."

"Tom told me about some of the stuff you've been getting into, Stephen."

"Oh, did he?"

"Yes, he did. Are you sure you want to be dabbling in that kind of thing?"

"What kind of thing? It's just stuff that interests me. Keeps my mind occupied."

"Fine, but we don't want you to end up like Tom, do we?"

"We were just having a few beers and messing about. No cause for concern."

"Just don't get too caught up in it, Stephen. Besides, Jane's going to need you more than ever now."

"Yeah. Perhaps you're right."

My acquiescence was all nonsense of course and I felt bad about lying to her, though I doubt she believed a word of it anyway. But I didn't want to talk about all that here, with Janie so close and still so vulnerable. That was hoodoo-voodoo shit that had to be kept outside. If it was out there, well away from Jane, it seemed somehow less threatening and easier to control, though control was probably the wrong word. I was stupid to think that I had control of anything – the events of the past few weeks had taught me that. But, as daft as it might seem, this hospital had become to me almost a sacred place. It was the place where Janie followed her vocation. She fought disease here, eased pain, kept death at bay, at least for a little while, or else attended to it in an orderly and civilised fashion, though I know that disease and death are neither of those things. But Jane and her fellow sisters of mercy nevertheless kept watch and, when necessary, rang in the changes. So, fanciful or not, in my mind this building was the nearest I had to a medieval monastery, convent or cathedral. A place of sanctuary.

"So, do you think she'll sleep for a while?" I said, trying fairly obviously to change the subject.

"I would think so, though it's difficult to say. Her parents are on their way over, but they've been told that they'll not get much from her for a while. We just have to wait and see."

"Ok, I'll get away then. I'll pop in again tomorrow. You'll keep me posted on how she's coming on?"

"Of course."

"Thanks, Lydia. See you later."

"Take care, Stephen. And get some rest."

I nodded, turned away from her and headed down the corridor, my echoing footfalls sounding somehow alien and intrusive in the dim and otherwise silent corridor.

CHAPTER TWENTY-FOUR

My journey home that evening from the hospital was so different from the usual sorry ritual I'd gone through during the previous weeks. The hundred or so yards to the tube station, the train-ride to Lambeth North and the long walk down Kennington Road seemed both less desperate and without that mixture of guilt and helplessness that were my usual companions on the way home.

Home. That was another thing that was different. Leaving Jane lying there on those previous occasions, lost in unconsciousness, the journey back to St. Ragnulf's was one that I knew I had to take but one that I never wanted to finish. It was not truly a going home for me since it was no longer a place that felt familiar, comforting, or safe. Not without Jane. Tonight, though, the word meant something again. Home. A place that you look forward to. Fuck me, yes, looking forward was another thing that I would have to learn how to do again. To a time, maybe not too far off, when Janie would be coming home with me. Such a thought was a winter warmer indeed, more than enough to take the edge off the chill of the evening and the strange tone of my conversation with Lydia.

I shook such wet blanket thoughts out of my head as I walked down Kennington Road. The Imperial War Museum looked grand in the dark and, passing shops and offices I also noticed, for the first time, the tinsel and holly and fake snow stuck to or sprayed on the windows, the trees and decorations on display, the flashing lights reflected in the glass. It was going to be Christmas in a week or so, for fuck's sake. All this festive paraphernalia had been around for weeks, of course, but I'd managed to block it out, to not really notice it because, like home, Christmas had been something that I had not been looking forward to. Without Jane, it was just another reason to feel lonely and lost. But not now. No, now I could see and feel it all around. Holy shit! I'd have to buy us a tree. And presents. Once again, I felt thankful, and my eyes welled up a little.

I was also looking forward to telling the folks in St. Ragnulf's the good news. I would speak to Michael first, of course – I almost rang him on my way home but decided I'd rather tell him face-to-face. As I turned off the main road, though, I thought of Eric and the warm, welcoming glow of The Ship. I decided to call in to see him and share a drink in thanksgiving. 'Twas suddenly the season to be jolly.

It was around six-thirty by the time I stepped into The Ship, so the place was pretty quiet. The jukebox was playing *Are You Lonesome Tonight?* while a couple of locals threw darts at a board in the corner and two fighters, probably long dead, pummelled each other in black-and-white on the tv. There were no Christmas decorations in here, though. No, Eric the Red's beliefs forbade such festive frivolities. If his customers wanted to partake in such a meaningless, and frankly capitalist, celebration, they had to do it elsewhere, outside the walls of his establishment.

Eric smiled when he saw me and started to pour me a Guinness. When he heard my news, he took a bottle of Ardbeg from his fine selection of single malts on a special shelf above the bar and poured one for both of us.

"Cheers, Eric," I said, as I took a sip of Islay's finest.

"To your very good health, son. And to the Princess too. I can't wait to pour her one of these when she's back in here again. We'll have a party that night, I'll tell you."

"Can we chalk that up as a miracle then?" I said, with a smile on my face.

"I would chalk it down to the strength of your woman's spirit and constitution. She's a fighter, that one. I'd also give a nod to plain old good luck, but I'll put it down to no more than that, just in case you think I'm going soft in my old age. In the end, it doesn't really matter. She's back and for that we must give thanks."

"But who do we give thanks to, Eric?"

"That doesn't matter either, son," he said, grinning. "Thank the good distillers of Islay, if you must – there's a miracle in that glass there if you're looking for one. You just take care of that girl of yours with everything you've got. Love her and let her know that you do. Don't give her any reason to doubt it, even for a second. She's the nearest thing to an angel I've seen in all the years I've been kicking around, and I don't ever expect to see the genuine article, whether they exist or not."

I could feel the Ardbeg working its magic, the liquor

gradually warming me up inside while its smokiness lingered in my nostrils and its peaty flavour enlivened my taste buds. On the jukebox, *I Still Miss Someone* by the Man in Black was playing now. Obviously, one of the darts players was a melancholy bugger, though with impeccable taste in music.

"So, how come you never married, Eric?"

"How do you know I never did?"

That stopped me in my tracks, since I didn't know and there was no good reason for me to presume one way or another. I'd known Eric for a good few years now and we'd talked a lot on a range of subjects – football, politics, literature, religion, the NHS, the general state of the world – you, know, all the big stuff. I'd always been struck by the range of his knowledge and the astuteness of his thinking, even though I didn't always agree with his views. But he'd never before discussed his personal life with me, or with anyone else, as far as I knew. Oh, there were rumours that he'd been married and divorced, maybe that he had kids somewhere, but he was never forthcoming when anybody plucked up the courage to probe him on his past. He just avoided answering, albeit in a light-hearted way, so it became a bit of a standing joke. It also added to the aura of mystery that surrounded Eric.

"So, Eric, were you ever married?" I said.

He looked impassive. I didn't know whether he was annoyed, or whether he was just having me on. Then, after a long pause, he put me out of my misery with a slight nod and a dry smile.

"Well, son, it's not the kind of institution I would patronise. That whole property thing. And the vows. It's just another form of state control. No, not for me, thanks very much."

"Right," I said, nodding. Not the biggest of revelations, I grant you, but still something of a breakthrough, for the reasons I've already mentioned.

"But I did live with a woman, once."

"Oh yeah?" Now this was gold dust, believe me.

"Yes, yes. A long time ago now. Naomi, her name was. A committed socialist – very active in the union. A lovely little body too, boy I tell you. And really tough in a debate. Very tenacious."

I was feeling giddy now. Jane coming out of her coma, the Ardbeg and these revelations were all combining to make me feel a little heady and off-balance. I tried hard to suppress the incredulity in my voice.

"So, what happened, if you don't mind me asking?"

"Well, if I did, I wouldn't be telling you about it, would I?" He gave me a little wink and smiled. "Oh, what the hell, let's have some more of the right stuff."

He opened the bottle and poured us each some more of the Ardbeg. I hadn't even touched my Guinness. He raised his glass.

"Tote that barge," he said.

"Lift that bale," I responded, lifting my glass too. We both took a drink.

"We were together for, oh, I don't know, maybe five years. Then I let myself get provoked on some demonstration – middle eighties, just after the miner's strike. A copper was winding me up and I threw myself at him, managed to rough him up pretty badly before they pulled me off. It was a bloody stupid thing to do, and they put me away for assault. Two years. She wasn't there when I came out. Found another bloke. Don't blame her."

"Shit, man."

"As I said, bloody stupid thing to do and I paid for it."

"And there's been nobody else since?"

"No, not really. Getting too old now. Don't have the energy or the inclination."

"How old are you, Eric?"

"You've had your spell in the confessional with me today, lad, and that may have to last you a lifetime."

"Fair enough, Eric. Fair enough."

We continued to talk, more generally now, sipping the Ardbeg slowly to the accompaniment of more sad songs from the jukebox – *Ode to Billie Joe*, *Always on My Mind* and *It's Over* amongst them. Then my mobile phone started to ring. I didn't recognise the number, but I answered it anyway.

"Hello, Floyd speaking. In the pink."

"Stephen?" A woman's voice. A little shaky and out of breath.

"Yes?"

"It's Sammy."

"Right. Hello Sammy. Nice to hear from you."

"I'm outside your house."

"You're outside my house now?"

"Yes, I needed to see you. Sorry, I should have called you first."

"It's ok. I'm nearby. Anything wrong?"

"Not really. I just need some company."

"Right. I'll be with you in a couple of minutes. Just wait there."

"Alright."

Eric gave me a concerned look.

"Problem?"

"No, not at all. Someone's turned up on my doorstep. A

friend. Just wasn't expecting it. Anyway, I've got to go. Thanks for the drink, man."

"Don't mention it, son. You're very welcome, as always."

"Catch you later," I said, as I headed for the door.

CHAPTER TWENTY-FIVE

The fresh air and the Ardbeg both hit me as I soon as I stepped outside – a double whammy, for sure. My head spun a little, but I blinked my eyes and shook my head a few times to try and clear the fog in my brain. I may have managed to do so to some extent, but my head was still all over the place as I made my way home. There was obviously something wrong, I knew that, despite what Sammy had said – why else would she trail all the way over to Lambeth to call on me? I mean, I could flatter myself that she'd been overcome by an overwhelming desire for my company, but the idea just didn't take. Moreover, the tone of her voice on the phone suggested that she had been shaken by something. What it had been I could only imagine, and I've got a pretty good imagination so you can guess the sort of things that were going through my mind.

When I got to St. Ragnulf's, the place was quiet – curtains closed, people locked up cosy and warm for the night. The lighting out front was not great but, as I headed up the path towards my door, I could see her sitting on the front step smoking a cigarette. She jumped up when she saw me.

"I'm so glad you're here," she said quietly.

"No problem," I said.

"Can we go inside?" She was looking back along the path, towards the street.

"What's the matter, Sammy?"

"I'll be fine. I just want to get inside. Out of the cold."

"Yeah, fine. Ok."

I took out my keys and opened the door. She took a last drag of her cigarette and threw it away. After a quick look down the path towards the street, she moved inside. I looked back myself, seeing nothing but my own breath on the chilly evening air.

When we got into the front room and I put the light on, I soon realised what the matter was. Her face was bruised, and her bottom lip split.

"Shit, Sammy. What happened?"

"Things have got out of hand. I don't know what to do."

"Is it Jason? Did he do this?"

"It's not...it's difficult to explain. Things are bad. They've just got really bad."

"Just tell me. Please."

"I just need a place to stay. I need to rest, to get my head together." Her voice was trembling now. "Please don't ask me questions. I'm too tired. It wouldn't come out right. I don't want to make things worse than they already are."

"Don't blame yourself for this. It's not your fault, whatever happened. But, if you give me some idea of what's gone on, I can maybe figure what to do about it."

"There's nothing to do. There's no point."

"Maybe I should call the police."

"No!" She glared at me now, her face flushing up.

"Ok...ok. Forget I said that."

"I don't want anybody else involved."

"Alright. I understand."

I tried to put a comforting arm around her. That was a big mistake.

"Don't touch me!" She moved over to the fireplace, rubbing her shoulder.

"Shit, I'm sorry."

"No, I'm sorry. I shouldn't have come here. This is not your problem. There's nothing you can do. I'm so sorry, Stephen."

She was breathing heavily, tears running down her cheeks. My head was pounding – I felt angry and confused, but also powerless.

"Look. Please sit down," I said. "We just need to think this through."

I already had an idea as to what I should do, but I needed her to sit and calm herself down first.

"I'm glad you came here and of course you can stay," I said. "That's no problem at all. You don't have to tell me anything if you don't want to. But please...just sit yourself down."

She took a deep breath and wiped her face.

"Do you mind if I have another cigarette?"

"No, not at all."

She ruffled around in a coat pocket and took out a packet of cigarettes and a lighter. She pulled a cigarette out of the packet and put it into her mouth, watching me the whole time. Then she sat down and lit the cigarette. She kept her coat on.

"It's cold in here," I said and moved over to the fireplace. I turned the gas fire on.

"Can I get you something to drink? Coffee, t...oh shit, sorry, you don't drink tea or coffee or alcohol...sorry."

"What are you having?"

"I'm going to have a black coffee."

"Then I'll have a cup of hot water. Please."

"Ok, hot water. I can do hot water."

I moved along the corridor to the kitchen and put the light on. Nana didn't seem to be around. She normally came to greet me. Probably off on a wander outside somewhere. I put the kettle on, then picked up the phone. I got through to the police station and asked for PC Swann.

"Hello, Mr Floyd. What can I do for you?"

"Look, I've got a bit of a problem here."

"Yes?"

"A friend of mine looks as if she's been beaten up. She won't tell me anything about it – who did it, anything. She just turned up on my doorstep. She's still in shock, I think, and a little unpredictable. She could run out at any minute."

I moved over to the kitchen door, so I could keep an eye on the corridor.

"Sorry, I'm having to keep my voice down."

"So, she doesn't know you're making this call?"

"No, and she probably won't thank me for it either, but I couldn't think of anything else to do."

"Well, I'll come over and talk to her but, if she's unwilling to talk, there's only so much I can do. I can't force her to make a complaint."

"Anything you can do will be fine. But she's not keen on involving anybody else so I'd appreciate a softly-softly approach."

"Of course, Mr Floyd, I am aware of both the concept and

the late sixties TV programme of the same name. I'll bring another policewoman, but I promise that we'll both be wearing our standard issue kid gloves."

"Yes...thanks. Sorry for trying to tell you how to do your job."

"Not at all, Mr Floyd. I understand your concern. We'll be over soon."

I hung up and headed down to the front room to see how Sammy was doing. She was still sitting on the sofa, smoking her cigarette. I sat down on a chair across from her.

"I really believed, you know," she said softly. Her voice was like a child's again, her face pale and drawn. "I thought that I was with people who knew what was really going on. People who stood for something in a world that's lost its way."

"It's good to believe," I said, trying to tread lightly, "and just because the people who run the show turn out to be dodgy, it doesn't mean that the ideas are."

She smiled, a smile that somehow managed to be both wistful and ironic.

"I appreciate your tact and diplomacy. Do you really think I'm that fragile?"

She stubbed out what was left of her cigarette in an ashtray on a table beside the sofa.

"I think that we all are," I said. "More than we realise, sometimes. But I think we can also be pretty resilient too when we have to. That's why it's important to have something to believe in."

"And what do you believe in, Stephen?"

"I believe in the people that I care about. I believe in music, in the power of art to change our hearts and minds, and to enrich our lives. I believe that we're here to try to know ourselves, who we really are, but that we might never achieve that, maybe never even get close. I believe that the universe is a big, scary proposition. A mystery that we can never hope to understand. And I believe that the world is a strange place without love in it."

Her smile was more natural now.

"Is that something you have memorised, for occasions like this?"

"No, just came off the top of my head, though the last part is a lyric from a song I wrote. Pretty lousy song, actually, but I like the line."

She shook her head, though she was still smiling.

"You are funny, you know."

"It's why I'm here. To amuse and...yes, to make hot drinks when required."

I jumped up and clapped my hands.

"Hot water?" I said, pointing at her.

"Yes," she said, taking another cigarette from the packet in a slightly exaggerated fashion. "Hot water."

She smiled again and lit the cigarette. I smiled back and headed to the kitchen. I turned the kettle on again, got out a couple of mugs and looked around for the coffee. I thought I caught something moving outside the kitchen window in the darkness. I moved over to get a closer look. There was a knock at the front door.

I headed down the corridor. Sammy was standing in the doorway of the front room.

"Don't answer it," she said quietly.

"I have to. Don't worry. I'm expecting someone. It's ok."

"Stephen..."

As I opened the door, it was pushed into me, with some force, catching me in the face and forcing me to one side until I hit the wall and couldn't go any further. Something hard struck me across the side of the head, and I felt my knees start to buckle. Sammy screamed and ran up the corridor, but she didn't get far. One of them caught up with her and lashed out at her with the thing in his hands, catching her on the back of the head. She fell to the floor like a marionette whose strings had been cut.

I saw all of this – or imagined that I saw it – in cruel flashes, like a strobe light had been turned on. Then he hit me again, in the chest this time, and I doubled up, coughing and retching. The strobe was switched to a slower setting now and I didn't see much of anything anymore. I only had the sense of being dragged into the front room and dumped on the sofa, jerking with pain, and gasping for breath.

The left side of my face was sticky, and I had the taste of blood in my mouth. My head was pounding, and my body ached all over. I could hear voices – men's voices – in the room, muffled but malign. I turned on to one side and began to make sense of what was going on around me, to fill the void in my perception. My vision began to clear a little, the reception getting slowly better. There were two of them – Jason and another guy I had never seen before. They seemed surprisingly calm and composed. They spoke to each other in measured tones, though there was an eerie harshness to their words. I raised my head slightly. I could now see Sammy. They must have dragged her into the room too though I don't know quite when – maybe I'd blacked out for a little while. They had dumped her in a chair by the window. She was unconscious and there was a stream of blood coming from her nose. I felt a terrible, sickening sense that everything was fucked, totally and utterly, way beyond the point where it could ever become in any way unfucked.

But it all still seemed unreal. As intense as the fear and the pain were, there was something about the situation that lacked substance or even meaning, something that rendered it abstract and absurd.

Jason knelt down beside me. I caught his movement out of the corner of my eye and then I heard his voice, close to me – his words clear, though they were spoken in a thick whisper.

"Where is your laurel crown, Stephen?"

I could see his face clearly now.

"Where are your three stones?"

"I have no fucking idea what you're talking about," I said.

"St Stephen. The first Christian martyr. You should feel honoured by the connection, though you are clearly not worthy of it."

"Go fuck yourself," I said.

He smiled. A patronising smile, though barely concealing the malice I could see in his eyes.

"Your words are crude, shallow and obvious. They betray the same qualities in yourself, the cheapness and hollowness that characterise your very being."

"Beat me up if you want to," I said, "but please spare me the fucking sermon." My words were slow and heavy, each one uttered with a degree of discomfort.

"It's too late for that anyway. I'm going to make you come to grips with fate."

"Of course you are," I said wearily.

"You think that you're so clever, don't you? So rational and in touch with what's going on around you. You poke fun at those who look for something else and those who can actually see it. The bigger picture that people like you always go on about but which they rarely ever get a glimpse of. Blinded

253

by intellectual arrogance, crippled by the leg-chains that shackle you to this Godless world. You have no idea what's really at stake. What's coming and what needs to be done."

"For fuck's sake, man," I said. "Just listen to yourself. You can preach at me and quote scripture until you're blue in the face but you're nothing but a deluded thug who is using God as an excuse for acting out your own twisted fantasies."

He punched me in the face. I felt my nose break and blood begin to pour from it.

"And you are a vexatious spirit," he said, with a barely suppressed snarl. "A godless piece of trash who is reaping what he's sown. You've interfered in business that was not your concern. You've tainted one of my flock – turned her against me and caused her to stray. It is one thing to resist God and to turn your back on your own salvation, but it is far worse to stand in the way of someone else's. A special punishment is designed for those who choose to do that, believe me."

"I don't believe you," I said, wiping blood from my nose and mouth. "You're a liar."

He lashed out at me again, but I grabbed his hand this time. His friend with the baseball bat moved over to us and landed a blow to one of my arms that was a little haphazard and didn't fully connect – I guess he was trying not to hit his guru. Whatever he hoped to achieve, neither of them, nor me, for that matter, were aware that the other person in the room had regained her wits. Sammy launched herself onto Jason's back, grabbing his hair and clawing at his face, until he lost balance and they both tumbled to the floor.

I kicked out at the other guy, and he tottered back towards the fireplace. I pulled myself up from the sofa and threw myself at him. I don't know how I managed it, but I do know that it hurt like hell – in my head, my ribs, pretty much all over. I connected with him, and we plunged into the fireplace, both of us grunting and cursing.

We struggled, his head jammed up against the bars of the fire and suddenly his hair was alight. He started to scream – a horrible sound – and, breaking my grip, scrambled away. I instinctively reached for the knob on the fire but, as I tried to turn it off, I was grabbed from behind, and jerked backwards. The room span around me as I fell onto the sofa, and Jason was suddenly on top of me. His friend was still screaming, and I caught a glance of him rolling around on the floor, desperately trying to put out the flames in his hair. Everything was unravelling now and all I had to hold onto were blurred snapshots of movement and garbled messages from my other senses – mainly jabs of pain all over my body, the taste of blood in my mouth and the smell of gas, which was very strong now. Jason tried to claw at my eyes with the fingers of one hand; I felt him scrabbling around in a jacket pocket with the other. There was a sharp, searing pain in my chest. Jason pulled back from me, a terrible grin on his face. I continued to hold onto him, gripping his arm, the hand of which held the knife that was stuck in my chest.

I loosened my grip on him and, with whatever strength I had left, pushed upwards under his chin, sending him sprawling backwards. He jerked the knife out of my chest and took it with him as he went staggering back towards the fireplace. It was then that the room burst into flames. Jason let out a scream and flailed his arms around in the air, like a demented banshee warrior, suddenly unleashed from hell. The whole far side of the room was burning. I had lost sight of Sammy in all of this but, as the flames began to fill the room, I saw her scramble to her feet, stopping for a moment at the door to look back at me, her eyes wide with fear.

"Get out, Sammy," I croaked, the blood gurgling in my throat – God, what an ugly sound! She turned and ran and, as the pain and heat intensified, I could only think of Jane, lying in her hospital bed, waiting for me.

And then everything was fire and burning and pain and nothing.

CHAPTER TWENTY-SIX

Well, maybe nothing is an exaggeration. I can't really be sure how or why but, for the time being, I'm still here.

And it wasn't Janie that died – though I pretty much tipped you off to that. No, that would be me. Really. Perhaps it's no surprise to you, maybe you saw it coming – I certainly didn't.

So, how am I telling you all this? How can you hear a voice from beyond the grave? Well…I don't know – you tell me. Maybe some things need to be communicated and find a way to do so, against all odds or indeed rational explanation.

All I know is that this is my story, my piece of string. I have to tell it; I have no choice. But now, as I come to the end and prepare to make my final cut, it's up to you to decide what else it is – or can be.

I can tell you that, in the middle of the inferno, the world, or what was left of it, slowed down. Maybe I was in the eye of the storm, or maybe I was just past caring. Whatever it was, I saw everything in slow motion – or, maybe, in no motion. I saw the world, unburdened by cause and effect – a room where all the burning has stopped, the oxygen sucked out so a kind of clarity can be achieved.

I just know that, in the still, quiet centre of that terrible scene, everything froze and somehow didn't belong to me anymore. I was not implicated or responsible. Flame and charred bone and the life lived here melted beyond recognition.

And that was when he appeared in the doorway – black helmet reflecting the frozen chaos around it. That reflection played for a while on the shiny surface of his visor, like a TV transmission from a room that once belonged to me but that I didn't recognise any more. He walked towards me and held out his hand. I took it and he helped me up, out of the sofa. I could have sat there forever, to tell you the truth – I had hardly any energy left – but nevertheless, I was suddenly up on my feet. Ace gave a little sideways jerk of his head towards the door and headed out of the room. I followed him, my legs unsteady, my body crumpled and ill fitting, as we moved along the corridor and outside, into the night.

Strangelove Place was burning. The fire service had arrived, and their men were engaged in battling the flames. The Place had thankfully been cleared. Ace and I walked down the path towards Cherry Tree Avenue, happily released from the struggle.

Out on the street, the inhabitants of St Ragnulf's were standing around, expelled from their dwellings, caught without comfort or cover, wrapped in blankets, exposed to the wind. They were still beautiful, though. All that they were meant to be.

And we passed them, Ace leading, me following close behind. We passed Michael – his face looking towards the place that he had made his kingdom. He did not look sad. He did not look happy either. He was Michael, with a spark inside him that he had ignited in me and everyone else who he came into contact with, and for that I thank him. He had his arm around Maddy, who huddled close to him, shakily lifting a cigarette to her lips, taking a drag then leaning her head back slightly and letting the smoke pour from her mouth, into the cold night air. We passed Tom and Lydia and Grace, also looking towards the flames. Tom, not without sadness, stared into the fire, no doubt seeing all the conspiracies in his head coming home to roost, leaving him still no closer to the truth. As we passed the three of them, Grace reached into a pocket, produced her harmonica, and started to play. Lydia, meanwhile, seemed to bristle, ever so slightly, and grasp her daughter's hand just that little bit tighter. I also could have sworn that she glanced at me out of the corner of her eye, just for a moment.

Further on was Sammy, wrapped in a blanket and being comforted by PC Swann – my cavalry who arrived too late. Never mind, I forgive her. As she asked her questions and got together the facts, such as they were, Sammy stood shivering and staring off into the distance – her face blackened by smoke but still beautiful and once more open to possibilities.

It is fair to report that there were no casualties in Strangelove Place that night, other than those at number twelve, chez Floyd. That much was a blessing, at least.

The fire service worked through the night to put out the flames, but they could not save Strangelove Place. It is no more. The people, however, are another story. They are a whole bunch of stories, in fact, waiting to be told. A precious fucking library, vast and wonderful.

Ace led me to his bike. He handed me a helmet and I put it on.

"Are you ready?" he said.

"Where are we going?"

"Oh, just for a ride. We'll see when we get there."

We got onto the bike, and he started it up. The machine moved off and onto the main road, off up towards – I don't know where. Pretty soon we had left Lambeth behind, then London – shed without complaint or regret, like a skin we no longer needed.

Then we were on the motorway, though one that was quiet and deserted, with only us on the road. The roar of the bike and the howling of the wind mixed together, filling my ears like the sound of the ocean in a seashell. Sound but not sound. Imaginary. Implied.

Was I going to meet Elvis, you may ask? Or Syd Barrett, Johnny Cash, Nick Drake? Would Kurt and Hank be there? I honestly don't know.

I can't tell you where I'm going. All I can see is the road stretching out in front of me. Even the view on either side is obscured. I have no idea what is at the end of this road, what my destination might be. Perhaps there will be no end, only the next stage of a journey I started nearly forty years ago. Or perhaps that too was not the first stage of the journey either. Maybe there is no end – only a continual movement onwards.

As I speak to you now, I feel that all I am, or have ever

been, may cease to be at any second. That all the words and thoughts, feelings, experiences, and imaginings that I've tried to describe to you here, and all the others I've had no time to mention, will dissolve and be absorbed into the ether. Maybe it is only my words, my story, as I tell it to you, that is keeping it together anyway and, when it ends, so will I. Maybe you, receiving this story, all that's left of me, are the thing that is holding me here, in place.

What are we anyway? Are we just the sum total of all our experiences – the people, places, sights, sounds, sensations, and thoughts that together form the strange, tenuous patchwork that we call our 'self'? If so, how is this held together and, once that hold is released, does it all fall apart and fly away, to disappear on the wind? Or does it become something else? They say that about energy, don't they – that it cannot be created or destroyed, it simply changes from one state to another. Maybe Dylan was right – perhaps people don't live or die, people just float. That's both a comforting thought and a scary one too, but it'll have to do for now.

As the road stretches out before me, rolling like a movie without any clear ending, I can see Jane – still alive and in the world, as I prepare to leave it. I don't know if I'm really seeing her or if I'm only imagining it. Perhaps I can be in two places at once, magically linked to people or places that mean something to me, a port where a connection already exists. Maybe that's just bollocks, I don't know – I've been through a lot lately and, if it turns out to be wrong, I hope that you'll forgive me. But I can see Jane, as close to me as ever though I'm not actually there. She's sitting up in her hospital bed, a little sleepy and dazed. As I watch her, she reaches into a drawer in a cabinet by the bed and, almost absent-mindedly, takes out a packet of cigarettes and a box of matches. She pulls a cigarette from the packet and, putting it into her mouth, lights it. As she savours her first drag for what seems like an eternity, she looks me straight in the eye though, as I've already mentioned, I'm not there. She carries on staring out at me, perhaps daring me to go away but realising that I've already gone.

And so, I continue to see Janie sitting there and, as we move on down the road, my head is filled with snatches of songs – a lyric here, a melody there – all rattling round in my head like sounds from a dying jukebox. Fragments of everything I've listened to and loved, songs written by others but so personal to me that they seem like mine, like an autobiography. Out of this swirling mess, one song gradually becomes clearer, slowly cutting through the static until it is the only tune that I can hear.

The song is called *When I Paint My Masterpiece*. It's a Dylan song, covered beautifully by The Band – a song that, in some ways, became my own theme song, the promise of how much better things were going to be once I got my act together and showed the world what a fucking genius I was. Waiting around for lightning to strike, for that time when the stars would be in perfect alignment, when it all fell magically into place, just like Janie said to me, that day we argued. All that time waiting, and the masterpiece never did come. Or maybe it did but I never noticed because I was looking in the wrong place. Maybe my life was my work of art, the love and friendship I found and my experiences along the way, my greatest achievement. Maybe it is for all of us – our canvas and the beautiful mess we make of it.

Well, this is my piece of string. What do you think? I'm about to make the final cut, but I'm too close to it to make any kind of judgement right now. Maybe there'll be time for that later, wherever I'm going. Or maybe there won't.

So, the bike moves on down the road, a road that's become an abstraction, a journey that seems like a dream, a hallucination, along with the wind that isn't a wind, the sense of movement fast becoming illusion. I can't even feel Ace in front of me anymore, though I sense his presence. I feel both scared and elated, though the two sensations seem so strangely intertwined that they become interchangeable to the point where they don't mean anything anymore. I hold my breath and close my eyes, tightening my face against what is, or is not, to come.

And, in my mind, deep inside what's left of my consciousness, with the world disintegrating and remaking itself around me – crackling like static that is both ancient and newly-born – I see one thing, and one thing only.

I see Janie's face.

THE END

If you enjoyed this book,
please visit us at:
www.rombapress.com
Sign up for our newsletter and receive
notification of forthcoming
titles and promotions.